KU-496-973

THE NO.1 BESTSELLING SENSATION

NICOLA MAY

WELCOME
TO FERRY LANE
MARKET

HODDER

First published in Great Britain in 2021 by Hodder & Stoughton
An Hachette UK company

I

Copyright © May Books Ltd 2021

The right of Nicola May to be identified as the Author of the Work
has been asserted by her in accordance with the Copyright,
Designs and Patents Act 1988.

A CIP catalogue record for this title is available from the British Library

Paperback ISBN 978 1 529 34644 2
eBook ISBN 978 1 529 34645 9

Typeset in 10.75/13.5 pt by Palimpsest Book Production Limited,
Falkirk, Stirlingshire

Printed and bound in Great Britain by Clays Ltd, Elcograf S.p.A.

Hodder & Stoughton policy is to use papers that are natural,
renewable and recyclable products and made from wood grown in
sustainable forests. The logging and manufacturing processes are
expected to conform to the environmental regulations of the
country of origin.

Hodder & Stoughton Ltd
Carmelite House
50 Victoria Embankment
London EC4Y 0DZ

www.hodder.co.uk

For Emma

WELCOME
TO FERRY LANE MARKET

'Every flower is a soul blossoming in nature.'

Gérard de Nerval

WELCOME
TO FERRY LANE
MARKET

Chapter 1

'I bet even the real Sid Vicious didn't shit in his bathwater.'
Kara Moon stared down at the noxious poo in the terrapin's
tank.

'Ooh, I bet he did,' her boyfriend Jago murmured whilst
flattening down his dark-brown Beatles-style haircut and
patting his khaki jacket pockets in turn. 'Seen my keys, Moo
Moo?'

Kara cringed inwardly at her once much-adored nick-
name. Then, retrieving the keys from the orderly rack in the
kitchen, she came back through the open archway into their
compact living space.

A lone beam of golden sunlight made its jittery mark
across the wooden floor as it seeped through the open crack
of the balcony door. The sounds of mewing seagulls and
creaking yacht masts in the estuary harbour rose up from
below, comforting and familiar, yet they did not ease the
gnawing feeling in Kara Moon's stomach. Hoping for a
different answer to the one she was expecting, she asked
casually, 'Where are you going this early, anyway?'

As Jago reached for his battered Beatles key ring, Kara
caught a whiff of the Gucci aftershave she had given him
for Christmas. He looked at her with a perplexed expression.
'It's Jobcentre day. You know I always go over to Crowsbridge
on a Friday.'

'How could I possibly forget?' Kara said sarcastically. 'Oh yes, maybe because it's been eighteen months and you still haven't come back with a job.'

'Don't start.'

'It's just, James Bond needs his flea stuff and I'm not sure if there's enough money in the blue pot and—'

Ignoring her pitiful plea, Jago went to the open hallway, jumped down two stairs at a time, then looked back to say in a patronising tone, 'My little Ginger Princess. You look quite pretty when you forget to tie your hair up in that stupid ponytail.'

Fighting back tears, Kara put her hand to the back of her long, messy auburn waves as her errant beau of eight years stalled again to say nastily, 'And why aren't *you* at work? Or did you stupidly forget about that too?'

Kara sighed deeply and held her palm up to him. 'Just go, Jago. You mustn't be late now, must you.'

She loves you, yeah, yeah, yeah. The famous Lennon-McCartney lyrics that Kara had chosen for his special key ring followed after Jago as he hurried down the stairs, jumped down the last three and went out, slamming the door.

To try and regain a modicum of inner peace, Kara stood still for a minute and stared out of the window at nothing in particular. Here she was, at thirty-three years old, living with a jobless, feckless, twenty-nine-year-old youth, with no mention or hope of plans for the future. And despite her working her butt off to support the two of them, she seemed to barely make ends meet, let alone save any money. The more cash she put aside in the blue ceramic savings pot for unseen eventualities and 'nice things' like holidays or week-ends away, the more excuses Jago Ellis found to dip into it. In fact, tragically, the only holiday they had ever been on together was a long weekend to Liverpool where she was dragged around every street and tourist attraction to satisfy his insatiable hunger for anything and everything relating to his precious obsession: the Beatles.

Deftly avoiding a bite from Sid Vicious, Kara swore loudly and continued to hold back the tears she had been gripping on to. Then, gagging as she pulled her pink rubber washing-up gloves up as far as they would go, she scooped up the offending smelly mess in the tiny net bought for the purpose.

It was five years ago when Jago had arrived home drunk, carrying a huge tank up the steep stairs, slopping water as he went. And five years ago when the job of looking after this poor little reptile, first seen by Kara hanging on to a rock for dear life, had become *her* responsibility. She lifted her head in thought. Had they been getting on then? She couldn't remember.

Their living room with a view offered an optical illusion of space but despite the long bay window seat and door out on to the balcony, there was barely room for their table/desk with a couple of dining chairs and a sagging, two-seater sofa. Jago had cack-handedly fixed a TV far too big for the room to the wall above the fireplace. And the glass shelf that was eventually put up for the tank to sit on was placed at such an angle that when poor Sid wanted to get out of the water and bask under his heat lamp, it took him several attempts to scrabble his way up the slope to his rock. A canvas of the iconic *Abbey Road* Beatles cover hung on the wall above him; it was as if the Fab Four were taunting the little terrapin with their ability to walk in a straight line.

Despite the lack of space in the two-bedroomed flat, when

Kara had caught sight of the Painted Turtle's cute little prehistoric face, she didn't have the heart to say he had to go back to the pet shop from whence he came. And by the time she had got around to googling 'How long do terrapins live' and realised it could be up to thirty years, it was too late: Sid Vicious, the most aggressive reptile in Cornwall, along with James Bond, the skinny twelve-year-old black-and-white rescue moggy, with his furry white tuxedo and 007 air of nonchalance, were now very much part of their dysfunctional little Ferry Lane family.

Grimacing, she emptied the terrapin's mess into one of the big terracotta flowerpots on the first-floor balcony. Then, taking in the fresh sea air, she looked down to see the welcome sight of her father opening the metal gates of the ferry float and Jago running across the road towards it at full pelt so as not to miss its prompt departure.

As if sensing his daughter's sad eyes on him, Joe Moon looked up, smiled, waved, then turned his attention to beckoning the queuing cars on to the beloved car and passenger ferry service – the thriving business that had been part of the Moon family's life for as long as Kara could remember.

Chapter 2

Kara scraped her hair back into its customary loose ponytail, pulled the one remaining ten-pound note out of the blue pot on the kitchen windowsill, took her own keys from their usual place on the rack and headed down the flight of stairs to the front door of their flat. As she reached it, James Bond screeched in through the cat flap, stopped briefly to scratch himself frantically and then, as if sensing that a vet's visit was due, he tore up the stairs straight past her without so much as an acknowledgement.

'You stay in now, you hear me? Or I'll be in a whole lot of trouble,' Kara warned her beloved feline in her faint Cornish accent. She paused. Then she did something she never did. She locked the cat flap shut. Feeling a surge of guilt, she quickly ran back upstairs, pulled an old baking tray out from under the oven and filled it with some compost from one of the flowerless pots on the balcony. 'Just in case,' she said aloud as she placed it under the cat flap and shut the door behind her. 'I won't be too long,' she warbled through the letter box.

The door to Number One, Ferry View Apartments opened out on to the bottom end of Ferry Lane. Kara tentatively looked left, then right, then scurried around to the front of the Victorian block and began to walk along the crazy-paved promenade to work.

Up at the top of the hill, Ferry Lane Market was bursting into life. Every Friday and Saturday since she could remember, all market dwellers would set up outside their fixed, covered premises and sell their wares to not only the inhabitants of Hartmouth and its plethora of second homers, but also to the many seasonal visitors to the small, historic town. With the market having a reputation for being the best in the area, tourists would make the short journey across from Crowsbridge, some by foot, but most by car on her dad's ferry.

Nobody could deny that there was something magical about the community feel on open-air market days. Stallholders and customers alike would mingle and chat. Fresh, locally grown produce and original handmade items and gifts were beautifully displayed and sold. And despite Kara having worked her stall for the past fifteen years, she had never tired of the theatre of it all.

The late-spring breeze today was carrying the regular sales banter from the Dillons' fruit and vegetable stall. 'Come on, ladies, here's your early rhubarb, two quid a kilo. Make the old man a nice crumble with that; put a smile on his face. Give him a bit – no madam, I don't mean that bit. Here, feel my asparagus. Plump and juicy. Have a little squeeze if you like – I won't tell if you don't. Bananas, as long as you need 'em, madam.' And so on.

Despite the miserable start to her morning, Kara managed a smile, then turned to look at Nigel's Catch fish stall – which was so colourful that local artists would often paint pictures of it to sell to visitors. Squid, spider crabs, scallops and clams were arranged in glittering beds of ice, next to the most recent catch of fish; and when she closed her eyes and focused, above the fishy aroma Kara could smell tempting wafts of savoury Cornish pasties coming from a stall up the hill.

Ferry Lane Market was her life. She had started working at Passion Flowers, the florist shop and stall run by Lydia Twist, on her eighteenth birthday. But before that, from just twelve years old, she had worked on other stalls at many open Saturday market days. Joe Moon, Kara's dad, was Hartmouth born and bred, as were his parents before him, and with the ferry crossing being essential to everyone, he knew most of the locals. So, he had put the word around that his younger daughter would like some work and if anyone needed an extra pair of hands, then Kara Moon was their girl.

She had been happy then. With her sister Jenifer already away studying business and finance at Leeds University, for a while Kara felt like an only child. She didn't miss the bolshie, forthright Jenifer Moon one bit. With a seven-year age gap, the siblings had never been close. Kara had always been made to feel like an inconvenience, with Jen's bedroom door being slammed shut on her on many occasions and their mother rarely bothering to react to their shouting matches. In fact, if it didn't involve her directly, Doryty Moon had rarely reacted to anything.

At least with her mother walking out long before she had received her A-Level results, Kara didn't have to face the disappointment of her non-reaction. And with the little study she had put in, she had not only been elated to get such good results for all three of her exams, but with the cash that her dad had given her for doing so well, she was also at last brave enough to get her teeth fixed.

With an infinite fear of the dentist and after years of being called Bugs Bunny, she had finally allowed her father to gently persuade her to see an orthodontist. Oh God, how she had hated those painful restorative sessions! But the result had been worth it. Thanks to her hair colouring, she continued to get the odd 'Ginger' labelling, but she could just about cope with that now that she had a set of Hollywood veneers to beam back at the perpetrator. So it had been with a renewed feeling of confidence that she had turned up for her first day of work at Passion Flowers at the tender age of eighteen – until she saw the bright pink top she was expected to wear, and knew at once that it would clash dreadfully with her colouring. She also realised in that moment that she was as green about floristry as her sparkling emerald eyes.

Today was another first – the first time in fifteen years that Kara had ever taken some last-minute time off work. When Kara had asked Lydia, her boss, the inflexible florist had huffed, 'I cannot *believe* you are asking me this on the day before market day too. Really, Kara, can't you rearrange the vet appointment? And a *whole* day? Surely you can come back when the cat has had its bloody injections!'

Lydia's furious reaction was thoroughly predictable, as it meant that she herself had to get up at 4.30 a.m. to drive over to the flower market in Penrigan, the place where they were certain to purchase the finest and freshest flowers for the shop and stall. For the past five years, this weekly task had been entrusted to Kara, who quite enjoyed doing it and wasn't afraid of the responsibility – not that she got any thanks. Since handing over the keys of the company van for

Kara to use at her leisure, Lydia felt justified in demanding that she work ridiculous hours. And Kara, used to the many unreasonable requests from her uptight fifty-year-old employer, just complied for the sake of a quiet life.

But today, for once, Kara had held her ground. Taking James Bond to the vet wasn't a full-on lie, as he did need his annual cat flu injection. The fact that she had told Lydia he always got a weird reaction afterwards was, on the other hand, a downright stinker. But as Kara didn't know how she'd feel once she'd done what she needed to do, rather than take the chance of getting upset at work, she had decided that the best tactic was to just not be there.

With funds so tight, she couldn't afford to take James Bond to the vet any more unless it was an emergency. Her old family cat, Bawcock, had lived to the venerable age of twenty-two and he'd never had an injection in his life. The one and only time he'd had to go to the vet was when his ear was hanging off after a fight with the next door's tabby. Kara's mother had insisted he be treated right away, but Kara's grandad Harry had been round and said that the battered moggy was as brave as old Tom Bawcock, his name-sake, and that animals healed themselves quite ably. Grandad Harry would have been quite happy to clean up the raw bits with disinfectant and put a plaster over them. But Doryty Moon had got her way, as she always did. The beloved pet was patched up and to this day Kara still hadn't found out who the old tom's namesake was and what he had done that was so great.

Chapter 3

Frank's was a stand-alone oblong brick building located right on the estuary-wall edge. It had a gaily striped awning and a pink neon sign saying plainly, Frank's Café. To the right of the building there was a roped-off concrete area housing fixed wooden table benches with red and white sunshades for use in the summer months. Now that the weather was warming up, the side hatch where you'd queue for delicious home-made Cornish ice creams would soon be opening up, too. At the end of the day, seven days a week, market stall-holders and visitors alike would companionably unwind at Frank's and watch the sun go down over the sea as boats of all shapes and sizes plied the busy waterway.

Kara loved looking down to the estuary mouth, where the left point of Crowsbridge, scattered with its white dots of houses and open green fields, stared almost belligerently across at the rugged cliffs and big posh houses of Hartmouth Head. From Frank's, the gap out to sea appeared just a few metres across. Up close, it became a wide window to the infinite ocean stretching ahead.

The café wasn't licensed, but Big Frank Brady, the muscly tattooed Irishman who ran the place, brewed his own magnificent dark ale, serving it in iced-tea bottles straight from the under-counter fridge. His sloe-infused gin also passed perfectly as a blackcurrant cordial; poured on ice with refreshing tonic water, it made for a perfect illegal summer cocktail. Inside the café was an old-fashioned jukebox, where hits mainly from the 1950s and 1960s blared inside and out, rain or shine, in an attempt to encourage customers to come in. In fact, Big Frank had been known to turn the volume up full blast if he suspected anyone of even daring to walk past and across the road to the Ferryboat, the white-painted pub on the corner.

Frank's was set out in the style of an old-school American diner, sporting red leather booths, white Formica tables and a jazzily tiled floor. There were six high metal stools where you could prop yourself up at the bar and, if not wanting some hooky booze, you could choose one of the milkshakes, hot drinks, or plentiful juices on offer. As for the snack menu, everything on it was freshly made and moreish. The walls were adorned with black-and-white prints of the Hollywood stars of yesteryear. Kara particularly loved the one of Audrey Hepburn in *Breakfast at Tiffany's* – the famous one in which she is wearing a gorgeous, tight black dress and seductively holding a cigarette holder. Kara sadly acknowledged that even if she signed up a personal trainer of great ability for the rest of her life, she could never look like that. Her double D-cup boobs would not fit on such a tiny frame, for instead of being blessed with Audrey's waif-like figure, her own body sported ample thighs that led up to a large, round bottom. With a slim waist, she was in perfect hourglass proportion – just not the proportions she'd have chosen. The older locals of the estuary town of Hartmouth didn't much care for change, so when Big Frank Brady and his long-term partner Monique had arrived in a flurry of paint tins and extravagant interiors, there had been a bit of a to-do. But as with anything, time is not only a healer but a leveller as well, and despite the completely random concept of a Hollywood-themed café in a Cornish town, pretty soon Frank's and its renowned all-day breakfasts and frothy coffees were as much a visitor pull as the stalls and stores of Ferry Lane Market.

The owner of Frank's took up a lot of space. Six-feet four of it, in fact. Big Frank Brady had a brooding gypsy-type look about him, with black collar-length hair and brown eyes so dark they were impossible to read. His full lips were the envy of many of the young girls who insisted on paying fortunes for false fillers. His tattoo sleeve was a work of art, displaying angels, birds, and at the top a young, naked Monique with one arm in the air and pouting red lips of her own.

Kara found something very sexy about good tattoos on a man. Her boyfriend, Jago, hated any kind of body art. 'Tramp stamps' he would call them. With her love of flowers, she had always wanted a tiny rose tattoo, somewhere discreet, but he had been drunk when she had mentioned it and, slamming his hand down on to the table, he had labelled her a slut for even thinking about it.

The early morning rush had subsided, and Big Frank greeted Kara with his lopsided grin. 'If it isn't the lovely Kara Moon. It's not like you to be down here at this time on a market day.' He carried on wiping the glass counter.

'I've taken a day off.'

'Have you, now. Bet that's got old Twisty Knickers' knickers in a bigger twist than usual.' He laughed. 'And try saying that after a Guinness or three.'

'Yes,' was all Kara could manage, her face falling instead of smiling.

'Who or what else has been upsetting you now, then?'

'I don't want to talk about it.' She sighed deeply, then looked away quickly to stop tears from falling.

Seeing this, Frank reached his big hand over the counter and gently stroked Kara's cheek.

'I've got your back, Kara Moon, you know that, don't you?'

Kara's throat began to burn. She nodded. When her mother had abruptly decided to up and leave her family when Kara was just thirteen years old, Frank had only just arrived in Hartmouth – but on finding out what had happened, he had been a silent helper. The best kind. Additions to his orders from the big cash-and-carry place had been delivered straight to her dad. And many a lasagne or bag of cakes would be handed to the distraught man to take home to his family after a long day working on the ferry. Both her dad, Joe, and her Grandad Harry had a lot of time for Big Frank Brady. A mutual respect.

'Coffee?'

'Yes, to take away please. One for Dad and I'd better get Billy one, or I'll never hear the end of it. Oh, and a couple of bottles of water too, please. And, um, two of those custard doughnuts.'

'Coming up.'

Frank quickly returned with takeout cups in a cardboard holder. 'So, that's one white, no sugar, and one extra milky with three sugars for the lad. Two chilled waters and the cakes are in here.' He balanced a bag between the cups.

'Memory of an elephant you've got, Frank Brady.'

He then gestured at his flat wide nose. 'Not quite the trunk though. Too much boxing.' He winked.

Kara reached for her purse and paid. 'No Monique today, then?' she asked.

'She's gone to Paris to see her sister. Got to let her have a break sometimes.'

They both laughed. Half-French, half-English, Monique rarely spent much time at the café. In fact, she rarely spent much time in Cornwall. Rumour had it, Monique had been working in Las Vegas when she had met bad boy Frank there on a gambling weekend. She had subsequently saved him from a violent lifestyle by moving him to Cornwall, where her great-aunt from the Cornish side of her family had just left her a wonderful large and sprawling four-bedroomed house on the edge of the town.

A formidable woman, Monique still did the odd bit of directing dance shows around the world, and if not doing that she would be either relaxing in their beautiful home or visiting family and friends. The couple spent little time together but when they did, they made it count and for them, the arrangement somehow worked.

Kara picked the cardboard tray up from the counter. Just as she was about to leave, Frank turned from the customer he was serving and said in her ear, 'I had a young lad in here earlier. Gutted he was. Been dumped by his girl.'

Kara wasn't quite sure where Frank was going with this.

He finished up with: 'I told him to get over it. That some break-ups are meant for wake-ups.'

A watery smile was all she could manage in return.

Chapter 4

Kara couldn't help but smirk at the loud wolf whistle that greeted her on arrival at the ferry quay. It was Billy Dillon, the handsome assistant ferryman. As she made her way past the line of cars waiting in the queue for the next short trip over to Crowsbridge, he winked and waved at her. He then deftly opened the metal gates, causing a flurry of engines to rev to life and the vehicles on board to drive off the flat ferry float, after which they would head either to the main road out of town to their left, or straight up the steep incline of Ferry Lane towards the market.

Meanwhile, Kara's dad was carefully manoeuvring the ancient tug that pulled the ferry float. It came to rest with a small thud against the buoy on the side of the creaky platform on the quay. On finishing this task and seeing his daughter, he let go of the boat's wheel and waved at her with both hands.

Oh, how Joe Moon loved that old red and yellow tug, named *Happy Hart*. The very same one that had been used since her Grandad Harry had taken over the ferry business from the Trevelyan family in the 1950s and had stayed in the Moon family ever since. The joining of the car ferry float in the 1960s had created the iconic shape of the ferry on the River Hart, the old-fashioned charm of which had become a tourist attraction for those visiting Hartmouth and Crowsbridge.

Billy came to Kara's aid and took the coffees from her. 'Kerry baby,' he said. Only three special people in her world called her Kerry, and Billy was one of them. Her mother had wanted to christen her plain 'Kara', the short form of Kerensa, the Cornish name meaning Love, but her father had insisted, and on a windy 13 September in Hartmouth General Hospital, Kerensa Anne Moon, a second daughter to Joe and Doryty Moon, was born. 'Better be one for me, or I'll be having to slap that gorgeous aris of yours.' Kara was amused by both his whistles and unaffected lapses into cockney rhyming slang. The word 'aris' had a complicated history: 'bottle and glass' to rhyme with 'arse' had been shortened to 'Aristotle' (to rhyme with 'bottle') and then shortened once more to 'aris'.

For one glorious second, Billy's cheekiness had made her forget the reason why she was here. But she couldn't let this go unanswered. Kara turned around and, keeping her face dead straight, she bent over and did a quick twerk, shimmying her denim-covered booty in Billy's direction.

Billy tutted. 'You're such a little tease.'

'And you're so immature.' Kara smirked. 'One of these days, Billy Dillon, someone will slap your face for being so rude.'

'And one of these days, Kerry Moon, you *will* go on that date with me.'

The 'date' joke had been a long-standing banter between Billy and Kara ever since the lad had started working on the ferry as a teenager. A compact five-feet nine, with dark brown hair cut short with a floppy fringe, he had long-lashed, almond-shaped eyes that were a unique, almost violet dark blue, and the ferryman's uniform of long black shorts and white T-shirt and hoody suited his lean but honed physique. His face was already deeply tanned from the lovely weather they had been having. He had dimples to die for, which not only made him look younger than his twenty-five years, but also made him a big hit with the ladies.

'Come on, lad,' Joe Moon said with a smile on his face. 'Stop flirting with my girl and get these cars on, will you.' He jumped across on to the float and kissed Kara on the cheek. At sixty-one, he was fit for his age. Kara had got her height and colouring from her mother, for her father stood at an average five-foot ten and his once fair hair had turned white overnight – the night his wife left. With his cheekbones set high on a ruddy face, and light blue eyes framed by wrinkles, you could see that he had been an extremely good-looking man in his youth. His thin frame was, however, proof of his broken heart never quite mending.

'I just gave Billy coffee and cakes for the pair of you.'

'Thanks, love. What do I owe you?'

'Don't be silly. If I can't buy my old dad a coffee some-times, then what's the world coming to?'

Joe put his thumbs up to Billy to shut the metal ferry gates ready for departure. 'Why aren't you working today? What's going on?' he asked his daughter. But before she could answer, a black and white Smart car screeched in, nearly knocking Billy over in its rush to take the eighth and final space on the ferry. 'Now I am confused,' Joe went on. 'It's market day, after all – and yet look, Star is here, too. All at the last minute, mind.'

Kara sighed with relief at her friend's arrival, since Star was not known for her timekeeping.

Joe checked his watch again. 'OK. We need to get going. I'll see you on your way back.' Respecting her silence, he placed his hand on her arm. 'I love you, Kerry Anne.'

'Remember to eat those doughnuts, won't you?' Kara

ordered. She was forever trying to feed her dad up. She then headed over to her best friend's car and climbed in.

'All right, Mr M?' the pretty, long-haired, blue-eyed blonde shouted out to Joe from the car window. He lifted his hand to her and headed to get behind the wheel of the *Happy Hart*.

Knowing that Star wasn't the best driver, Billy pointed to the DON'T FORGET TO PUT YOUR HANDBRAKE ON sign and shouted down the float to them: 'Ladies. Hope you've got yours hard up?'

Joe Moon shook his head in disbelief.

'No, but I bet you have.' Star laughed, then turned to her friend. 'Ready?'

Kara made a little groaning noise. 'As I'll ever be.'

Chapter 5

Billy blew exaggerated air kisses to them both as Star revved her little car's engine and they drove off the ferry, heading towards the road that ran through the centre of Crowsbridge.

Steren (Star) Bligh had been Kara's best friend since primary school. It had been a sheer coincidence that a girl with a name meaning Star should partner up with a girl called Moon – and so far, it had proved to be a match made in heaven. Later on, a dream came true for them both when the unit next to the florist's became free and Star was able to set up shop as STAR Crystals & Jewellery and move into the flat above with her seventeen-year-old daughter.

'Did you see Lydia this morning?' Kara asked, worried.

'No. I deliberately kept out of her way. I heard her rattling on about how tired she was and I didn't want her to ask me any questions in case I said the wrong thing.'

'Tired?' Kara scoffed. 'That's the first time in five years she's had to get up to go to the flower market.'

'Well, that's a good thing,' Star said. 'It's about time she remembered how much you do for her.'

Kara screwed up her face. 'I'm so sorry to pull you off your stall at such short notice, but my work van is so recognisable, and, well . . . I just need you with me today.'

'This is where having a daughter when I was still at school

does have its advantages. And you know how much Skye loves working my market stall on her own.'

Kara pulled one of the bottles of water she'd bought earlier out of her bag and wedged it in the holder by the gear stick. 'For you. Nice dress, by the way.'

Star was wearing one of her trademark flowery maxi-frocks. Her long, poker-straight hair, so fair it was almost white, was pushed back with a silver hairband with a tiny diamanté butterfly clipped to it. Dangly silver seahorse earrings finished her look.

But Star wasn't having any of Kara's small talk. 'Why today, Kar?'

Kara suddenly gestured frantically for Star to pull over. 'We can't be getting there early.'

As they parked in the lay-by just up from the ferry, Kara began to explain. 'Today, because, well . . .' She sighed.

'Take your time,' Star said kindly.

'You've told me to leave him so many times, but you did also say that it had to be the right time for me and – well, last night he came in drunk again and he was being his usual vile inebriated self.'

'He's such an arse.' Star spoke her mind.

'And then – I can't believe I'm telling you this . . .' Kara paused. Then with pain in her voice, she went on, 'James Bond came rushing in as he does, made Jago jump and the bastard only went to kick him. How I managed to stop him, I don't know. It was so awful. I didn't dare say anything then as I just wanted him to fall asleep without a load of verbal abuse.'

'Oh, Kara.'

'But what I did do once he was asleep, I checked his phone. And you know me – I've never gone there, not once. Not once in eight years, to be exact. I've never been through his pockets, either. But last night something snapped. I'd had enough. Nobody hurts an innocent animal.'

'And nobody should hurt you,' Star replied gently.

'To be fair, he's never touched me.'

'But he has hurt you with his words and the way he controls you, which in my eyes is just as bad.' There was a silence between them, then Star added, 'I can't believe his phone wasn't locked.'

'It was, but I had watched him open it enough times to work out the code.' Kara's voice was unsteady. 'I must have been ready to find out.'

Star became animated. 'Yes, yes you were – you *are*! Bloody hell, it's hot for April.' She pressed the button that took the black cloth roof of her little car right back and down.

'He *has* been seeing someone and he's meeting her today, and what's more, it looks like he's been doing so for the past umpteenth Fridays and beyond.'

'Mate, you seem incredibly calm in the circumstances.' Star undid her water bottle and took a sip.

'Last night I felt sick, but this morning I'm strangely fine. The signs were there, I just didn't want to see them. We haven't had sex for months – and who wears Gucci aftershave to the bloody Jobcentre? This is well overdue, Star. I've been hanging on to this ridiculous relationship for years.' Kara added determinedly, 'I can do this.'

'Yes, you can.'

'I checked the savings account, too.' Kara made a little moaning sound. 'You know, the one *he* told me not to tell him the password for as it could be our little secret nest egg and he didn't want to touch it?'

'Go on.' Seeming to guess what was coming next, Star placed her hand on Kara's as her voice began to crack.

'Anyway – nada. Zero. He's had the lot. So not only has he been clearing the blue pot, he's spent all that too – and on *her*, no doubt, whoever she is. Why am I surprised? I've been such a bloody fool.'

'No, no you haven't. Sadly, love is stronger than pride sometimes and that wanker is a sneaky dick of a sociopath. I don't know how you didn't go crazy.' Star bashed her hand down on the steering wheel. 'I'm getting cross for you. I'd have had his bollocks off. Where did you put all that anger? I'm the one who preaches peace and love, but I don't think even I could have coped with all this as calmly as you are.'

'I sat up half the night and wrote him a letter. I cried, I ranted. I want him to read it. It's the best way.'

Star thought that only dear sweet Kara would write a letter in a situation like this. 'Please say you are telling him to leave.'

'Yes, but I don't know how I'll manage on my own.' Kara's strength suddenly vanished. She blubbered, 'He's always told me that I would be lost without him.'

'Look at me.' Star took her friend's face in both hands. 'You will be fine. The cock has been spending all your money anyway.'

'I'll have to pay the council tax on my own and bills and—' Kara panicked.

'You will be eligible for a single supplement on the council tax and bills will probably be less with him not in the flat all day,' Star replied practically, then added, 'And he'd better be taking that stinking terrapin of his.'

'Depends where he goes, I guess. If he goes to his mother, she's far too uptight to take on the both of them.'

'Well, neither Sid Vicious nor Jago Ellis will be your responsibility any more. Imagine how good that will feel – getting not one, but two reptiles out of your life.'

'What if he doesn't have anywhere to go?' Despite everything, Kara was still programmed to think of Jago's welfare.

'It's tough shit, Kara. It really is.' Star's Cornish twang became heightened in frustration. 'He's been playing you for a fool for years and he's far too wily to be without a roof for long. He's made his own bed – in another woman's house! Let him lie between her sheets now. She can put up with him, poor cow. Now, where are we going?'

Chapter 6

As it was such a lovely day and he needed to stall for time, Jago Ellis had decided to walk the two miles from the Jobcentre to the end of Crowsbridge High Street and on to Crowsbridge Hall, the Cornwall Trust property and previous home to the past six generations of the Penhaligon family. With the Easter holidays upon them, queues had already started to form along the winding drive that led up to the grand Queen Anne-era white mansion set within stunning gardens.

It had been a year ago when he had first met Rachel Penhaligon, twenty-six-year-old daughter of Lord and Lady Penhaligon, the current owners of Crowsbridge Hall. It wasn't long before he'd learned that Rachel was heiress to an exceptionally large fortune. He'd gone to the Hall to enquire about a gardening job in order to keep both the Jobcentre and Kara happy. And when the promiscuous beauty had made it quite clear that she could show him something far sweeter to bed in the lodge at the bottom of the drive than the begonias he'd been tasked to plant by the head gardener, he couldn't believe his luck.

And from that day forward, every Friday without fail, Rachel Penhaligon had got the bit of rough she had been craving for. And Jago Ellis had embarked on an illicit tryst with a filthy posh heiress. Rachel was content with their once-a-week arrangement, not wanting anything more than fun and good sex. She hadn't even asked whether Jago had a girlfriend, thinking that as he always had to get the last ferry home to Hartmouth, he probably did.

Today, she had grudgingly promised her parents that she would oversee the busy visitors' café in the morning as they were short-staffed, and not knowing what time she would be free, she had suggested Jago make his way there. She could sit and have a coffee with him and would warm him up with a mistress-gardener role play, *Lady Chatterley's Lover*-style – the very same scenario that had turned her on right from the start.

Their normal weekly routine was that Jago would go straight to her lodge, where the door would be left on the latch. He would creep up the stairs to find Rachel more often than not in stockings and suspenders, teetering precariously on high heels on her huge queen-size bed whilst brandishing a riding whip. Today, with her parents away at their holiday home in Puerto Banus, Jago was hoping she might even be able to take him up to the main house where there was a private pool and Jacuzzi to add to the fun.

Rachel winked at him as he strode towards the counter. Then, leaning forward to show a hint of cleavage, she whispered in his ear that she wasn't wearing any knickers and that he should wait for her on the bench nearest the lake where she would be taking down his credentials sooner rather than later.

Chapter 7

Joe Moon pulled two faded red fabric fold-up chairs from the old tug and set them on the Hartmouth quayside. The ferry crossings had kept to the same timetable since he had started working with his dad as a teenager. He knew them off by heart and could recite them like a mantra – something he had to do on a regular basis.

'Eight until dusk, January to December. Nine until four on a Sunday. Closed Christmas Day. Weather dependent, o' course.'

His daughters had shown no interest in taking the helm and if he was honest with himself, Joe was quite glad they hadn't. With his old-fashioned values, he felt it wasn't the right work or acceptable hours for a woman to undertake. So, he was rather hoping for a grandson to be born to one of them, a sturdy lad who would want to continue the family business. However, so far, the signs were not looking good. Jenifer, his eldest, had turned forty, and was more in love with her international banking career than she had been with any man – that he knew of, anyway. And with his youngest stuck in a relationship with that useless good-for-nothing Jago, his hopes weren't high for the continuation of the Moon name, and that made him very sad. He had always thought that his second-born, with her kind heart and generous nature, would make such a marvellous mother, too.

It was a glorious day. The sky was home to not a single cloud; the still expanse of the wide estuary offered twinkling reflections from the warm April sun and the seafaring sound of yachts' halyards clanging was carried on the soft breeze. Joe sat down with a joyous little sigh at the prospect of a moment's peace. Market mornings were always busy. There were the same number of crossings, but always a full ferry.

Looking across to the Crowsbridge quay, he could just make out a couple of cars already queuing to take the ferry across to Hartmouth. They would have to wait; they were early. He was never late. Tipping his head back and shutting his eyes just for a moment, he could also hear the faint murmur of the bustling market away at the top of the hill. He slowly opened his eyes, took a deep breath, then signalled Billy to join him.

When Harry Moon, Joe's dad, had reluctantly retired in his late seventies, it became obvious that running the ferry wasn't a one-man job. And with Billy Dillon not wanting to be stuck behind a fruit and veg stall for the rest of his life, the then teenager had snapped up the opportunity to work on the water.

Billy did his final safety checks, then sat down next to Joe. Peering into the paper bag his daughter had given him, Joe licked his lips. Custard doughnuts, his favourite. One of these would do him until teatime, now.

He offered one to Billy. 'Here, lad. Elevenses.' Joe then poured coffee from his Thermos flask into the now empty takeout cups that Kara had given them earlier. Taking a sip, the young ferryman winced then quickly ran his tongue over the sugary doughnut to make up for the lack of sweetness in his warm drink.

Joe spoke with his mouth full. 'Is my Kerry all right, do you think?'

'I don't know, Joe. Something's up. It's odd for both those girls to be going over the water together on a market day.'

Joe frowned, then said, 'There are times when I just want to go round and scream at that bastard she lives with. She never seems happy now and she was always such a smiley child.' He cleared his throat. 'Well, until her mum left, that is. Old Cora Blunt, who lives a few doors up from them, delights in telling me that she often hears them rowing – my Kerry and Jago, that is. And sometimes things are thrown.' Joe clenched a fist. 'If he ever so much as laid a finger on my girl, I think I would kill him.'

'Do you think he does? Hit her, I mean?' Billy was horrified that this might be the case, and at the same time he was surprised to witness this outpouring of feeling from the usually private Joe Moon; the older man was very close-mouthed where his family were concerned. The young ferryman knew that Jago's reputation wasn't a particularly good one, in that he was known to smoke weed and be job-shy, but he seemed too much of a wimp to be a bully. Kara often looked unhappy, but Billy had never suspected there was any kind of violence involved in their relationship. He did, however, continue to live in hope that the girl would see sense and the couple would split up. Something that would please both himself and Joe, but for different reasons.

He said aloud, 'Because if he does ever hurt her, I would be right behind you in giving him a good hiding.' A short silence then, 'Joe?'

'Yes, lad?'

Billy hesitated for a second. 'Tell me to piss off if I'm being too nosy, but what did happen with Mrs Moon? Kerry freezes up if I even dare to mention her name.'

'I know that look,' Joe nodded. 'The same way she clams

31

up when I try and ask her about that bastard.' He then sighed deeply. 'It's a bit of a long story.'

Billy checked his watch. 'We've got some time.'

Joe sat back in his chair and began his sad story. 'It happened twenty years ago, and yet I remember it like yesterday. Granted, I worked long hours on here, but she never went without, Doryty, my missus.' He paused. 'I met her right here – on this spot, actually. She had a week in Crowsbridge with her sister and came over on the ferry to check out the market. Just one catch of those piercing green eyes and swish of those long auburn locks and I fell for her hook, line and sinker.'

'I can imagine,' Billy replied softly, knowing the effect that Kara had on him whenever he caught sight of her.

'We didn't mess about. She was twenty-one then, so old enough to decide,' Joe went on. 'We married within a year of meeting and she seemed only too happy to move down here and escape the rat race. She did sometimes say she missed the faster pace of London – that was where she was brought up, see, lived in a block of flats near Marble Arch – but she never seemed to fret to the extent I should worry. I showered her with jewellery, gave her money for clothes, funded visits for her to go by train to visit her sister in London. Gave her anything she wanted, really.' Joe took a drink of his coffee. His doughnut remained untouched.

'It was when our Jen went away to university that she started to get itchy feet,' he resumed. 'My Kerry had always been a daddy's girl. Doryty wasn't that enamoured with motherhood and would have been quite happy with just our Jen. In fact, if it weren't for me, she wouldn't have had any kids at all, I don't think. When an unplanned Kerry came along, the thought of more nappies and sleepless nights threw her slightly. She didn't even want maternity leave from the job she had taken in Penrigan when Jen had started school, either. We had a few tough years. Then when Jen flew the nest, Doryty became really agitated. Not because she'd lost a child, but I think more likely because if we hadn't have had Kerry, she would have been free to leave here. She'd always harped on about going abroad, so I decided to surprise the two of them – our Kerry and the wife, that is – and booked a hotel in Majorca. Beautiful it was, four stars, right on its own private beach with wall-to-wall sunshine.'

'Nice one,' Billy said, interrupting Joe's sorrowful soliloquy.

'Our Kerry was thirteen then and excited that at last we were venturing abroad.' Joe took a big mouthful of coffee. 'As for Doryty, it was as if she had had her eyes opened to a whole new world, and I suppose she had. You get used to being down here, by the sea; neither of us had travelled a lot and where I couldn't wait to get home to the ferry and our comfy cottage, something switched in her.'

'So, I guess you all came back, and she realised life down here wasn't enough for her.'

Joe shook his head. 'Worse than that,' he said in a low voice. 'She did a proper *Shirley Valentine* on me and went off with the hotel manager.'

'Shirley Valentine?' Billy looked bemused.

'I forget how young you are, lad. It was a film from the eighties. I'll let you google it. It's about a wife who leaves her husband and goes to live abroad. She's bored at home, see.'

'Blimey. That's so harsh,' was all the lad could manage, knowing that if the look of distress on his boss's face wasn't so great, he might have burst out laughing at the absurdity of it all.

'Yep. Didn't even come home with us. Said there was no point in trying to persuade her otherwise and that her mind was fully made up. She kissed our Kerry on the cheek, promised she would be in touch and walked out of the hotel room. Just. Like. That.'

'And was she? In touch, I mean?' Billy finished his doughnut and licked the remaining heavenly sweet custard from between his fingers.

'We never saw her again. Obviously, smarmy Jesus – yes, that really was his name – had something far greater than bread and fishes on offer,' Joe said bitterly. 'It didn't affect our Jen so much as she was up and away, but Kerry became a different girl after losing her mum like that. It proper shook her up. Terrible thing to do to a youngster.'

Billy let out a soft whistle. 'I'm so sorry. And . . . is your wife still with this Jesus fella?'

'Don't know, don't care. She sends a birthday card every year to our Kerry. I don't know about Jen. I haven't asked and she's never mentioned it. It adds insult to injury, really. I still to this day don't understand her actions. I loved that woman.' Joe scratched his head. 'Maybe she'd had it all planned, I don't know. I get it that she could have fallen out of love with me, but to leave her own daughter like that. So bloody selfish,' he muttered. 'I've been worried about my sweet girl ever since. I'm sure one of the reasons she hasn't ventured abroad is that she is still scarred by that awful bloody holiday. I blame myself for arranging it now. I don't want what happened to ruin both of our lives.'

'Oh, Joe. That's so shit.' And Billy meant it. 'Have the girls not seen or spoken to their mum at all, then?'

'No,' Joe replied. 'Well, Kerry hasn't, I know that. It's as if they came from different pods, those daughters of mine.

Jen is more like her mother, a magpie, attracted to nice things and as secretive as a squirrel. Whereas my Kerry is as gentle as a dove – sometimes to her detriment.'

'So, you didn't divorce Mrs Moon, then?'

'No . . .' Joe's voice tailed off. 'I couldn't face corresponding with her and she's never come to me.'

'But what if you found someone decent who you wanted to marry, Joe?'

Joe laughed. 'Me with another woman? Despite all of this, Doryty is still the love of my life. I don't need anyone else.' Suddenly he switched back to work mode. 'Right, this car ferry isn't going to cross the water itself, is it? Come on, lad, we'd better get going.'

The young ferryman jumped up and put the folded chairs under his arm.

'And Billy?' Joe added.

'Yes, boss?'

'I'd rather you didn't discuss this with anyone, especially not my Kerry. You said yourself, she doesn't like to talk about it.'

'I swear.'

And knowing Billy so well, Joe Moon knew that his words would be safe behind those wise, albeit young lips.

Chapter 8

Twenty minutes later, Kara ran back across the car park to her friend's little convertible and leaped into the passenger seat, her face sallow with anguish.

'Quick, drive! Let's get the hell out of here,' she said. Her hands were shaking.

The barrier to the Cornwall Trust car park seemed to take an age to lift and once it had, Star turned left and drove along the main road towards the ferry crossing and home to Hartmouth.

Kara put a hand to her forehead and pushed back her fringe. Tears slowly fell down her face. Star squeezed her friend's knee gently. 'In your own time, darling.'

'I've done it.' Kara pulled a pack of tissues from her bag, removed one and blew her nose loudly. 'I've bloody done it.'

'I'm proud of you, mate.' Star removed her hand to change gear and allowed her friend to speak again when she was ready. It felt good to have the wind rushing through their hair, Star's flowing behind her in a long, white-blond stream, like a pair of Afghan Hound's ears.

'There was no drama.' Kara had to raise her voice to be heard above the road noise. 'He was sat with a woman, around my age. Quite pretty, dark hair in a sleek bob, nose too big for her face. And so skinny! I recognised her from somewhere, then realised it was from an article I'd seen in a copy of *Cornish Living* magazine I'd been flicking through at the dentist the other week.'

'Oh! That's weird.'

'Not really. She's only the posh bloody daughter of the Penhaligons – you know, Lord and Lady Penhaligon who own the house. Her name's Rachel, the one who is always online on the arm of a Hugo or Bartholomew at various celebrity haunts.'

'I've heard of her. I thought she lived in London?'

'She did, until her drug habit caught up with her, evidently.'

Star became animated. 'I can't bloody believe it! No disrespect, Kar, but what would she want with someone like Jago, then?'

'Exactly what I thought. But there they were, sitting opposite each other at the edge of the lake on one of those fixed wooden bench things. I've been here a couple of times with wedding flowers, but never actually in the grounds. There's an ornamental lake with swans swimming around and willow trees overhanging the water. I think maybe the Penhaligons were trying to replicate Monet's paintings of lilies as there is a Japanese bridge over the lake and the most gorgeous water lilies beginning to open.'

'Kara, just get to the point,' Star said kindly but firmly.

'I'm getting to it,' Kara sighed. 'I watched them for a second and could tell from their flirty body language that they are definitely at it.'

'Oh my God! What did you do?'

'Jago was sitting with his back to me, so I walked calmly over to their table. I say calmly, but my heart felt like it was actually going to explode out of my chest and I nearly did projectile vomit over the pair of them.'

Losing concentration in anticipation of the expected revelation, Star veered over to the wrong side of the road and was tooted at loudly by an oncoming white van man, who waved his fist at her.

'Mate! Be careful.' Kara took a large swig from her water bottle.

'Sorry, go on.' Star fixed her eyes back on the road as her friend then began to talk at a hundred words a minute.

'So, I tapped him lightly on the shoulder and said, "Excuse me, sorry to disturb you two, but I saw this fall out of your pocket in the café." On hearing my voice, he just spun around; his eyes were so wide, like a startled rabbit. But even then, he didn't say my name out loud. He just stood up from the bench, took the envelope on which I had plainly written *Jago*, then waited for me to erupt.'

'Shit, Kar, what did you say?'

'I said nothing, just lifted my head, pushed out my boobs – he always did love my big boobs – and walked away without uttering another word.'

'You're amazing. Did he not say anything, anything at all?'

Kara attempted a laugh, but it came out as a sort of squeak. 'He pathetically called "Thank you" after me.'

'What! Jesus. So, he didn't even come after you?'

'No. Of course he didn't. Jago Ellis would want to keep all options open.' Kara's voice had a slight shake to it now. 'When I got back up to the café I glanced round and there he was, still sitting in the same place, and to make it even worse, it looked like they were both laughing.'

'Oh, Kar, I'm so sorry. You do realise you just gave him a complete Get Out of Jail Free card, though?'

'Not really. Just seeing the look of terror on his face was

enough.' Kara put her head in her hands and then lifted it to scream into the warm air as they sped along and back to the ferry: '*Eight years of my life!* Eight years I've wasted, Star.'

'You can't look at it like that. Time to move forward now. Focus on you, that's what matters.'

But with her gut still doing somersaults, Kara couldn't take in the sense of her friend's words. She carried on, 'The only thing that gave me a slight bit of satisfaction was what you said about letting him lie in someone else's bed. Because I would put a bet on it that when he tells Lady snooty bloody Penhaligon that he wants her for more than just a fling, he won't be lying in her bed for too much longer.' She then took a deep breath and giving it ten decibels, shouted, '*Deluded fucking wanker!*' Then promptly burst into tears.

A shocked Star, unused to hearing her normally placid friend swear so vehemently, veered to the left this time, only just managing to avoid a cyclist.

Chapter 9

Ferry Lane Market was situated at the top of the hill at the far end of Ferry Lane. The market consisted of twelve brick-built Victorian terraced houses, six per row facing each other on either side of the lane. Each house consisted of a ground-floor shop unit with a flat above. The shops were open daily, but on a Friday and Saturday the shopkeepers brought their wares out for sale into the open air, setting them out on their individual stalls. And that was when Ferry Lane Market and the historic town of Hartmouth really came to life.

Some of the stallholders lived above their shops; others rented their flats out as residential or holiday lets. A car park, convenient for unloading goods, sat at the back end of Ferry Lane. The rest of the street, which led down to the ferry crossing and the Ferry View Apartments, was made up of more terraced houses, cottages really, with different-coloured front doors opening directly on to cobbles. It really was very quaint. The sense of a place untouched by time, plus the history of the ferry crossing and the view down to the sea, made Ferry Lane Market worthy of its tourist attraction label.

As you walked up the lane from the ferry, on the right side of the market was Passion Flowers the florist's, STAR Crystals and Jewellery, then the Hartmouth Gallery, where local artist Glanna Pascoe sold her own work and that of other artists (for a commission). Next to the gallery was a wonderful artisan bakery where you could buy scones as big as saucers. Clarke's the butchers and a stall that sold old books and vinyl records completed that side of the road. On the other side, the units were made up of the Dillon family's fruit and veg stall, a clothes stall that sold all sorts of wonderful vintage items, Nigel's Catch, the fishmonger, a stall selling home-made fudge and local honey, and one stall that was loaded with antiques. To finish off, right at the end of the lane was Tasty Pasties, in Kara's opinion quite possibly the most aptly named of all the stalls, and on which she often blamed the size of her thighs.

Last year, Philip Gilmour, the eccentric owner of said pasty shop, had hinted that he was hoping to expand his tasty empire to a small café on the side as well. However, rumour had it that after a meeting with Big Frank to discuss the matter, the subject was swiftly dropped, and Philip had since been seen driving around in a brand-new Mini estate.

As Ferry Lane Market was always busy, rain or shine, the independent owners were able to sell their wares at competitive prices. A unit on Ferry Lane Market was hot property, and should one come up for sale – a very rare occurrence – there was usually a multi-enveloped auction.

'Don't tell me: after his visit to the vet's, old James Bond is shaken but not purred,' was the witty quip made by Charlie Dillon, owner of the fruit and vegetable stall, when Kara arrived the next morning to set up her stall.

'Very good,' she replied, only just managing to keep a straight face. 'Almost funny, in fact.'

'Oi!' Then Charlie tapped his nose with one meaty finger. 'Watch out, the boss is in before you, for once,' he whispered, pointing up at the Passion Flowers' pink and white fascia board, then went back to arranging broccoli on to his green display grass matting. Kara noticed that his bald head was slightly pink from yesterday's sunshine, and his cheeky smile was the same infectious one that his son Billy had. To her mind, Charlie could easily pass for a gangster in a Quentin Tarantino film.

Now she rolled her eyes at him, said, 'Wish me luck,' and pushed open the glass shop door.

The interior of Passion Flowers was painted all white. There was a tiny office, toilet and kitchen to the back, then a middle section with two large tables, where Lydia and Kara made up the bouquets and displays, and the front area, which contained an array of beautiful blooms in pretty metal buckets. The smell was intoxicating. The window display was always simple, with the same white-twigged tree depicting the season or an occasion. Today it was decorated with various Easter-themed floral baubles and fluffy yellow and white chicks.

Other gifts, including ornate pots and vases in varying sizes, colours and materials were also up for sale, displayed on shelves throughout the shop. From the back of the kitchen, you could walk out into a small oblong garden, which weirdly, despite it being connected to a flower shop, had no flowers in it. It was plain and uninviting, a bit like its owner, and housed a tiny patio with a small round table and two matching chairs. An area of artificial lawn led up to a back gate and driveway, room enough to park the sign-written Passion Flowers' van, which Kara mainly used. Alongside it was parked Lydia's fancy new black Mercedes.

With Lydia not short of a penny or two and not wanting 'dirty strangers traipsing around my property', she didn't rent out the flat above the shop. Instead, she used it as a storage area for when they had big events like weddings or funerals; the flowers could be laid out in the cool corridor, ready for delivery. Plus, if a big order of vases and gifts came in, the new stock could be taken upstairs and not left to block up the shop floor. As with some of the other flats along Ferry Lane, Lydia's had an exterior metal fire escape. Handy if she ever changed her mind and did decide to rent it out.

The front room of Lydia's flat upstairs was carpeted in a deep cream shagpile and housed a big, comfy crimson-velvet sofa with matching satin cushions. An impressive bay window overlooked the market area. There was a huge free-standing, shabby chic French mirror leaning against one of the clinically white walls, and the open Victorian fireplace with its ornate tiled surround was in full working order. Star had gone up there once when Lydia had been on holiday and had likened it to a whore's boudoir. It was Lydia's 'breakout room', if she was feeling a little tired. A luxury that eluded the over-worked Kara, whose suggestion to take on an extra member of staff at busy times like Valentine's Day or Mother's Day consistently fell on her boss's deaf ears.

'Oh, Kara, you're here early too. Good.' Lydia Twist started as she generally carried on. 'We've had loads of orders for Easter flowers, so it's going to be a busy day, *not* helped by you not being around yesterday. I can make the bouquets up, so you can stay out front on the stall and then I'll give you a list so you can deliver them all later. That will allow you to make up some time, won't it?'

Fuelled by her anger from the day before, Kara stood up for herself. 'Make up what time? I took yesterday as holiday.' Then, cementing her own lie, she added, 'And James Bond is fine, thanks for asking.'

'Well, of course he is. He's a cat,' Lydia replied dismissively, hurrying back into her tiny office to answer the phone.

Lydia Twist rarely appeared to experience moments of real happiness. In fact, Kara didn't think she'd ever heard the woman laugh. Her boss did manage a Mona Lisa-type smile when taking money from customers, but that was about it. Her frame and features defied her fifty-year-old age ticket and she had a toned, boyish figure aided by her yoga practice and vegan diet. She was particularly proud to announce that she hadn't eaten a refined carbohydrate for twenty-five years. Her black jeans fitted her tight little bottom snugly and her small but perfectly formed breasts sat upright in her pink Passion Flowers T-shirt. Her hair was dark brown, styled in a neat elfin cut, and today she wore a sticky red lip gloss. Old Twisty Knickers was so ordered and officious that Kara often had the urge to stick a thickly buttered French baguette down her throat, to forcibly remind her of what having a large dose of carbohydrate felt like. *Bloody wonderful.* This also led Kara to ponder what life would be like without eating another carb ever again. A *serious nightmare!*

Lydia's grown-up son, Felix, lived in Berkshire, where Lydia had originally come from, and even after working for her for the past fifteen years, that was all Kara knew about the Twist family. Well, apart from the fact that Lydia lived in one of the posh houses on Hartmouth Hill, overlooking the mouth of the estuary – alone, most people assumed, as there had never been any sight nor mention of a man, aside from her son.

'Probably buried a few blokes under the patio,' Charlie Dillon had once guffawed, making Kara wonder for a split second if maybe he was talking from experience.

Lydia appeared from the office and began issuing instructions in her faux posh voice. 'We need to shift those yellow roses today and I got extra tulips and daffodils. A pound a bunch on the daffs and three for two pounds fifty. Keep a fiver on the tulips, regardless of colour. No offer on those today. Plus, put all the spring planters out that we made up last week – they should go today. Oh, and we've got a wedding next Sunday. Evidently the bride was using a freelance florist who's had to pull out due to illness.'

When Lydia paused to take a breath, Kara whispered, 'Please and thank you,' under her breath, whilst thinking: *Why not stick a broom up my backside so that I can sweep the floor at the same time?*

'I know Sunday is your day off, but I thought you wouldn't mind picking that up for me. It's just the bride's bouquet and the seven white birdcages we've got upstairs stuffed with gypsophila for the tables. Oh, and ten buttonholes, but they just want a yellow rose, with a bit of gyp and green for those. You've got no plans, have you? The venue is doing the rest up there and they don't want anything in the church. It's in the Oak Room at Crowsbridge Hall. OK?'

Kara breathed in deeply, then exhaled for a count of seven. This small but effective calming tactic had got her through many years of tolerating Lydia Twist.

'No plans, no,' she replied stoically.

However much she felt like rebelling, especially at the mere mention of Crowsbridge Hall, she couldn't rock the boat. She needed this job, even more now Jago's benefits were no longer coming in. Despite his lazy, thieving ways, she had always managed to bag a percentage of the mortgage from him before he frittered the rest, and some. But she wouldn't be doing that any more. She had half-hoped he would return last night with his tail between his legs to maybe offer some sort of apology, but he hadn't. Not even a text message to say when he was coming home to collect his stuff – including Sid – let alone everything else she had cited in the letter. It was no doubt for the best, but it hurt nonetheless.

She had awoken this morning after a short and fretful sleep, feeling both sad and lonely and with James Bond standing with his tail in the air and his bum within two inches of her face. She had had a little cry, wondering out loud whether a single life was really what she wanted. But later, when Sid Vicious caught her unawares and bit her palm hard enough to draw blood for the heinous crime of putting food in his tank, it not only caused her to sob uncontrollably, but also brought her to the beginnings of acceptance of the sham that her eight-year relationship had been.

Kara struggled out to the marketplace carrying a vase full of particularly tall gladioli.

'Morning, darling. How's it going today?' Pat Dillon enquired from the stall opposite. In her mid-fifties, and as wide as she was tall, Patricia Dillon was salt to her husband Charlie's pepper. Since the much-loved characters had moved down from the East End of London twelve years ago with their twin boys, they had been immediately accepted and soon became renowned amongst the market dwellers for being not only all-seeing and all-knowing, but all-swearing, too.

Despite earning a particularly good living from their shop, Pat's appearance wasn't a priority. Her bleached, shoulder-length hair quite often had dark roots showing. She rarely wore make-up to accentuate the small features in her round, rosy-cheeked face. Her huge tortoiseshell spectacles were quite often covered in smudges, and her uniform of tatty jeans and baggy T-shirts was standard. However, for what she lacked in self-care, she gained in that rare quality in a person where beauty and joy radiate from their soul. She was also one of those women that if she were to lose weight, she wouldn't be who she was any more.

Clonking the vase down, spilling water on her black trainers as she did so, Kara knew that the minute Pat got a glimpse of her face, she would know that Kara wasn't all right at all. Remaining silent was her safest tactic.

Pat continued, 'Don't let that frigid cow get you down. We all know she just needs a damn good seeing to. Go on, tell your Auntie Pat: what's up, darlin'?'

Charlie squeezed Kara's arm affectionately, telling his wife, 'Leave the kid alone, Pat. You're such a nosy old cow, you are.' He carried on arranging some shiny aubergines in a row.

'Mind your own business, Colonel bloody Rhubarb, and get back to what you're good at.' Pat slapped her husband's bum. 'Silly old sod.'

But Charlie was right. Kara wasn't ready to open up to anyone else today, so was glad for the crashing diversion of Darren Dillon.

'Forgot to charge my bloody phone, didn't I?' The lad

came rushing down the metal backstairs of the flat above *Dillon's*, which he shared with Billy, his non-identical twin.

'How many times do I have to tell you that you should get an old-fashioned alarm clock like me and your dad,' his mother nagged. 'And why didn't your brother wake you when he left? You've got an army of deliveries to do today.'

'Too many questions when I'm not yet with it, Ma. And Billy did wake me, I just fell back to sleep.'

Darren 'Daz' Dillon had a shaved head like his father. He wore a tiny diamond stud in his left ear, which glinted brightly in the sun as he started to dart about getting boxes ready to load in his van. Preferring the pasty shop to the gym, his body shape was not as lithe or muscly as that of Billy. He was, however, just as smiley and amiable, and with his magnetic charm, a hit with the ladies, too.

'All right, Moony?' Daz called as Kara appeared, this time with a flat box of beautiful double-headed daffodils. She put them down on the cobbles in front of her and managed something that resembled a smile.

'Leave her alone a minute, Daz,' Pat said behind her teeth, as if she was holding a ventriloquist dummy rather than a tray of asparagus.

Darren was about to say he hadn't understood a word of what his mother was saying, when Lydia, struggling to wedge the florist's door open, clocked him talking to Kara. The vase she was carrying slipped through her hands and fell, smashing into a hundred pieces. Infuriated, and swearing loudly, she shouted across to Kara, 'Stop dawdling and get yourself in here now and answer the bloody phone to that useless boyfriend of yours!'

Chapter 10

A few days later, Kara pushed open the wooden side gate, shut it carefully behind her and made her way up the garden path of Bee Cottage, the white-painted thatched dwelling where she had spent the first twenty-five years of her life.

Despite it only being April, the air already smelled of summer to her. The lawn had been freshly mowed and several bees were flying around, busily doing their work amongst the bright tulips and pretty forget-me-nots in the lower flowerbeds. Chattering birdsong from the now fully leaf-laden trees would have been music to even the unhappiest of ears. Looking back down the hill, she could just make out the estuary teeming with Easter holidaymakers.

She knew exactly where her grandfather would be and there he was, at the allotment end of the garden, next to a pile of grass clippings, pouring a small amount of yellow liquid into a water container. She could hear the hypnotic buzz of more bees flying in and out of the hives at the back of the shed.

It had been a sad day when her loving and vivacious Granny Annie had died. Grandad Harry had suggested almost immediately that he move out of his bungalow and in with his son, stating that he could live out his retirement tending to the bees, chickens and the garden with its view of the sea. Though he never said it, Kara had been astute enough to realise that her selfless grandfather was not doing this for himself, but for her and Joe. Now that his father was living with him, Joe was much less lonely. And with the money that had been gifted to her from the sale of her grandparents' cottage, she had put down a deposit on Number One, Ferry View Apartments. On top of all this, with her dad and grandad now keeping each other company, Kara didn't have to feel guilty about wanting to move out and start to build her own life – even if it was just around the corner from their cottage.

When she had turned the key to her new home, Kara had felt free for the first time in years. To be able to live in such a gorgeous location looking right over the water was a dream come true. It was to be a short-lived freedom, though. Aware that finances would be tight on her own, when Jago had insisted that he move straight in she had agreed, thinking he could share the bills. How wrong could you be! In hindsight, it had been far too early into their relationship. But as everyone knows, hindsight is a wonderful thing.

Harry Moon was a stout man with an air of contentment that the acceptance of old age had brought along with it.

'Here she is, number two.' The old man walked with a slight limp towards her and as he leaned down to kiss her forehead, the rim of his orange bucket hat brushed her cheek. Kara had never known him not to be wearing a hat or cap of some sort to cover his wispy white-haired head. His snowy beard was always trimmed to perfect precision.

'You all right then, Grandad?' she asked, kneeling to say

hello to Henrietta and Daisy, the brown and white speckled chickens who were clucking and scratching contentedly in their long wire-mesh run.

'Of course I am,' he said cheerily. 'Now the sun's out, I'm out. You know me – I couldn't be happier. Chooks, bees, and lots of planting to do. Spring – it's my favourite time of year in the garden.' His deep Cornish accent enveloped her in love and familiarity.

'What's that?' She pointed to the bottle in her grandad's hand.

'Apple cider vinegar. A bloody fox was prowling about last night. There was a right old commotion. I got up and came out here with my big torch to scare the little blighter away.' He handed the bottle to Kara. 'It seems to de-stress my girls.' He smiled and looked right into his granddaughter's emerald eyes. 'Maybe you should try some.'

Kara looked away; she could feel her eyes filling up.

'Come to my office,' he said gently, 'and you can tell your old grandad all about it.'

Harry Moon let out a loud, 'Oof!' as he plonked himself down on the threadbare green armchair in his large shed. The open door offered a perfect view, back past the chickens and down the long, beautifully tended garden to the pretty cottage at the end. He turned off his portable radio, which was now blaring out the local news, took the vinegar from Kara and put it on the shelf next to him. Shifting to get comfortable, he looked with satisfaction at the purple flowering wisteria that covered the left side of the cottage. It was getting ready to fade now, but the beautifully scented old-fashioned pink climbing rose was already starting to take its place. The arch over the back doorway would soon be rampant with fragrant honeysuckle, a favourite of both Kara's and the bees. All these blooms created an enduring track of the seasons and moments in life for the Moon family.

Kara took her usual place on the old red fold-up chair that her grandad had just placed outside for her. Despite the sun now going down in a blaze of glory, she was glad to be shaded by the little shed porch so as not to burn her pale skin.

'Don't mention anything to Dad, will you?' she said. 'You know I don't like to worry him.'

'Oh Kara, I do wish you'd stop this.' Harry Moon took a breath. 'Family is where life begins, and love never ends – and don't you ever forget that.'

'It's just—'

Harry interrupted and went off on a tangent. 'I was thinking back as I was checking the hives about why this Queen bee called Kara didn't go to floristry college. What went wrong, my girl?'

Kara sighed. 'That was years ago, Grandad. And I told you before, I would have been homesick.'

'For a few weeks maybe, child.'

'And I knew that Lydia would train me up, like she said she would.'

'Train you on the job maybe, but she's never paid for you to go to college and get a proper qualification, has she? She's shrewd, that one. Got you right over a barrel.' Harry took his hat off and placed it on the bench beside him.

He was right. It had never been spoken about and Kara would never admit it to her father, but she had been so worried that he wouldn't be able to cope living alone that when she had finished her A levels, she had turned down a place to study floristry at Bishop Burton College. Instead of moving the four hundred miles away and following her dream, she had stayed home in Hartmouth to keep an eye on him. Her grandad was right: despite Lydia making continued promises with regard to her studying for her BTEC in Floristry, it had never come to anything, so if Kara were to move on, she would only have the experience behind her and not the all-important qualification.

Harry, who was well aware of his granddaughter's constant shielding of his son, shook his head and said softly, 'He's a big boy now, you know. He can take it. He would hate to think he was holding you back, love. And what happens when I'm dead and buried? You'll have to talk to him then.'

'Don't say that,' Kara mumbled, pushing her bottom lip out and reverting to her five-year-old self. In that moment she remembered all the times she had sat in exactly the same place over the years, rubbing ice on to her palm to ease a wasp sting she'd got from picking up half-rotten apples from the grass or hiding after one of the frequent rows she'd had with her mother whilst growing up.

'I'm eighty-three – and yes, I do feel like I'm firing on nearly all cylinders, but I'm also realistic.'

'Nah, you'll be like the Queen Mother, riding around the village on that old trike of yours until you're at least a hundred and ten.' Then, 'Poo! Grandad, was that you?'

'No, it bloody wasn't, you cheeky mare.'

Kara noticed the scruffy little bundle on the dirty dog bed in the corner of the shed. 'Oh Bert, how could I forget you? I didn't even think to ask where he was – how awful is that! Too bloody wrapped up in my own woes.' As though the ancient Jack Russell knew he was being talked about, he let out a contented sigh, then, continuing to snore, let off another vile whiff. Kara carried on ignoring the real issue and fanned the smelly air. 'Well, *he's* definitely firing on many cylinders by the stench of him.' They both laughed, then a short silence followed whilst Harry waited for his obviously troubled granddaughter to speak her mind.

Eventually, taking a deep breath, the words simply flew out. 'Jago's been cheating on me and he's spent the little money I did have saved.'

'OK.' Harry nodded matter-of-factly. 'Is he still at the flat?'

'No, I told him to leave.'

'Did he go?'

'Yes. He came the other night and got his stuff. The woman who he was . . . well, you know what . . .'

'Banging, you mean?'

'Grandad!'

'The birds and bees are my forte, you know that.' He laughed. 'You youngsters. Your dad didn't get here by a stork, you know. Now, go on.'

'Well, the woman he was . . . banging . . . well, she doesn't want him living with her.'

'Someone's got some sense, then.'

'The Penhaligons' daughter, can you believe that!' Kara managed a stifled giggle.

'Yes, I can. I read she's a right old tart.'

Kara shook her head and smiled at her irreverent grandfather. 'Jago pleaded for me to let him stay until he sorted himself out. I nearly wavered but found the strength from somewhere and said no.'

'Halle-bloody-lujah.' Harry shifted his fat backside again in his sagging chair. 'He is a cad, that one, but whatever amount of telling, we have to see it for ourselves. How are you feeling about it though, love?'

'I'm OK. I look back and don't understand why I didn't

just have the sense to chuck him out before now.' Kara sighed.

'Well, you've done it now and that's what matters.' Kara felt herself welling up again as her grandad went on. 'One of the few things I do remember from the reading at my wedding all those years ago, is that real love *is* patient and kind and it does not dishonour others. And I held that belief with your dear old gran till, sadly, death did us part.'

The wise old fellow cleared his throat then continued, 'I do also believe that love comes in many guises and you did love Jago, in a way, and he you. But it wasn't right. It wasn't true. And I know that there is somebody out there who will be so much more in tune with my beautiful, kind, self-sacrificing granddaughter. Your gran used to say that there's a lid for every pot, you know.'

Kara smiled at the memory of dear Granny Annie's funny sayings. 'I hope so.'

'I know so. And by the sound of it, you've let the fool go with such dignity that he will look back with both regret and fondness for you.'

'Drama is not my style.'

'No, it's not. Try not to let him back in though, Kerry.'

Kara said quietly, 'No, I've done it this time.'

Her grandfather leaned forward and asked her straight out: 'Do you need some money?'

'My goodness no, that's not why I'm here.'

'Because I can help you out a little bit.'

'I'm thirty-three, I need to stand on my own two feet, and I've been thinking about how I do just that. I've decided that although my place is small, I may get a lodger . . . maybe.'

'Hmm . . . hmm . . .' The old man stroked his beard in thought.

'Hmm what, Grandad?'

'Firstly, you're still a youngster. What is it with the obsession with age these days? I see it in every newspaper or magazine. Well, all I have to say on the matter, Kerensa Anne Moon, thirty-three, from Hartmouth, is that age is just a number and that everyone's time comes differently in life. The second hmm was: don't do anything rash, my lovely. It's only because me and your dad have separate living spaces that we've continued to live in peace and harmony. Think carefully about it. Go home tonight and imagine the scenario of sharing that little space of yours – especially a bathroom – with someone you don't know.'

Pushing himself up from his armchair, he groaned. 'Bloody seizing up, I am.' He reached for the spectacles that were on a chain around his neck, looked down to check Bert was still breathing, then pulled out a book from under a mass of seed packets, scattering them on to the floor as he did so. He turned around and handed Kara a wedge of ten-pound notes. As she went to give them back, he pushed her hand away, then put his index finger to his lips and made a shushing noise. 'Love always protects, too.'

'But—' Kara went to protest again.

'It's only a couple of hundred quid. I won it on the horses last week, but don't tell your father that, either. You know he thinks I'm squandering his inheritance.'

Kara grinned at the preposterousness of his latter statement. 'I love you, Grandad Harry, and thanks for always being there for me.'

He smiled, then patted his granddaughter gently on the hand. 'That's my job, isn't it?'

At that moment, a barking Bert shot past them and started careering down the garden.

'He may be an old dog, but he's got selective hearing on him, that one,' Harry grinned.

'Are we talking about you or Bert here?' Kara laughed.

'Oi, young 'un. You're not too old for a clip round the ear.' Kara linked arms with her grandfather. 'That'll be your dad coming in from work now.'

On reaching the back door, Harry lifted his stick to the clear evening sky.

'My dear Kerensa Anne, before you go, did I tell you that every soul is a flower blossoming in nature?' He picked one of the large pink roses that had just come into full bloom on the side of the cottage and held it up.

'Agatha Christie,' he said.

'Sorry?' Kara looked puzzled.

'The name of this rose.'

'Ah. In all these years I never knew that.'

Harry went off on another tangent. 'Your gran. What a joy to behold that woman was.' He handed the prickly stem to Kara, who put the bloom to her nose and breathed in its sweet aroma as her grandad added dreamily, 'So vibrant, so brimming with life. Full-figured with soft pink cheeks, and she always smelled so beautiful to me, with or without her favourite scent on.' He paused and ran his finger across the petals. 'Just like this perfect rose.' His voice quietened. 'My Annie.'

Chapter 11

'No Skye this morning, then?' Kara greeted Star who was busy setting up her stall for the Saturday market.

'A teenager up before midday? You've got to be joking. She was at the park last night with friends and a few too many bottles of cider. And all the while, here I was, Norma No-Mates, sitting up making these with some old crystals I found in my cupboard under the stairs.' Steren started hanging some delicate silver chains looped with varying coloured crystals onto her star-shaped display stand.

'They're gorgeous – you are clever.' Kara picked a blue-stoned one up and put it up against her neck.

'Oh – and yes, I also found this,' Star added nonchalantly, reaching down behind her. She handed Kara a pretty peach canvas with grey wording on it. 'I want you to have it.'

'What is it – a picture?'

'Read it,' Star said gently.

Kara started reading under her breath.

The Guest House
This being human is a guest house.
Every morning a new arrival.

A joy, a depression, a meanness,
some momentary awareness comes
as an unexpected visitor.

Welcome and entertain them all!
Even if they are a crowd of sorrows,
who violently sweep your house
empty of its furniture,
still, treat each guest honourably.
He may be clearing you out
for some new delight.

The dark thought, the shame, the malice,
meet them at the door laughing,
and invite them in.

Be grateful for whatever comes,
because each has been sent
as a guide from beyond.

Rumi

Kara had tears in her eyes. 'Wow! That is so true and so beautiful . . . are you sure I can have this? I bloody love it. It can fill the faded square that Jago's *Abbey Road* picture left.'

Star smiled at her friend's pleasure, saying, 'Rumi is my favourite master of the spiritual world and yes, of course it's for you.'

'"Clearing me out for some new delight" . . . Let's hope so!'

'Kara, Kara! Can you come inside for a minute, please!'

The anything but delightful tones of Lydia Twist broke their moment.

'Maybe not today though, eh?' Star laughed.

'Kara Moon and Miss Bligh? To what do I owe this pleasure?' Big Frank greeted the young ladies at the door of his café with his lopsided smile and soft Irish accent.

'It's Saturday evening, the sun is shining and I've missed you, of course,' Star flirted, as did most of the women who frequented the charming Irishman's establishment.

'How was the market?'

'Bloody busy, actually.' Star yawned.

'Yes, thought so, it's only just quietened down in here. So, ladies, sorry but today you've got time for just one drink as my Monique is home from Paris tonight and I'm cooking her a special dinner.'

'You spoil her,' Kara teased.

'She deserves to be spoilt. As do you, Kara Moon. Feeling better now?'

'Yes – well, I will be. It's early days.' Kara knew no further explanation was needed. She added, 'One each of your special cocktails will help.'

'Grand, grand.' Frank went behind the counter to make up the drinks. He plonked two tumblers of fizzing purple liquid with ice down in front of them. 'Double blackcurrant cordial with tonic on the house.' He winked. 'Now, go outside and relax.'

Kara and Star walked outside to find a free bench amongst some of the other market traders and handful of visitors enjoying the early evening sunshine. The various annual holidays brought with them those with second homes and tourists alike; this, combined with today's beautiful weather, ensured the estuary was alive with boats and, this evening, windsurfers. Kara could see the car ferry touching down at the Crowsbridge quayside. Sometimes she worried just how hard her dad worked. But on the upside, he enjoyed it and even though keeping busy was an excuse for him not to focus on anything else in his life, he didn't seem unhappy. Or if he was, he never showed it. And with Billy being such a grafter, she knew that he would be taking as much of the strain as he could.

It certainly had been a successful market day. Lydia had managed at least two Mona Lisa-type smiles and was so pleased to see the money rolling in that she had even taken the time to prepare all the wedding flowers and buttonholes for the next day. They were all now nicely laid upstairs in the cool ready for Kara to load into the van and take over to Crowsbridge Hall early in the morning.

Kara put her new canvas containing the Rumi poem down on the bench beside her and patted it, saying, 'Thanks again for this, mate, it's so bloody poignant.'

Star took a big gulp of the strong gin cocktail and winced slightly. 'I know.'

'It's weird,' Kara went on, 'but remember the bit about "violently sweeping your house"? Well, I know the words didn't have anything to do with this, but the other night after Jago had gone, instead of moping around, I got the rubber gloves on and I sorted, tidied, bleached and scrubbed in a frenzy – and after it was done, I felt a sense of serenity and calm. I can't explain it.'

'I can,' Star said knowingly. 'Your body is your home. If

your mind is chaotic, if you're not treating yourself well, eating bad food, not exercising, not cleaning up after yourself, et cetera, then you won't feel settled. By cleaning up your exterior space, you've also cleaned your inner rooms.'

Kara took a gulp of her gin. 'That's very deep, my friend.'

But whatever it meant, Number One, Ferry View Apartments was now spotless and every last bit of evidence of Jago Ellis had been removed – bar one thing . . .

'It was so busy today I didn't even get the chance to ask how you're feeling about everything now.' Star rubbed on sun cream. It had been a constant annoyance to Kara over the years that Star wanted to keep her pale skin pale, whereas Kara with the inherited translucent and freckly skin wanted nothing more than a deep, rich tan.

'I'm actually feeling surprisingly good. I miss having someone there for company, but I realise now that "someone" could be anyone. Jago was only ever half with me, when he *was* with me, if that makes sense. He's a strange one, that man.'

'Most of them are.' Star kicked off her shoes and put her head back to the sun.

'I actually spoke to Grandad Harry about getting a lodger the other night.'

'That's a great idea, Kar. But if you do go for it, I insist that we only interview tall, dark handsome men who are around thirty years old.'

The strength of the gin was already getting to both of them. Kara laughed out loud. 'Yes, and someone who wants to procreate within the next five years and adores ginger women with rotund derrières.'

At that moment, Big Frank appeared at the table. 'What's the craic, ladies?'

'I'm just setting Kara up with some potential suitors.'

'Grand, grand. I'm locking up now, but you can sit here as long as you like. Just pop the glasses down behind the dustbins when you go, can you?'

He ruffled Kara's messy ponytail.

'Enjoy Monique,' she shouted after him. Then sighed. 'He's one in a million, that bloke.'

'Yes, he is. Quite the stud, too.' Star had a vision of placing her tiny rosebud lips on his wide, full ones and committing herself to gay abandon in the café's back kitchen.

'I don't look at him that way, he's more like an uncle to me.'

Star took another sip of her drink. 'He doesn't realise quite how sexy he is, nor that he's really spiritual. I can feel his aura.'

'I bet you'd like to feel more than that.' Kara even surprised herself with this comment. It was as if her true self and wit had been submersed for far too long.

'He's a bit *too* good looking for me,' Star carried on, 'but those arms are a real turn-on.' She giggled. 'So, back to the serious stuff: are you really thinking about getting a lodger?'

'It does seem a good idea in principle, but I only have one bathroom. And I'm a bit worried about the toilet business.'

'Oh, Kara, we're all human, just leave the window open and put a good air freshener in there. It depends what job they do, I guess. You're up with the larks every morning except Sunday anyway. Someone who works nights may be the answer?'

'Yes, yes. That's a great idea. Now that Jago's vinyl collection is out of the spare room it does look bigger, but whoever came in would have to take my room as it's facing the sea.

I could ask for more money then, maybe? I don't know, it's all new to me.'

Star then bashed her palm on her forehead. 'I've got it – of course!'

'Got what?' Kara screwed up her face at her friend's eureka moment.

'It's Rumi to the rescue: a Guest House! Rather than commit to a smelly lodger full-time, just offer your place as an Airbnb. You're right on the water, you're in a tourist town. You can pick and choose when people stay and you'll make as much money doing that, if not more, as you'll be charging on a daily basis rather than a set monthly rent.'

'So that's when people just book per night, like a hotel or bed and breakfast, right?'

'You've got it, sister! I'm definitely going to do it when Skye flies the nest.'

'But I wouldn't be able to give them breakfast as I leave so early in the morning.'

'You could leave cereal or bread to make toast out for them, or no . . .' Star started flapping her arms around excitement. 'I've got it – maybe do a deal with Big Frank and buy them a breakfast voucher for here? That would help him, too!'

'Do you know what, Steren Bligh? You are not just a dumb blonde with a pale face. This is a genius idea!'

They clinked glasses and Kara suddenly grinned. 'Guess what? There's something else I did that was genius.'

'Go on.'

'You know how Jago used to love my home-made lasagne.'

'Yes.' Star had no idea what was coming.

'Well, the night he came to collect his stuff, I defrosted one, mixed in some of the dirt I had used for James Bond's litter tray that day and popped it in a Tupperware.'

'Kara Moon! I can't believe you did that.'

'Well, I did,' Kara replied triumphantly. 'My last words to him were that I was letting him go "with love and a lasagne".'

Chapter 12

Kara woke groggily to her alarm, stared at the ceiling, and sighed. She had never been much of a drinker and Big Frank's ridiculously large gin measures on an empty stomach made you want to stay in bed for the rest of the next day. She turned her head on to a cold bit of pillow and let out a whining noise. There was no chance of a lie-in. She had flowers to deliver and not just any old flowers or any old venue, but wedding flowers to Crowsbridge Hall, home to 'Adulterers United'.

James Bond had been sleeping soundly on her feet at the end of the bed but as soon as he saw her open eyes he ran up and started kneading her stomach in his usual demanding breakfast ritual. It was weird that, even if he were outside, he seemed to know exactly the moment she woke up and would come tearing through the cat flap and run upstairs to disturb her. He also had a very strange habit of dragging in random things through the cat flap. This morning, a coffee-cup lid from Frank's. Last week, a bit of pink ribbon and a blue rabbit ear from a soft toy. She checked her watch and pushed him off gently. 'In a minute, mister.' His indignant miaow, followed by furious scratching, reminded her that she really must get him some flea stuff with the money that Grandad Harry had given her.

She was happy that freshly changed sheets and an injection

of alcohol had made her feel comfy and relaxed enough to drop off to sleep last night without her usual fretful tossing and turning. Also, the idea of making some money by opening up her room to guests had momentarily taken away the anxiety of her finances.

This morning, she also felt strangely used to waking up alone. Probably because over the past few months Jago had so rarely even rolled over to cuddle her or touch her in any way. She had also discovered the joy of having a double bed to herself, stretching her legs and arms right across as if reasserting her dominion over it. She'd had one good sob on the night Jago had come home, tail between his legs, to try and schmooze his way back in, but she had done so much crying beforehand that she felt done with it now. She was also enjoying having her flat all to herself. No one stealing her space, time or money. If she didn't want to clean or cook dinner, she didn't have to. She could lounge around in her own mess and enjoy the peace. No more having to constantly listen to the Beatles or be clearing up dog ends from the balcony. Even James Bond seemed less skittish.

From now on she could please herself, do what she wanted when she wanted. There was no longer the worry of Jago coming home drunk, either. Sometimes he had been so awful to her that she would walk up and down the estuary promenade in the early hours, not returning until he had fallen into a drunken coma. He would always do this before a busy market day, too, which made sense now that she knew Friday was when he would have been shagging his lover! You'd have thought he would have been a happy drunk after that. 'Selfish bastard!' she said aloud.

Running a market stall meant seriously early mornings, so it was bittersweet having to be up this early on a Sunday.

At least it was Easter Monday tomorrow so she could have a lie-in. And to be fair, as Lydia had surprisingly made up the decorations and buttonholes, it wouldn't take her long to load the van, then deliver the wedding flowers to Crowsbridge Hall. She would be back in time to enjoy the afternoon sun, and planned to stretch out on her small balcony like a lizard and doze off.

Looking around her, she realised how basically she had been living. The old IKEA metal bed she'd had since they had moved here eight years ago was all right, but the mattress could do with being replaced. The single pine wardrobe in the corner was marked with James Bond's scratches. The chest of drawers, on which stood a small flat-screen TV and an unlit candle they had got from the market a couple of years ago, was still OK, but nothing special, just like the matching bedside tables. She hoped that her guests would be able to overlook these slight flaws as she would have to wait until she had enough funds to replace anything.

What she would never tire of, and what was priceless, was the gorgeous view of the estuary below; when the old sash window was pushed right up, you could lie in bed and look out over it. If it was a good day, you could even feel the breeze and warmth of the sun on your face. Kara loved just as much when it was stormy and the howling wind and heavy rain buffeted against the window; at those times she would snuggle under the duvet feeling all cosy. Simple pleasures that Jago didn't appreciate. Simple pleasures that she could now enjoy without interruption or complaint.

She got up, pulled on joggers and a T-shirt, went to the bathroom, then through to the lounge.

'Morning, Sid.' The Painted Turtle was basking on his rock under the heat of his lamp. It had taken all her resolve to refuse when Jago pleaded with her to allow him to come back; so when he asked if she could mind the little creature until he sorted himself out, Kara didn't have the heart or mental strength to say no. And as much as his biting was bloody annoying, she had to admit she really was quite fond of the pretty terrapin. Her sporadic spiteful thoughts of leaving the lid off the tank for James Bond to have a plaything had eased. She had even given Sid a new under-water hiding place: the blue pot – another part of her old life with Jago. She would have thrown it away during her cleaning mission, but then she remembered that Granny Annie had given it to her one Christmas with a mini-Poinsettia in it.

She threw the little reptile a couple of dried floating sticks of food, then after emptying a sachet of wet food into a whingeing James Bond's bowl, she made herself a coffee and went and sat out on the balcony. She checked her watch: just time for a few minutes of glorious sunshine before going to the shop to collect the flowers and the van, then make the dreaded journey to the big house.

Tipping her head back, she shut her eyes – only to be immediately disturbed by the familiar whistle of Billy Dillon. Then his calling up from underneath her balcony with, 'Kerensa, Kerensa, wherefore art thou, Kerensa?' She looked down to see the handsome ferryman grinning up at her.

'Shut your traps, the pair of you! It's early on a Sunday morning!' Cora Blunt shouted down from her balcony of the building four doors down as she lit her first cigarette of the day then erupted in a deafening round of coughing.

Billy put an out-of-sight middle finger up at a now laughing Kara who tried and failed miserably to whisper her reply over the racket.

'You've got it the wrong way around. Juliet summons Romeo from above. And there's little chance of that happening.'

'It's only a matter of time.' Billy smirked. 'Can I pop up for a second?'

'I'm not dressed.'

'Kerry Moon, you really do leave me open for innuendo.'

'Get a room!' Cara Blunt shouted hoarsely then disappeared inside.

The buzzer sounded and Kara went back inside to press the button to release the ground-floor entrance. Opening the flat door, she could hear Billy's footsteps running up the stairs.

'Coffee? I'm just making myself another one.' Her back was to him; he took in her firm round bottom and womanly thighs housed in her grey jogging bottoms.

'Yes, please. Three sugars, milky.'

'I know that.' Kara turned around, scratching at her hair, which was stuck up in the air and tumbling messily over her shoulders.

Trying hard not to stare at her braless breasts, Billy kept his gaze at eye level. 'I hear Dickhead's gone, but surely he didn't take your hairbrush with him?'

Kara checked herself in the mirror to the right of the balcony door, wiped away a remnant of black mascara and pushed her locks behind her ears. 'Leave me alone,' she instructed him. 'I've just got up and I'm a bit hung-over. Are you not working the ferry today, then?'

'No, I've just been briefing Daz. He's agreed to run the float for me every Sunday from now on. He only works three days on the market anyway, lazy bastard. He won't go in the tug, like I can, but your old man is cool about that as it's early finish day.'

'Good for you. Maybe if Daz likes it, you can both give

Dad a day off sometimes. It does worry me, the hours he works.' Kara went through to the kitchen to make their drinks. Billy followed.

'Your dad's sound, Kerry.' He started eyeing up his surroundings and the impressive view. 'Nice up 'ere, innit.'

'I forget you haven't been up here before. Saying that, not many people have. I'm only just learning how few people liked my ex.' The word 'ex' didn't slip easily off her tongue yet.

For once Billy thought before he spoke. 'I didn't mean to be flippant then about – you know – you being on your own now. And nobody told me. I saw him leaving with all his stuff, so kind of assumed it was over.'

'It's all right. I don't really want to talk about it.'

'Blimey, that's a bit deep.' Billy had swiftly diverted to reading the *Guest House* canvas, which now had pride of place above the terrapin tank. Sid was happily basking under his lamp.

'Ah. Here's old Sid. He's so cool.'

'A bit like you. He has his moments.'

Billy was annoyed to feel his face reddening at Kara's lukewarm compliment. 'I guess you're wondering why I'm here?'

'Yes. Please do tell me and break the suspense.' Kara carried the steaming mugs of coffee out on to the balcony. She indicated with her head for Billy to sit on the bench next to her.

'Well, it was Star, actually. I saw her yesterday. She said you've got to go to the Cornwall Trust place today and deliver some flowers, and she suggested you might need a hand. She can't help as she'll be busy working – reckons business will be good as it's a Bank Holiday.'

It was for that very reason that, as much as Kara would have loved Star's help, she hadn't asked her. Bless her kind heart for suggesting that Billy might, and how sweet of him to do this for her on his precious day off.

Kara took a sip of her coffee, then looked into the handsome face of the young ferryman, considering his offer. If nothing else, they'd get the job done in double time and Billy would at least be an entertaining diversion.

'Well, Kerry Moon? Do you want me or not?' He winked and it was Kara who felt herself slightly reddening this time.

'Always.' She laughed, then, 'Come on, let's drink these and get it over with.'

Chapter 13

Harry Moon was just rinsing his mug at the kitchen sink, when a yawning Joe appeared.

'Morning, son. Kettle's just boiled,' the old fella said.

'You off out, Da?'

'Yes, just going for a ride with Bert to Duck Pond Park and getting my paper on the way back.'

The scruffy Jack Russell, curled up in a ball, lifted an ear at the mention of his name, then promptly put it down again with a whimper. He was sixteen now and still working on being the oldest Jack Russell to have ever lived. At this great age he felt he deserved his privileges, so being pulled behind Harry's trike on a lead at zero miles an hour wasn't his idea of fun. He much preferred it when he could sit in a basket on the front and pop his paws over and see what was going on.

'You worry me, you know, charging about on that trike of yours.'

'Hardly charging.' The old man laughed loudly. 'And if it was a superbike I was on, you'd have a right to be concerned. More worrying is you working seven days a week without so much as a break. You're sixty-one, not twenty-one now, lad.'

'I like working.'

'You don't like stopping, you mean. I'm not daft.'

'I don't want to discuss it, Dad.' Joe put the kettle on and took a mug from the cupboard.

'Why don't you try dating again, son? You never know, you might meet a nice woman, rather than having to put up with an old codger like me all the time.'

Joe poured boiling water on to his teabag. 'I'm content as I am.'

'What about Celia Dunsford who works at the paper shop? She seems lovely. And her husband's been gone at least two years now. She's probably a bit lonely without someone too.'

Joe made a face. 'Dad! Give me some credit. She must be at least seventy and it looks like she's growing a beard.'

Harry laughed. 'Well, that could be a conversation starter, at least.'

'I'm actually quite pleased you're going out on your trike now. Bugger off.' Joe flicked his hand at his dad as if to shoo him away, but smiled. 'I'll see you tonight. I'm hoping our Kerry might pop in for a roast dinner.'

'How lovely we have her to ourselves for a bit now.' Harry pulled Bert's lead from the coat rack in the hallway.

'Yes – at last. I thought she was never going to get rid of that bastard.'

Chapter 14

'Stop being a back-seat driver!' Kara shouted at Billy as they drove off the ferry and headed for Crowsbridge Hall.

'I'm next to you, if you hadn't noticed,' he replied drily. 'In the death seat.'

'Ha ha – funny.'

'Someone's a bit tetchy today, isn't she?' Billy realised he'd gone too far when he looked at a now silent Kara and noticed a lone tear falling down her left cheek.

'Oh God, Kerry. I'm sorry, I was joking with you. What's up, Doll?'

'I'm just hung-over, that's all.'

'If I cried every time I had a few too many beers, I'd be sobbing every weekend.'

A hint of a smile crossed Kara's face.

'That's better. I'm so insensitive, I keep forgetting you've just split from your fella.'

'I've been fine, but . . . look, the real reason Star suggested you came with me is that my Jago is currently shagging the Penhaligons' daughter and I just can't bear the thought of bumping into her or worse still, both of them, so the plan is for us to get in and out of there as quickly as humanly possible.'

'Oh . . . my . . . God. Well, our Rachel certainly does like a bit of rough. I know Darren's no stranger to her "hunting lodge".'

Kara gasped. 'No! No wonder she didn't want Jago moving in with her.'

'Yeah, the dirty slapper probably has a rota of bad boys.'

'You haven't, you know . . . have you?' Kara's voice dropped an octave.

Billy's face was a picture. 'No, I bloody haven't. I'm actually quite selective in my choice of women.' He paused and his voice softened. 'As you well know.'

'You're such a joker,' Kara said dismissively, winding down her window. 'Phew! The air con in this van is so rubbish.'

'So, do you know where Jago is living then?' Billy asked. 'I haven't seen him about.'

'He told me he's with his mum in Crowsbridge. He'll hate it as she's such a clean freak. That's the reason I'm still stuck with the care of Sid Vicious. Mrs Ellis wouldn't have him in the house.'

Kara drove in silence for a bit, until Billy put his hand gently on her knee.

'OK, so tell me what I need to do when we get there. You can just stay in the van, if you want.'

'I'll have to go in or Twisty will kill me. I'm meeting the events manager in the reception in the main room. The car park is right next to where Rachel lives, so I'm probably better being out of the van. If you can just help me carry everything in, it'll save me some trips.'

'OK, well, just show me what you need me to carry, and I'll make sure we are in and out of there in no time.'

They pulled up in the car park near to the main entrance to the Oak Room, where the wedding was taking place within Crowsbridge Hall. There were a couple of other vans there: the DJ by the look of it, and an events theming company.

Kara opened the back doors of the van and was just about

to start handing out the ornate metal birdcages full of gypsophila to Billy, when she put her hand to her forehead and said, 'Shit!'

'What's up?'

She rummaged around in the van. 'Yes! I did put them in. Here, can you put one in each of the birdcages, please? Just tuck them in the middle.' Kara handed Billy a few stems with the sweetest-smelling little bell-shaped white flowers on them. 'They mustn't show.'

Billy stood by the side of her and did as he was told. 'I don't get it,' he said. 'Why are they hidden? They're lovely.'

'The bride didn't ask for this, but I always like to add a little something to all of our special orders. Lydia loves using gypsophila as it's so cheap, and as it's a wedding, prices are always inflated so she'll make a bomb on it, anyway.'

'Ah, so she doesn't know you're putting these in?' He held up one of the stems.

'You've got it. It's Lily of the Valley, the scent is SO gorgeous, I love it and it's perfect as they are having an unscented flower in the cages.'

'You're so sweet.' Billy smiled.

'And let me tell you more, Billy Dillon.' Kara giggled. 'The smell is only part of why I do it. Grandad Harry told me the other day that every flower is a soul blossoming in nature. Now that *is* sweet! I didn't know that, but what I do know is that every flower has a meaning.' She stopped to put the last stem of fragrant Lily of the Valley to her nose, before tucking it into the miniature birdcage. 'And this one represents Pure Love. Perfect for newlyweds, don't you think?' She wiped her hands down the side of her jeans. 'Right, let's do this.'

She gathered up some of the birdcages. Then she turned, and it was as if she had stumbled into the most awful slow-motion movie she hadn't even auditioned for, because who should be walking across the car park but the two people she especially didn't want to bump into? And they were heading right in their direction.

'It's OK,' Billy soothed, immediately recognising the Beatles-style haircut of Jago Ellis. 'I'll handle this.'

It was as if the cowardly Jago had heard him, as at that moment he stopped walking, leaving Rachel Penhaligon to carry on marching with gusto towards the white Passion Flowers van and a now shaking Kara.

'Be calm, be calm.' Kara said to herself, doubting that the heiress would recognise her in the pink Passion Flowers uniform. And even if she did, Kara wasn't the one in the wrong! She whispered to Billy, 'Honestly, don't say anything, it's cool.'

'Oh hi.' The skinny Rachel sounded as if she had a punnet of Charlie Dillon's plums in her mouth. 'You must be the florist's assistant. Tara in events said you were coming.' But Kara wasn't listening. Instead, she was staring at the neat little tattoo of a bluebird that was very apparent on the top of one of her pert little breasts. A bolt of anger shot through her whole body. A tattoo. She had a tattoo!

'Just pop them in the main door like a good girl, will you. Tara is waiting for you.'

Kara, now breathing like someone in the throes of child-birth, just replied with a faint, 'Sure.' She stared over at Jago. Knowing the cheater's body language so well, she could sense his dropped-shouldered relief when his lover Rachel started to walk back towards him with not a hint of drama in sight. Kara could also quite plainly see that he was not looking at his new fancy piece, but was instead staring right back at her.

Putting what she was carrying down on to the ground and without any word of warning, she clumsily pulled Billy towards her and started to kiss him. A kiss so long and passionate that it would have made the cut in any Hollywood blockbuster movie.

'How bloody unprofessional – but they do work for Passion Flowers, I suppose.' Rachel's guffaw and plummy voice could be heard a mile off.

And whilst a shocked Jago tried to compute exactly what he was seeing and feeling, a breathless and very turned-on Billy Dillon thought he had died and gone to heaven.

Chapter 15

'You did *what*?' Star stopped looking at the new delivery of vases that had just come into Passion Flowers.

'I kissed Billy. Only because I was SO angry that after all the times Jago would go on at me about tramp stamps and how he hated them – and there was Randy Rachel with a perfect little bluebird tattoo on her perfect little titty.'

'I thought he liked big boobs,' Star stated innocently.

'He's a man, Star, he likes boobs, period.'

'So what happened then?'

Kara said in a rush, 'Billy got excited, by the feel of things. And Star, this is the thing: so did I, a bit, and I don't know if it's because I haven't had any sexual contact for so long or whether I do fancy him. Anyway, he's only twenty-five, far too young for me.'

'And . . . breathe,' Star said calmly as Kara carried on putting flowers into the birthday bouquet she was working on.

'I've never looked at Billy in that way before,' Kara went on. 'I like him, we get on so well, but . . .'

'He is kind of cute though, Kar.'

Kara bit her lip. 'No. What I need now is a bit of space, not more dramas.'

'And I guess throughout all this carry-on, Jago the shallow shark did nothing?'

'Not at the time, no. Saying that, I was far more engrossed than I should have been. He did actually text for the first time since we split to ask if Sid was OK. His weird way of showing it bothered him. I know him so well. He's such a cock.' Kara sniffed. 'I just ignored it.'

'Good girl! So, wasn't it awkward with Billy on the way back from Crowsbridge?'

'No, I just told him straight I was using him to get back at Jago.'

'What's happening to you?' Star laughed. 'Saying that, eight years is not that big a gap, Kar.'

'Don't even go there. I think it is if the woman is older and wants to have children. It could get very tricky.'

'Bloody hell, mate, you've just kissed the bloke and now you want his babies,' Star joked.

'You know what I mean,' Kara tutted.

'Well, they do say that to get over one bloke you need to get under another.'

At that moment, Star's daughter came into the shop. 'Hey, Auntie Kara.'

'Hey, Skye.'

Skye Bligh was almost the same height as her mum, and with her beautiful straight white-blond hair and baby blue eyes, the spitting image of her, too. As Star had given birth to her when she was just sixteen, the teen and Kara, her mum's best friend, had also developed a natural and close bond over the years.

'Mum, there's a man in the shop who wants to book one of your crystal gridding-session things and I can't find the prices.'

'I'm coming now.' Star headed towards the door.

'One sec.' Kara stopped them in their tracks. 'I know what

I meant to ask: could you help me with my Airbnb advert sometime soon, please, Star? I need to start getting some money in and want to make sure it's really appealing.'

'Sure, sure. Pop in later and I'll let you know when's good.'

The shop bell signalled Star and Skye's departure.

Kara carried on placing some ferns into the pink and white birthday bouquet she had been creating, then stood back to admire her work. She knew she was a proficient florist, even if she said so herself, with a natural eye for colours, shapes and design. Some of the hoteliers on her delivery round who booked weekly flowers quite often pulled her aside and said they much preferred her arrangements to Lydia's. Deciding that the bouquet needed an extra touch, she hunted through the metal flower buckets and was relieved to find a couple of bunches of pink-and-white, April-flowering sweet peas. She carefully removed one fragrant stem and concealed it within the birthday bouquet, since sweet peas were the birth flower for the month of April. It gave her a little buzz knowing that she had added her own special touch without subjecting the purchaser to the Lydia-Twist Added Tax. Star had also just dropped in a tiny fragment of Rock Crystal, one of the April birthstones, which Kara had hidden inside one of the white lilies. Perfect.

At that moment, Lydia appeared from the flat upstairs and clocked the stunning pink and white bouquet on the workbench.

'Lovely job, great colour mix.'

Kara felt faint. A compliment from Old Twisty Knickers?

Expecting a well-endowed stallion to follow her uptight boss down the stairs at any moment, Kara just about managed a whispered, 'Thank you.'

Chapter 16

'Wheee!' Grandad Harry deliberately made the handlebars of his trike wobble as he came to an abrupt halt on the drive outside Bee Cottage, just missing Kara in the process. Bert, with tongue out and paws resting over the front of the basket, looked like he was smiling.

Kara laughed and chided him, 'Grandad, be careful.'

'Being careful doesn't make for a fun life, young 'un. We've had a lovely time, haven't we, Bert?' He slowly hoisted his large frame off the trike and parked it under the covered area to the right of the drive.

'Where have you been?'

'Just to Duck Pond Park and we go to a class up at the church hall for a couple of hours on a Tuesday, don't we, my boy?' He lifted the Jack Russell from the basket and put him gently down over the other side of the gate.

'A class?' Kara screwed her face up.

'Come on in. I need to get the dinner on, or we'll be eating at midnight. Why don't you stay and eat with us?'

'I've just come from the market and I need to feed James Bond.'

'He's an animal, duck, he'll be all right for a couple of hours and I've got a bit of mackerel you can take home for him.'

Henrietta and Daisy came running up to Kara as she opened the door of their run and threw some cabbage leaves on to the grass for them to peck at. Their incessant 'tuk-tuks' denoted their pleasure at both fresh food and another balmy evening for them to scratch around in. Harry was pottering about in his shed. Back inside, vegetables had been prepared and a ham hock pie was cooking in the oven.

'Would you mind changing their water too, please, Kerry, my love? And pop a bit more of that apple cider vinegar in. When it's warm, that stuff encourages them to drink, evidently.'

'It probably tastes like real cider, that's why.' Kara filled the water container then joined her grandad in the shed. She picked up some sticky labels that were on the side: *Harry's Honeysuckle Honey*. 'I can't wait for a new batch,' she said. 'I used up my last jar on my toast just this morning.'

'Me too,' Harry agreed. 'I've already had an order from Alicia at the market. It'll be a few weeks yet, though. It's all looking good, mind. I've checked the frames all the way through; the queens are there, and the bees are healthy.'

'It certainly looks like they're bringing the pollen in,' Kara said, pointing to the flowerbeds that had a few yellow-and-black striped visitors buzzing around them.

'Yes, we will get some lovely honey in this summer, I think.' Harry turned his kettle off at the wall and checked to see if Bert was still breathing in his basket behind him.

Kara picked up some felt-tip pens off the shelf and went to open them.

'Not those, duck, they are for my queens.'

'I didn't know they could write,' Kara humoured him. Then, 'What *are* they for?' She'd never really taken much time to understand the whole beekeeping process.

'I have to mark the queens behind the ear with a felt-tip pen every year.'

'No way! So, is there more than one queen, then? I didn't know that either.'

'We have three hives, so yes, three queens, one in each hive. It amazed me too, when I started researching it all, back in the day.' The old man plonked his bulky frame down in his armchair. 'Let me tell you quickly. You never know, you might want to look after some yourself one day. Open up your chair, duck.' He pointed to the one remaining red fold-up chair in the corner of the shed. The others had been taken to the ferry long before.

Kara suddenly went into a regular brief daydream of hers, in which she was living in a rose-covered cottage with a handsome and loving husband. Children and pets were running around her feet as she tended to her own bees and flowers. The beautiful smell of home-made bread escaped from the imaginary Aga and she felt as if she had not a care in the world.

Grandad Harry's voice startled her back into the present moment. 'So, young 'un, let me explain. There are five queen bee-marking colours that follow an internationally recognised colour sequence depending on the last number of the year that the queen was introduced. Since queens do not live more than five years, the colour code starts over in the sixth year.'

'That's mad!'

Grandad Harry went on. 'The pens are coloured white, yellow, red, green and blue, so a common mnemonic used by us beekeepers to remember the colours is, "Will You Raise Good Bees?"'

'Oh my God, I love that!' Kara repeated the mantra a couple of times.

'Each colour represents the number the year ends in; blue is for the year ending in a zero or a five for example.'

'Wow, you learn something new every day. Talking of learning, what class have you been going to at the church hall, then?'

Grandad Harry struck a Superman pose with his arms. 'Just call me the silver surfer. I, Granddaughter, have been learning how to use a computer.'

'Really?' That was the last thing she had expected to hear.

'Don't sound so surprised. There's life in this old dog yet. I even have my own email account, hmm . . . what is my email dress now?' He paused, and she didn't have the heart to correct him with the word *address*.

'Yes, I remember now: harrybgood@bmail.com. I am also getting a new mobile phone, which will enable me to not only text but to do that face video thing using something called What's Up.'

'*WhatsApp*, Grandad.'

'Nothing's up, duck.'

Kara smiled and gave up as the old man continued, 'So, no more of that sister of yours saying she's called me on the home phone, when she quite clearly hasn't.'

'That's brilliant.' Kara beamed.

'I'll be giving that Bill Gates a run for his money soon.' Harry's belly moved up and down as he laughed. It was infectious. When Kara managed to stop herself, she put a hand on his squidgy knee. 'I'm proud of you, Grandad, I really am.'

'The thing is, Kerry, there was another reason I've done this, and I do need your help now.'

'Go on.' Kara was intrigued.

'You see, I want to use your father's laptop to set up one of those dating things.'

'O . . . K . . .' Kara dragged out both letters to stop what she really wanted to say coming out wrongly.

'Your face.' Harry laughed again. 'Not for me, I can only just about ride that blinking trike without falling off.'

'Grandad!'

'No, seriously now. It's for your dad. I worry about him, Kerry. It's time he forgot about bloody Doryty and got himself a decent lady. I can't bear the thought of him rattling around here on his own when I'm gone.'

Kara took a sharp intake of breath. Even the mention of her mother's name rattled her. She had sparse memories of that fateful holiday. It was as if her brain had allowed her to forget it. She then thought about her father. In the twenty years since Doryty had left, he had never been on so much as a date. Instead he had initially put all his focus into bringing her up as best he could, whilst still ensuring that the ferry crossing kept its magnificent reputation. And when she did eventually fly the nest, he continued doggedly working his way through life, without so much as a thought for what might make him happy.

'I don't know if this is a good idea, Grandad,' she said doubtfully. 'I mean, how are you proposing to persuade him to do it?'

'I'm not. I'd like you to upload a photo of him – I was thinking the one when we are all sat outside Frank's on your birthday. He looks happy in that one. I'm not sure how it works but can we put up a few words about him and then just see what happens?'

'So, make up a dating profile for him, you mean?'

'Profile? Hmm. That's what they call it, is it? But you've got it, little lady.'

'And how are we going to get him to meet someone if

they agree to go on a date with him? Hmmm. I'm not sure about this.'

'The most precious thing in this life is uncertainty, young Kerry. Imagine if we knew what was going to happen in advance? We'd never get out of bed.'

'OK, OK.' Kara checked her watch. 'Dad will be home soon. Let's go inside and finish getting the dinner ready. I'll pop in tomorrow after work and we'll see what we can do.'

'Good girl.' Harry eased himself slowly out of his armchair.

Kara handed him his stick. 'I'm so happy to be a part of you.'

'Hmm. Depends which part. I'd skip the dodgy right knee, if I were you.'

Chapter 17

Star put her legs up on the rails of the balcony at Kara's flat and sipped from a large glass of chilled white wine.

'Your new boyfriend is looking up here,' she said. 'He's probably peering up your dress.'

Kara came to the doorway and tried to remain out of sight of the ferry. 'Billy's just a mate and I don't want to hear anything else on the matter, OK?'

'The lady doth protest too much, methinks.'

'Don't you go all Shakespeare on me. Billy was calling up at the balcony last time he was here.'

'See? It's all written, Kar. I can feel it, you know me. Little bit of the old white witch coming out today.' Star put her legs back down to ground level. 'Have you spoken to him since Snog Gate?' She blew noisy kisses into the air.

Kara remained serious. 'To be honest, I've avoided him, but I will talk to him. And talking of writing, come on, let's get this guest advert done.'

Star softened. 'You know I'm just joking with you. How are you feeling? It is still early days, I know.'

'I kind of miss Jago, if I'm honest, but then I think it may just be the company I'm missing. Eight years is a long time not to be alone.'

'I hear you. I guess I'm never alone as Skye has always been with me. And I vowed that unless I met someone who

95

would fit in around both of our lives, I would never invite them in. So, in a funny way, she allows me to be alone, as in partner-free, without me even questioning it. And being a free spirit suits me. Well, it does at the moment, anyway.' Star took another drink of wine. 'Did any of that make sense?'

Without waiting for an answer, she carried on, 'My crystal sessions quite often turn into counselling sessions. I hear so many people telling me their partners are holding them back. But no one can force someone to do anything. You are in charge now, Kara. You are free to be who you want to be and do whatever you want to do.'

Kara looked wistful. 'Sometimes I don't even know who I am any more.' She looked out across the water and, on noticing the ferry heading back to Crowsbridge, joined Star on the white metal bench. Seagulls were noisily cawing overhead and the estuary was alive with yachts and pleasure boats enjoying the Easter holiday break. The strong easterly breeze had encouraged a few windsurfers out to make the most of the early evening sunshine. A couple of kayakers were also heading towards the quay. The sound of chattering children could be heard from outside the ice-cream kiosk at Frank's and cars were already pulling up on the road below for the return ferry journey across the water. 'But what I do know is that I want to be able to do more than just work, eat, sleep, repeat.'

James Bond appeared and started weaving in and out of their legs, emitting loud, lawnmower-sounding purrs.

'So, let's get you to that place, Kara Moon. Come on.' With a delighted James Bond jumping up on the now empty bench and stretching his long, thin body along it, they made their way inside to the small table and two chairs where Kara had set up the laptop.

'Did you decide on yours or the spare room for your guests?' Star asked.

'Definitely mine. I'm going to move all my clothes and personal stuff into the spare room. I can use it as a dressing room now he's gone. So, when a guest does book, all I need to do is change the bedding in my room, as it will be clutter-free.' Kara paused. 'That's a thought – I'll get some new duvet sets and towels. I can use some of the two hundred quid Grandad Harry gave me for that. Shit, and tomorrow I need to get flea stuff for mad cat.'

After an hour of faffing and tidying, plumping pillows and straightening the duvet, standing on chairs to get the best camera angles of the harbour and several copy rewrites, an Airbnb listing for Number One, Ferry View Apartments was born.

Kara uploaded photos of the pretty Victorian block, Frank's and the estuary harbour, plus her now spotless bedroom and bathroom and a view from the big bay window in the lounge. She also reluctantly agreed on Star's insistence that including a host photo would make the listing more personal and would help to attract clientele. A nightly price of sixty pounds including breakfast was deemed by both to be acceptable.

Kara began to read aloud to make sure it all made sense before going live.

Location: Ferry View Apartments is situated overlooking the lively Hartmouth Estuary amidst the stunning backdrop of the Cornish coastline. Hartmouth is a thriving market town famed for its bustling Ferry Lane Market and narrow cobbled streets. It is a haven for yachtsmen and visiting tourists alike, offering fine restaurants, a bespoke floristry centre and a world-renowned crystal shop. The historic ferry crosses the

River Hart regularly to Crowsbridge, where you will find the impressive Cornish Trust property, Crowsbridge Hall.

They both then laughed. 'Loving our bit of free advertising there,' Star added.

Kara agreed. 'Let's add our websites on there too. If they get removed, so be it.' She cleared her throat and carried on reading at speed.

The space: Your room is on the 1st floor of this charming sea-facing apartment block. As you enter the room you are greeted by a stunning 180-degree view of the Hartmouth Estuary through a large sash window. The size of the room is very comfortable and it houses a king-size bed.

Bathroom: Directly opposite your room is a spacious toilet and bathroom, which is shared with the host, who will rarely be present at the two-bedroom property.

Notes: Must not be allergic to cats or reptiles.

'Me not being there isn't wholly a lie as I intend to go to Bee Cottage to shower, et cetera, when they are here,' Kara stated, 'although I'll have to come in to feed Sid and James Bond, and to give them a bit of attention.'

'It's sounding great. Go on,' Star urged.

Breakfast: Cereal, bread, milk, tea and coffee will be available, as well as one voucher per day for Frank's, the popular American-style diner just a five-minute walk from the apartment, where you can sample one of their magnificent traditional Cornish breakfasts.

'Ooh, it's sounding so good I might book it myself.' Star laughed, standing up from one of the uncomfortable wooden dining chairs and stretching out her back. 'Right, I'd better get going, Skye will be wondering where I am.'

The intercom buzzer rang.

'Maybe it's your first guest already,' Star joked.

The distinctive London accent of Billy Dillon rang through the flat.

'Kerry, it's me.'

'Shall I remind him to put the toilet seat down if he stays over?' Star winked and headed off down the stairs.

'Billy Dillon.' Kara formally greeted the handsome ferryman in the doorway of her apartment, slightly nervously.

'How's it going, Kerensa Moon?'

Kara bit her lip. 'Before you say anything else, look . . . about the other day.'

'I thought we'd covered that already?'

'It's just. I didn't want to—'

'Lead me on?' Billy interrupted.

Kara nodded.

'It's fine,' he shrugged. 'I wait years for a date, get snogged within an inch of my life and then discarded like an old rag. It's fine, really.' Kara had to double-check to see if he was joking. For a second, he had sounded serious but his smirk gave it away. 'I'll be your handsome decoy any day, darling, don't you worry.'

'Come in.' Kara shut the door behind him.

'So, has the toad been in touch since, then?'

'Only to ask how Sid was.'

Billy laughed. 'That bloke is such a twat.' He paused. 'And if he'd rather be with a posh stick insect with no tits over you, then let him, it's his loss.'

Kara smiled, absent-mindedly taking out her headband and shaking her head so that her long auburn waves settled around her shoulders.

'Whoa, girl, what are you doing to me now?'

'Will you stop it! You know you could have a choice of much younger girls with swishier hair and much slimmer thighs.'

'Maybe I could.' Billy waited. 'If I wanted to.'

Kara rolled her eyes, hoping he couldn't see the faint blush making its way up her cheeks. 'Anyway, what can I do you for?' She rustled around in her handbag for her lip balm.

'It was just that your dad mentioned you were opening up your flat to guests and I wondered if you needed any help shifting anything or whatever.'

'Aw.' Kara made a tutting noise. 'I probably will do, but not now as I need to get a move on as, talking of Dad, I'm meeting him and Grandad in the Ferryboat in a minute.'

'OK, well, you know where I am.'

'That I do, and Billy, thank you. That's really sweet of you.'

Billy put his finger lightly on Kara's nose. 'Sweet? *Moi*?' He winked. 'I think you hold the monopoly on that one.'

Chapter 18

Pearlette Baptiste was sweating as she rushed in through the front door of the Victorian semi-detached house she shared with her much younger sister, brother-in-law and their two children in Penrigan. Thinking she mustn't forget to throw her uniform in the washing machine, she tore up the stairs, nearly knocking her twelve-year-old nephew over on the landing in the process.

'Auntie Pearl, what's the hurry?'

'I'm so sorry, my little darling. Did you have a good day?'

'There's no school, so of course I did.' The lad sloped back into his bedroom to play on his computer game.

Pearl heard the bath running and the deep voice of her brother-in-law doing his usual Pavarotti impressions, oblivious to the world around him, and sighed. Oh, to feel that free and easy again, she thought.

There were of course many advantages to living with her sister and family, but having a house with just one bathroom wasn't one of them. She checked her watch and berated herself for not having had a shower at the hospital where she'd just finished her shift. Pearl had been a staff nurse for thirty years, but had only been working at Penrigan General for the past six months. Previously she'd worked in the busy Accident & Emergency department of a south-east London hospital, where stabbings rather than tractor injuries were the norm. But whatever the injury, compassion for her patients was always the same and, despite it still being a stressful and extremely draining job at times, there was nothing in the world she would rather do. And with her due to turn sixty later in the year, moving out of London and enjoying the slower pace of living in such a beautiful area of the country was also helping her to rebuild her life . . . after the accident.

Realising that she would be late if she waited for a shower, she took her toiletries bag into the downstairs cloakroom and gave herself the kind of strip wash usually reserved for her patients. She dressed, cleaned her teeth and then gave herself a critical glance in the mirror. She couldn't deny her platinum crop looked amazing against her smooth ebony skin, but her eyes, as well as having bags under them, had recently lost their sparkle.

'Well, just look at you – you look a picture, honey.' Her sister Ireany passed her in the kitchen.

'Let's just hope he likes big-bottomed girls with even bigger bags under their eyes.' Pearl laughed and then groaned. 'I'm too old for this dating malarkey.'

'Didn't I tell you that you should've got him to come here to Penrigan, not have you rushing around the county for him,' her sister scolded. 'That's not the way to start courting a man, you hear me?'

Pearl heard her, but didn't want to go into the fact that her date *had* offered to meet her locally; however, on learning that he wasn't finishing work until eight, she wouldn't hear of it. Instead she would jump on her beloved pea-green Vespa and go to him.

'Here.' Ireany reached for a perfume bottle in her bag and without warning sprayed Pearlette from head to toe.

'Poo!' Ireany's younger son came in from playing outside. 'That stinks!' His mother mock-swiped him around the head as he darted past her and up the stairs.

'Ignore him. That'll have him chasing you up and down them cliffs and back again.' Then Ireany added softly, 'Dear Don would have wanted you to move on, you know he would.'

With tears in her eyes, Pearl replied, 'I know he would, but that doesn't make it any easier.'

Chapter 19

'We never normally go out for a drink midweek and I'm shattered, Dad.' Joe Moon had only just kicked off his boots after a long day on the ferry.

'But I promised our Kerry we'd meet her in the Ferryboat. She must be a bit lonely at the moment and we don't have to stay for long.'

At the mention of his daughter, Joe rallied. 'All right, come on then. I'm starving so let's get some food there, too.'

Harry smiled inwardly; he loved it when a plan came together. 'Aren't you going to have a shower and brush your hair?'

Joe went to the mirror to briefly flatten down his snowy-white, collar-length hair with one hand. 'I'm sixty-one, not six years old, Dad, and it's only the pub not the Ritz.'

Just as Kara was ordering herself a drink at the bar, she noticed someone matching the photo of Pearlette, 59, known as 'Pearl', arriving at the bar opposite. As the potential date for her dad greeted the barman, Kara checked her out. Thankfully the photo of the woman matched her real self perfectly. Kara had read so many horror stories about Internet dating and her dad was so trusting, like her, that she was going to make sure she was behind him all the way on this.

Pearlette's wide and perfect smile took up half of her pretty face. She also could definitely match Kara on the boob front and her loud, infectious laugh, which was now echoing across the bar, was simply wonderful. Kara noticed that her hair was gorgeous too: silvery blond, cropped and stepped into her tight curls. She had a lime-green crash helmet over one arm. Even cooler, Kara thought. More important was the fact that Pearlette's profile had been so natural, honest and unassuming. She was also a nurse, which gave her further plus points.

Checking her watch, Kara prayed that her dad and Grandad Harry wouldn't be late. They had just five minutes left in which to get here. It was already bad form that they hadn't already been here when Joe's date had arrived.

Thankfully, there had not been much of an email correspondence to get to this dating stage and what conversation there had been, Kara had overseen it all. She just hoped that her dad would play the game and not run a mile when he knew they had set him up like this. Just then, her phone beeped with a WhatsApp message from her grandad. Phew. He'd remembered how to use it. They were here. Taking her drink outside, she saw Joe's van pulling into the car park, then smiled as she spotted a pea-green Vespa parked up in the corner. This woman had style too!

'Hello, darling.' Joe Moon kissed his daughter on the cheek as Harry, completely relinquishing all blame and responsibility, stumped his way over to one of the outside benches and sat down. There was no time for a long introduction.

Kara cleared her throat and blurted out: 'Dad, we've arranged a date for you.'

'You *what?*'

'Her name is Pearlette – Pearl; I think you may well get on.'

'Hey, no, when—? No, I don't think so. You did this without asking me? No, I—'

But before he had a chance to say anything more, Pearl herself appeared in the doorway and waved across at him.

'Joseph? Joseph Moon?'

'Er. Um. Yes, that's me.' Joe looked like a rabbit caught in headlights.

Kara whispered, 'You'll be fine,' as she hotfooted it over to her grandad.

'I'm Pearlette, but everybody calls me Pearl.' The large lady beamed at her date, then held out her hand. 'Lovely to meet you.'

'Um . . . yes, likewise. I'm Joseph, but everybody calls me Joe.' He caught a whiff of Pearl's strong, musky perfume. Kara, anxiously listening in from the sidelines, was immensely proud of her dad when he went on politely, 'I love your scent, Pearl. What is it?'

And was even more delighted when Pearl replied back in a deadpan voice: 'It's called desperation, Joe, but we can work on that, I'm sure.'

Chapter 20

'Welcome to Ferry Lane Market.' Kara felt like *she* was on a first date as she held out her hand to her very first Airbnb guest. For there in front of her was a thirty-something short man, with a wide face and bushy brown beard. His eyes were hazel and his handshake firm. She had suggested to 'Jack from New York' that it would be easier for him to meet her at Passion Flowers so that she could take him down to the apartments and show him how the entry system worked, etc.

'How very formal.' Jack laughed to reveal a slightly crooked set of bottom teeth.

'You're English?' Kara noticed.

'Last time I looked, yes.'

'Oh. I wrongly assumed that you were American as you said you were travelling in from New York.'

'It's complicated.' Jack yawned. 'Oh, excuse me, it's been a long day already.'

'Well, let's uncomplicate things now, shall we, and get you to your room. You must be knackered.'

'Wow, what a view – but you had me at not being allergic to reptiles, to be honest.'

Kara laughed. 'Yes, we just by-passed Sid Vicious. He's a terrapin who bites, hence the name – but you can meet him later.'

Jack grinned. 'This place just gets better and better.' At that moment her moody moggy, on hearing a new voice in the flat, jumped up on the freshly made bed.

'James Bond, get down this minute!' Kara shouted.

Jack's comical laugh sounded like he had a bad bout of hiccups. 'And you have a cat called James Bond? That's unreal. You wait until I tell Riley about this. She's always wanted a cat, but we're not allowed pets in our place in New York.'

'Riley's your girlfriend, I take it?'

Jack let out a big sigh and ran a hand through his thick dark hair. His face was all eyes against his bushy beard.

'Sorry, I didn't mean to pry.' Kara wasn't sure if she was overstepping the boundaries of an Airbnb hostess's attributes.

'You're fine. She's the reason I'm an Englishman in New York. For the time being, anyway. And no, Sting didn't write that song about me. Let's just say that a spoiled out-of-work actress and a writer who is just about to submit the most important screenplay of his life isn't a good combination.' He rested his wheelie case in the corner of the bedroom. 'This is a great place, Kara. Do you own it?'

'Yes – well, I have a mortgage. I've been living here eight years now, and was lucky to get on the property ladder early. But I'm having to rent my room out, so it's not all plain sailing, this homeowner – or relationship – lark.'

'I hear you on both counts.' Jack yawned again loudly and put his hand over his mouth. 'Sorry. You're not boring me, honest.' He went to look out of the window and called back, 'We're in the Dakota building, have you heard of it?'

'Heard of it!' Kara raised her eyes. 'My ex is a huge Beatles fan. Every year on December the eighth, I've been involved in many an outdoor candlelit vigil, rain or shine, to celebrate John Lennon's life, whilst listening to every track he'd ever written. It's been a long and winding road, I can tell you.'

Jack turned round, looking sympathetic. 'Oops, sorry to remind you of it and him.'

'Apology not required, it's fine.' There was a silence. 'So, New York to Hartmouth, that's a bit of a culture shock.' Without waiting for Jack to respond, Kara hurried on, 'Shit, *I'm* being a nosy cow now, aren't I? OK, Jack, here are your keys. There's tea and coffee in the kitchen, and a couple of bottles of water in the fridge. And if you're hungry, I can highly recommend Frank's, which is a five-minute walk to your right.' She pointed the way. 'Any questions, just call me on my mobile. In fact,' she went to the kitchen and came back with a Frank's flyer, 'tomorrow, just give this to Big Frank, the owner, when you go in there and it covers you for the breakfast of your choice with a drink.'

'OK. Cool. Could I also take your Wi-Fi code before you go, please?'

'Of course. The box is just behind Sid's tank. Don't put your hand anywhere near him though. I'm not insured for injuries of a reptilian nature.'

'You're very funny.'

Kara felt herself blushing. 'Funny peculiar, maybe.'

'Well, it's lovely to meet you, Kara, and I guess I may see you later? If I don't fall asleep, that is.'

'Just make yourself comfortable and relax. There's a key in the balcony door, if you want to get some air. Oh, and James Bond just comes and goes as he pleases, but make sure to shut your bedroom door as he does have a tendency to bring in presents, sometimes of a vermin-type.'

As soon as Jack heard the front door click, he took one of the clean towels that Kara had placed neatly on his bed and headed to the bathroom to use the loo and give his hands and face a thorough wash. Then, after getting himself some water from the fridge, he opened the balcony door and took in the beautiful vista stretched out before him. New York had felt almost as claustrophobically humid as his relationship situation when he had left. So, this morning's rain, bringing with it a fresh Cornish breeze, was already helping to clear his mind, as well as his senses.

The sea was calm apart from a few wrinkles when the very light wind hit its surface, and he noticed a quaint little tug pulling cars over on the ferry in the distance. Even with the most basic of facilities on offer, he could already feel the stress lifting from his mind. And if he was honest with himself, he felt as comfortable here as in any of the four- or five-star hotels he was used to staying in with his job.

He stepped back inside and was pleased to notice a power point under the table and chairs in the lounge. Leaving the balcony door open, he had a good look around him. Maybe simplicity was all you needed to be happy. The fancy trappings of a New York lifestyle were, on paper, what a lot of people might aspire to, but it was hard work to keep that lifestyle going and, despite being only thirty-seven, he felt tired and burnt out. He sat on the sagging two-seater sofa and shut his eyes for a minute. Absorbing the peaceful sounds of the estuary, he thought about Kara. She seemed so much cooler and more laidback than he had expected her to be, which made him and his main reason for being here feel all the more awkward.

Fishing out his laptop from his wheelie case, he sat back on the sofa, opened it up and put in the Wi-Fi code. Sleeping would have to wait; he had a job to do. He went into his email and began to type:

I'm here. You're right, it's not quite the Ritz, but Hartmouth is a beautiful place. I haven't had a chance to suss out everything yet, but I'll report back as soon as I can. Don't work too hard! Jack x

Kara got into the Passion Flowers van, which she had parked right outside the downstairs entry door. It felt so weird leaving a complete stranger in her own home. But Jack seemed nice enough. He obviously didn't want to discuss his personal life, but there had been no mention of two people staying in the room, so she assumed his girlfriend wasn't joining him. Kara was curious as to why he was here, though. There wasn't a lot of business to be had in Hartmouth, apart from shop work and tourism. Or maybe it was just that he wanted the peace and quiet to finish off his screenplay.

When she had set out to take in guests, she was purely thinking of the extra cash; she hadn't even thought about the social element of being an Airbnb live-in host – that people might actually want to chat with her. She had just assumed that people would mind their own business and want to stay in their rooms and out of her way. Being sociable was all right if they were nice, like Jack, but what if they were a bit weird? She shuddered at the thought. A knock on the van's window made her jump. It was Billy. She opened it.

'Did you know there is some kind of Neolithic man on your balcony?'

Kara laughed. 'Yes, that's Jack, my new fella. He's moved in. I don't like to waste time, as you know.'

'Oh yeah, you're a landlady now, I forgot,' Billy stated with a modicum of relief. 'Is everything to his satisfaction, madam?'

'I don't know, I didn't speak to him for long, but thanks again for helping me get everything sorted. By the way, Sid is hilarious. Even though you fixed the shelf straight and he no longer has to scurry up his rock for fear of sliding down, he still has a run up at it.'

Billy laughed, and then as if he had been reading her mind, he added, 'Kerry, be careful with a strange man in there though, won't you? I should have put a lock on your door.'

'I did kind of think of that. But Grandad Harry said in his matter-of-fact way the other day that there's not a rapist on every corner and anyway, everyone on the site is verified. It is very safe. I'll be fine.'

'There's always room for a little one in my bed.' Billy winked. 'But seriously, if you need me, you know where I am.' He then looked over to the quay. 'Uh oh, the ferry is nearly full. I'd better get back there pronto. Fortunately, your old man is in a really good mood today.' He thumped his hand on the van bonnet, blew her an exaggerated kiss, then made his way at speed back down to the quay.

Kara put the window up and then rested her hand on her heart. She'd forgotten what it felt like for someone to really give a shit about her. She had also forgotten what it was like to see her dad in high spirits.

Chapter 21

Darren Dillon's shiny shaved head suddenly popped up from behind the fruit and veg stall counter, like a curious meerkat.

'What are you doing, Daz?' Kara appeared from the shop with a vase of colourful gerberas in her hands.

He spoke in hushed tones. 'I thought you were Twisty.'

'She's on an early delivery, what's up?'

But her question fell on deaf ears as Daz had already shot back to his dad's van to unload fresh supplies.

Pat Dillon waddled out with a tray of early strawberries and looked up at the sky. 'Looks like bleedin' rain later, although they didn't forecast it. I'm going to have to tan that lovely young Tomasz Schaggernaker's hide for getting it wrong.'

'It's Schafernaker, woman, and rumour has it he'd rather I did that than you,' Charlie Dillon chipped in. 'I'll get the canopy down now, eh. Better that than scurry around like rats in a Stepney knocking shop later.'

'What are you two on about now?' Darren appeared, smelling of cigarette smoke.

'Oi, Darren! Will you stop putting that muck in ya!' his mum scolded.

His dad tried to explain. 'We're arguing about a bloke called Tomasz. He's some young BBC weather reporter, son, and your mother evidently fancies the thunder clappers off him.'

Ignoring the pair of them, Pat turned to Kara. 'All right, love? Hear you've got a sexy guest staying with you. At this rate, you'll soon be over that other waste of space.'

'Patricia Dillon! Whatever are you insinuating?'

'It might up the review rating,' Charlie noted sagely.

Star, who was busy filling her necklace display stand at the stall next to Kara's, overheard and said, 'But he is SO fit.'

'Really? I can't see that at all. All that hair and wonky bottom teeth.' Kara started to erect the pink-and-white awning above her stall. 'But you've always had a thing for ugly men.'

'I agree – and I like them short,' Star said. 'But he's far from ugly, Kara.'

'He's got a girlfriend.'

'That's not a wife.'

Kara shook her head. 'What are you like, Steren Bligh?'

'I don't even know why we're having this conversation.' Star stood back to see what her display looked like from the other side of the table. 'It must be at least three years since I've even been on a date with someone. I've probably healed over down there by now. Now, does anyone fancy a pasty?'

'Ew, not after that comment, thanks,' Darren said, then checked his watch. 'The nine a.m. ferry is just pulling in, so get ready for action, people.'

'Talking of dates, how did your dad get on?' Star was now sitting behind her stall, checking that the earring backs were safely on her new birthday crystal section of jewellery.

'He really liked her!'

'Oh my God, that's great, Kar!'

'She's a nurse, works at Penrigan General. Her husband was killed in London a couple of years ago.'

'Oh no.'

'Yeah. A stolen car knocked him over on a pedestrian crossing.'

'That's so sad. Does she have children?'

'I forgot to ask, but if she does they're probably grown up as she's just coming up sixty. She lives with her younger sister and family at the moment. She told Dad she couldn't bear to be in London any more, as the memories are too sad for her there now.'

'Aw. Bless her.'

'Billy said what a good mood Dad was in the other day, so it sounds promising. He's seeing her again tonight, actually.'

'I'm made up for him. What's her name?'

'Pearl.'

'Oh, my goodness. This is a *definite* sign!' Star reached excitedly for one of her crystal and gem leaflets, displayed on her stand ready for customers to help themselves. 'Listen to this.' She began to read. '"If you're single, Pearls signify that you will find love"!' She beamed and carried on. '"Pearls will make you a more dependable partner, and you will enjoy a more faithful and trusting relationship. There will be balance and harmony in your emotions."'

Lost in the moment, the pair of them jumped when a male voice interrupted, saying, '"The heart has its reasons which reason knows not." Sorry, I couldn't help but overhear you.'

'Blaise Pascal,' Star said dreamily.

'No, I'm Jack Murray, but pleased to meet you.' The bearded man grinned his wonky smile. 'Sorry for barging in like that.'

Star blushed. 'I love that Pascal quote.'

'Did you sleep well, Jack?' Kara enquired.

'Amazingly, thank you. No sirens, no traffic noise. Bliss. I'm fit to burst after a Frank's breakfast too. Thought I'd have a mosey around the market and then pop across on the ferry to visit Crowsbridge Hall just like a proper tourist.'

Without warning, Star's subconscious sprang into life and the words flew straight out of her mouth: 'So, do you have any plans for tonight, then?' she heard herself saying.

And in reply, Jack's expressive hazel eyes told her all she needed to know.

Chapter 22

Kara was relieved to kick off her shoes, make herself a cup of tea and sit back on the sofa. It had been a busy day and Lydia had left her to clear up on her own. Checking her phone, she gasped as she saw an email come in. A one-night booking for next Friday from someone called Angel from Barcelona. Were men really called Angel? Shuddering at the thought that her mother had run off with a Spanish man called Jesus, she guessed so. She checked out his guest profile and spoke to James Bond, who was now purring loudly on her knees. 'Look at us, getting the handsome Spanish men to come and stay with us, now.'

It was early days, but she was already finding this whole Airbnb thing quite exciting, and the extra money would come in so handy. In fact, she had picked up a vintage money box in the shape of a Puffin from the antique stall in the market, and it was now in pride of place next to Sid Vicious. Any floristry tips she received would be going in there. She had no idea how long it would take her to save for a decent holiday, but with only having to look after herself now – and the pets, of course – and with the guests covering some of the mortgage, she hoped it wouldn't be too long. Then she frowned. It was all very well saving for a holiday – but there was the small matter of finding someone to go with her.

Setting her auburn locks free from her hair clip, she rested her head back on the sofa and allowed the soft breeze from the open balcony door to caress her face. It was the first Saturday night when she had had time to just sit and reflect on what had happened. Since Jago had gone she had been rushing around, cleaning and sorting and getting the apartment ready for guests. It made her realise that when you were in a relationship you didn't have to make plans, because even if there wasn't a plan, you were together, doing nothing. But she and Jago didn't even do doing nothing together well. Most Saturday nights he would go off pretending to be taking a walk to clear his head, when really, she thought he was having a joint at Duck Pond Park with his friends. He would come back late, put his headphones on and listen to the Beatles, then fall asleep, usually on the sofa. She much preferred him stoned to drunk, though, as at those times it was Kara who had to take the walk, to get away from his ugly behaviour and verbal abuse.

A sudden thought lit up her mind: *she felt less alone without him.*

Still in recovery and wary of getting into the wrong relationship, she had decided last night that men could wait now. But this thought was overridden by the nagging doubt telling her that if she wanted to have a family, at the age of thirty-three, her body clock might not be so forgiving. As she lay there, Kara started to question herself. Why hadn't she pushed the baby thing with Jago? Why had she let things drag on for so long before she made the decision to kick him out? Despite her angst, the sounds of the estuary began to work its magic of soothing even the most troubled of minds and to the background of James Bond's contented purring, she fell into a deep slumber.

After what seemed like seconds, she awoke to a seagull landing and squawking at the top of its voice on the side of her balcony railings. Opening her eyes slowly, she moaned as she had slept in a funny position and her neck was painful. The room was dark. She checked her watch. Ten o'clock. How could that have happened? She then nearly jumped out of her skin as she heard a key in the lock and saw the lounge light go on.

'Jesus, Jack, you scared the life out of me.'

'Oh sorry,' he said, then added apologetically, 'I'm a bit tipsy.'

'Don't you be apologising to me. What sort of host am I? Have you eaten? Are you all right?'

'You're so sweet, Kara. Not how I expected you to be at all.'

'What do you mean by that?'

'Oh, er, nothing, nothing. Ignore me, it's the red wine talking.' He sat on one of the dining chairs. Kara, with squinty eyes, tried to tame her now completely wild sleep hair.

'And some advice to the host,' Jack went on, 'coming from someone who sometimes rents out a room in New York. You offer somewhere for guests to rest their head, but you don't have to be their cook, tour guide or confidante, not if you don't want to.'

'Maybe I do want to.' Kara stood up and groaned as she stretched out her back. 'This sofa needs to be changed too. I'm starving. There's a pizza in the fridge if you fancy some?'

Wearing coats to ward off the evening chill, the two of them sat side by side on the balcony bench, scoffing pizza and drinking coffee. Kara had lit a citronella candle and placed it on top of an upturned flowerpot by their feet. Even the seagulls were surprisingly quiet tonight. Only the noise of creaking masts and a couple of voices carrying from the outside smoking area of the Ferryboat occasionally broke the peace of the late-spring night as the full moon threw a shimmering pathway of light right across the estuary to Crowsbridge Quay.

Pointing to the twinkling stretch of water before them, Kara murmured, 'I love it when that happens. It makes me feel that anything is possible, that you could walk across the water on top of the guiding light and only happy things would be waiting for you at the end of it.'

'You're quite the romantic, aren't you?'

'I actually don't know any more. I've been in a bloody loveless relationship for so long.'

Jack put his hand on her arm. 'Well, from what I've seen so far, I think you're a great girl, Kara Moon.' He hiccupped. 'Ah, and I get it now.'

'Get what?'

'Why you like the moon, because you are one yourself . . . Miss Moon.' He laughed at his nonsensical statement. Then sighed, 'Riley would love it here.'

'You should have brought her along.' A brief silence. Then Kara went on, 'What are you doing here anyway? I mean, if you're writing a screenplay, Hartmouth couldn't be any further removed from Hollywood.'

'I'm here for *real* work, I'm afraid. Got a couple of business meetings in Plymouth next week, plus I needed time to think. A girl I work with suggested that coming here would be amazing.'

'What do you do?'

'Just boring old finance.'

'My sister works in finance. She raves about it.' When Jack didn't respond, Kara carried on, 'So, writing is your hobby then, I take it?'

'I'd like to call it my passion. My dream. I think we all need a dream, Kara. Something that helps us remove our minds from the rat race and enables us to escape it.'

'Yes. In which case, my passion is flowers.'

'*Passion . . . Flowers*! I see why you chose the name now.'

'I wish it was my shop.'

'Time to stop saying I wish and saying I will now, I reckon, Miss Moon.'

'I wish I could be as wise as you. Oh no!' Kara laughed. 'I'm doing it again already.'

'I talk a good sage, at least.' Jack smiled. 'I came here to clear my head about Riley too and tonight, I've just properly clouded every brain cell in it.' He ran a hand through his bushy beard.

Just as Kara was about to ask her guest what exactly he meant by that, they were interrupted by a rowdy conversation carrying on the still air. Two figures got to the corner of Ferry Lane and stopped under the lamp post. Kara instantly recognised the unmistakable silhouettes of the Dillon twins.

Billy looked up to the balcony and began beating his chest, calling out to Jack, 'Oi, Tarzan, remember she's just your landlady, not Jane, won't you?' He then proceeded to Tarzan yell his way up the hill.

Chapter 23

Kara heard an unfamiliar sound as she walked up the path to Bee Cottage. Laughter. Full-hearted, glorious peals of laughter, accompanied by the appetising smell of fresh baking and the velvety voice of Elvis Presley drifting from the open kitchen window. She also noticed that her dad's work boots were abnormally clean and had been neatly placed in the porch.

She opened the door to the kitchen to find Pearl Baptiste and her father struggling to fix the blind up above the kitchen window: the very same blind that had been lying dormant and dusty on the windowsill for at least six months.

'Here's your girl.' Standing on a chair, Pearl directed her magnificent smile at Kara as she came in. 'I love a bit of DIY, me.' She released her screwdriver. 'OK, that's it by the look of it. Job done.' Joe helped her down, then gently smacked her ample backside before turning down the radio.

'Kerry, meet Pearl. Pearl, meet Kerry, my second daughter.' Joe seemed a little nervous.

Pearl gave her an affectionate hug, saying, 'I hear you and your grandfather are responsible for me meeting this glorious man. I have a lot to thank you for.'

'Yes, and it looks like things are going well, then?' Kara managed, slightly thrown by the first public display of affection she had ever seen coming from her dad.

'They are indeed.' Pearl put her hand under Joe's chin and squeezed it. 'My Nana used to say that the best relationships are the ones you never saw coming – and I think she's proved it with us, don't you, my Joey?'

At that moment, Grandad Harry appeared in the doorway, with Bert carried over his shoulder. He raised his eyes knowingly to Kara behind the couple's back before saying, 'Have you got a minute to help me up the garden with some bits, Kerry?'

'Of course. I'll get your stick.'

Pearl checked the oven. 'So, sweet Kerry, as I knew you were coming I'm cooking us all a special roast-beef dinner. I've done the potatoes small, the way your dad says you like them. Plus for afters, we have my world-famous morello-cherry pie. Do you like cherry pie?' Pearl didn't wait for an answer. 'Actually, I've never met anyone who doesn't like my morello-cherry pie and quite frankly, I don't want to.' The curvy woman let out a deep, throaty laugh, which set all of them off again.

Harry and Kara sat in their usual positions in the shed at the bottom of the garden, Harry in his threadbare green armchair and Kara just outside on her faded red one. Bert had slowly followed them up from the cottage and was already curled up, sleeping on the old man's lap. The June afternoon was a dull one, but not cold. The birdsong was quieter than usual, and it seemed that even the gulls were having a Sunday siesta. Henrietta and Daisy were scratching around in the garden, making happy murmuring sounds at finding the broccoli stalks that Kara had just thrown down for them.

The pleasant hum of bees working away in their hives behind them caused her to gulp in a big breath of home.

Harry leaned back and shut his eyes for a second.

'Are you feeling all right?' Kara asked.

'It's a case of be careful what you wish for and all that. Three times they've met up, and as you can see, she's already got her staff nurse's feet well and truly under that kitchen table of ours, young 'un.'

'True, but she seems so lovely – and when did we last see Dad look so happy? Surely it can only be a good thing?'

'I know, love, and yes, she does seem to be so jolly and full of kindness. The complete opposite of that wicked mother of yours.' Kara winced at his comment. 'Sorry. That's not fair on you.'

She immediately changed the subject. 'I can't believe I'm asking this question but, er . . . did Pearl stay the night?'

'She pretended to reappear at eight o'clock this morning, but your dad has always underestimated my levels of selective hearing.'

'Ooh, I don't want to know any more. It makes me feel a bit funny.'

Harry laughed, causing Bert to make a little woof of annoyance at being disturbed from his doggy slumber. 'I mean, as in I heard her creeping down the stairs this morning, going out of the front door then knocking on it again to appear as if she was just arriving. That pea-green scooter of hers never moved an inch. They then went off together to the supermarket to get all the lovely lunch supplies.'

Kara couldn't have been happier. 'It's so great that Daz and Billy are working the ferry on a Sunday now, giving Dad some time off.' She felt her phone vibrate with a text message.

'Yes, it really is,' her grandfather agreed. 'It's time for

my Joseph now. He deserves every drop of happiness that's coming his way. And I don't want him to be creeping around the house like a teenager. So maybe it's time I did shuffle off this mortal coil.'

'Grandad! What are you talking about? Men with the heart of a lion don't escape this world that easily.'

'And I need to see that sister of yours first before I go anywhere.' Bert squirmed to get comfortable.

'Grandad!'

Harry ignored his granddaughter's indignation. 'Have you spoken to Jen lately?'

'Randomly, she did message me yesterday morning. Dad had obviously told her about Jago going and Pearl arriving. She didn't dwell on that, but did suddenly start showing a keen interest in my Airbnb venture and how I'm getting on with the one and only guest I've had so far.'

'Oh. She's a funny one, that one. I feel I hardly know her. Well, any of her good parts, anyway.'

'You and all of us,' Kara agreed. 'I'm surprised Dad didn't mention that she called, actually. It's such a bloody rare occurrence.'

'That's what love does to you.' Harry smiled. 'But it's great she's been in touch. I'm going to try that What's Up thing on her later, now I know how to use it and we know that she's still alive.'

'It's WhatsApp, Grandad.'

'What's Up, What Ever.' Harry took on the tone of a teenager.

'You've got funny bones, you have.' Kara stood up and went to kiss her grandad on the forehead.

'Old bones, more like. Here, take Bert, will you. We'd better not be late for lunch, as a lot of effort is being made, by the look of things.' Kara lifted the old Jack Russell from Harry's lap and put him on to the floor. She then linked her grandad's arm and helped to steady him as he stood up.

'What did you want my help with, anyway?' she wanted to know.

'Nothing. I just needed your ears and your sweet smile.' He ruffled her freshly washed hair. 'You have given me great joy throughout my life, Kerensa Anne. I love you, darling.'

'What are you getting all soppy for?'

As they walked slowly back down to the cottage, Bert at their heels, Kara checked her phone message and let out a sharp, 'Oh.'

'Everything OK, duck?'

'Yes, it's Jack, my Airbnb guest. His plans have changed, and he's had to leave suddenly.'

Pearl threw open the back door as they approached. 'Ta-dah! Our feast is ready.' Harry limped off to wash his hands in the kitchen sink, whilst Joe busied himself opening a bottle of red wine that had been sitting on the kitchen side for months waiting for a special occasion.

'Wow! Look at this.' Kara felt tears welling in her eyes as she took in the wonderful spread laid out on the long kitchen table in front of her. A huge joint of beef sat steaming on the willow-pattern meat plate that belonged to her grandparents and was only brought out at Christmas, and only then when Granny Annie had been alive. This was surrounded by a mountain of golden roast potatoes and huge crispy Yorkshire puddings. Another serving dish held mixed vegetables, and alongside that, a glass dish of creamy leeks in a cheese sauce next to a jug of delicious-smelling thick dark gravy. Each place setting was adorned with a colourful serviette. Kara also spotted Bert's bowl sitting on the draining board: it was full of neatly chopped brown meat. Altogether, this was a feast to behold and it had obviously been prepared with complete heart and soul.

Sensitive to the range of emotions that might be running through her new lover's daughter at this moment and holding back tears of her own, Pearl gently squeezed Kara's shoulder, saying lightly, 'My Nana also taught me that cooking is like love: it should be entered into with abandon or not at all.'

Kara automatically reached down and held Pearl's hand. 'Thank you,' she said. 'Thank you so much.'

Chapter 24

On Monday morning at the far too early time of 7 a.m., Kara was standing outside the florist's trying to find her keys when Darren appeared in a rush from the alley at the back of Passion Flowers, nearly knocking her over in the process. He was peering at the ground as if he was looking for something.

'Darren Dillon, you're up so early, you've either wet the bed or you're up to no good.'

'Assumptions are very dangerous things, Kara Moon.' With that, he tore across the cobbled street and up the metal spiral staircase that led to his and Billy's flat over the Dillon family's greengrocery shop.

So full was she from Pearl's amazing late lunch yesterday, that Kara had fallen asleep at 9 p.m. and slept like a baby until 6 a.m., when a seagull perched on the balcony railing had refused to stop squawking until she got out of bed. It had been lovely to see her dad so animated. It was as if another being had entered him and taken him over. His face even looked different. Amazing what your heart could do to your body and soul.

Despite Pearl having taken over the kitchen and much-needed DIY duties at Bee Cottage already, it somehow felt right. Everything she had done and said yesterday was thoughtful. Not only towards Joe, but also with regard to

Kara and Grandad Harry too. This might not have been obvious to everyone's eye, but to Kara, who had a larger empathy gene than most, it was clearly apparent. And when she had been pulled tight into the woman's soft curves for a goodbye embrace, she knew why her dad already liked her so much. Pearlette Baptiste was the embodiment of love and kindness. The terrible pain of losing her husband in such an untimely and tragic way had manifested into the greatest gain to the Moon family. And after just that one lunch with a woman so giving and full of good spirit, Kara realised sadly just how inadequate her own mother had been and still was.

Last night, she had felt slightly disappointed that Jack had had to leave without saying goodbye, but he had left her a lovely note, saying he had enjoyed his stay very much but due to personal reasons he was heading straight back to New York on an earlier flight. He said that he would leave her a glowing review on the Airbnb site, and on the table there had been a little package wrapped in pale yellow tissue paper sitting on a Post-it note, with the words *No more I wish x* written on it. She was so tired she'd forgotten to open it, so instead had thrown it in her bag to open with her morning coffee.

She texted Star to see if she was up. Monday morning was hotel flowers day, so she had plenty to be getting on with, but it was only seven and she didn't have to officially start work until eight. So with luck she could breakfast with her buddy first.

'At your service, Kara Moon and Miss Bligh. Anything else for you, so?' Big Frank placed two coffees and a plate of buttery white and brown toast in front of them.

Star shook her head.

'No, we're fine, thanks. Good weekend?' Kara enquired.

'My Monique is home so yes, a perfect one, thanks. She said she may even pop her pretty little head down here later, ladies, but you know what she's like, so don't be holding your breath on that one.' With that he went outside to start wiping the tables down.

Kara put her phone back in her bag and pulled out the wrapped gift, telling Star, 'Jack left this for me.'

'Did he now?' Star took a tentative sip from her steaming frothy coffee.

Pulling off the tissue paper at speed, Kara held up a pretty pair of pink-flecked earrings, set in a silver casing. 'Aw, they are gorgeous,' she said, pleased. 'Did he get them from your place? If so, he did that quietly.'

Star blushed. Knowing her friend so well, Kara opened her mouth wide.

'Steren Bligh. Have you got something to tell me?'

'They are Rhodochrosite. I thought they would be perfect for you. Just a minute.' Star typed something into her phone then began reading aloud: '"This stone can guide one in the quest for happiness, help one move forward after a period of doubt, and express love towards others without fear of rejection."' She met Kara's eye. 'The meaning is perfect for you.'

'That's very sweet of you and so kind of him to leave me a gift. Thank you, but it kind of all makes sense now too.'

Star hid behind her hair as she drank more coffee. 'What makes sense?'

'Jack arriving back to mine late on Saturday night, then him saying that something had clouded his mind.'

'He said that?' Star was looking slightly wistful; she bit her lip then said quietly, 'OK. I slept with him.'

'Shit.' Kara was surprised. 'I wasn't expecting that.'

'There was just an instant attraction and, well, Skye was at her friend's house until ten, so we had a few drinks and it just kind of happened. It was just sex, Kar; it's been a long time.'

'He's got a girlfriend.'

'Yeah, well, thanks for reminding me of that. It was what it was, though. No one need ever know. Needs were met. No real crime committed.'

'Really?' But Kara knew that her friend didn't give herself away lightly.

'Why did he hurry off?' Star asked.

'Said he had personal problems to sort back home.'

'Probably wanted to get as far away from me as possible.' Star attempted to joke as inwardly, her heart sank to her toes. She had been so looking forward to seeing him one last time before he left.

'Oh my God, you really like him, don't you?'

'Kar, I was with him for a few hours, that's all.'

'"The heart has its reasons which reason knows not."'

'Oh, shut up and put your new earrings in.'

Chapter 25

'I wondered why you had sunflowers on the flower-market list.' Lydia was being unusually polite this Thursday morning. She watched as Kara put the finishing touches to a tall and colourful display for a retirement party at the church hall. 'That looks beautiful.'

'Er, thanks, Lydia. I think these big boys are perfect for a farewell gesture. Sunflowers always make people smile – a bit like the real sun does. And they are said to attract good luck, too.'

'I wish I could feel the same enthusiasm as you do. You really do put the passion into Passion Flowers.' Then Lydia Twist snapped back to her usual self. 'Right! I need to pop home. I'll come back and drop those off. They need them by eleven, don't they? Don't forget you need to tidy out the storeroom, too.' And she left.

Kara finished off the display by sticking a minute piece of Malachite crystal that she had got from Star earlier, (also symbolising good luck), inside the middle of one of the sunflowers. She stood back and admired her work. Then she took a photo of it for her personal collection before carrying the display upstairs to keep the flowers cool and out of the way until Lydia came back to collect them.

Kara couldn't quite believe how normal her boss had been this morning. Almost pleasant, in fact, and there had been an element of sadness in her voice when she had used the 'I wish' words about keeping enthusiastic. Jack had really made her think about the need for passion in one's life now. And thinking of Jack reminded Kara that she must sort out her bedroom later, as handsome Angel from Barcelona was arriving tomorrow – on a market day, too. It would be fine if Lydia wasn't around; she could ask Skye to look after her stall for a few minutes. It wouldn't take her long to show him the flat then hurry back up the hill to work.

Kara placed the flowers in the cool corridor and then was nosey and poked her head into the front room upstairs that Lydia sometimes used to relax in. The sagging sofa seats looked like they needed a good plump, and scatter cushions were all over the floor. Streaming through the bay window, the sun suddenly caught on something on the sofa arm, causing it to glint in rainbow prisms. Curious, Kara blinked in the dazzling light and went to check out what had caused it.

She then put her hand to her mouth and began to laugh. No wonder Daz had had his nose to the floor this morning and why Lydia was being so charming. Putting the diamond ear stud carefully in her jeans pocket, she made her way back downstairs to the shop, still in a state of disbelief.

Chapter 26

'Welcome to Ferry Lane Market,' announced Kara to Angel, her new Spanish Airbnb client, as they stood under the bright pink Passion Flowers market stall awning and looked down towards the estuary.

'Bloody hell. I'll be renting out my place if they all look like that,' Patricia Dillon muttered from across the lane.

'Perving again, wife?' Charlie had overheard. 'You've got top rump steak at home, I tell ya. So, no paella required. Cheeky mare, you are.'

'Top rump? More like bloody minced beef, and that's if it's my birthday,' Pat said coarsely, causing Star to burst out laughing and even the usually very quiet and private artist Glanna Pascoe's lips to twitch on the next stall along from Star's.

'An apple a day keeps the doctor away!' Charlie Dillon suddenly bawled at the top of his voice, brandishing a box of crisp green Granny Smiths in the air. A couple of pensioners stopped at his stall. 'Morning, ladies. How about some fruit to help you look good in your birthday suit?' He grinned the infectious Dillon grin, causing Pat to feel an insurmountable surge of love for her husband and the old ladies to blush and titter with pleasure and to reach for their purses.

'Tomatoes from the Scilly Isles, sure to keep you in big

smiles,' Daz then added, followed by the ruder, 'Cucumbers only fifty pee, good if you live in a nunnery.' And he winked at Kara, which reminded her that she still had his earring in her pocket.

Managing to hide her amusement at the whole scenario, Kara decided to take her slightly bemused visitor away as quickly as possible, leading him down the hill to Number One, Ferry View Apartments; home to both her and the extremely handsome Angel Perez for the next couple of days.

Billy looked up from the ferry quay and waved as Kara showed Angel the view from the balcony and finally which key he needed for which door.

She waved back quickly, then said, 'I'm sorry to rush, Angel, but I have to get back to work.' Then, without warning, the words, 'Are you here just for pleasure?' flew out of her mouth.

The Spaniard went in and sat down on the sofa. He gestured for her to sit down next to him. At six foot, and with his perfectly groomed stubble, short sharp haircut and naturally dark skin, he was one of the best-looking men she had ever been in a room with. His aftershave was a mixture of musk and must-have. She then noticed for the first time the man's beautiful, dark brown and expressive eyes – and for fear of getting too close to him and doing something silly, she went and sat abnormally upright at the dining table.

She didn't know quite what to say next, but thankfully, with a loud miaow and a crash, James Bond came careering through the cat flap with an empty crab shell in his mouth.

'That is good service.' Angel laughed. 'I didn't even order my fish course.'

'Meet James Bond, current man of the house – and please don't put your hand in this tank.' Kara pointed to Sid. 'In here is a terrapin. He has been known to eat previous guests whole.'

Angel's film-star smile accentuated his perfection further. 'Funny, funny! It is such a charming flat. And as for pleasure, yes, that is my reason for being here. I play a little game, you see, Kara.' Kara's thought that he could play any game he wanted with her was cut short as he carried on. 'When I hit twenty-one, nine years ago, I decided that once a year I would take a short trip to a place in Europe that I hadn't visited before. What I do, with my eyes closed, is stick a pin in the map of a country of my choosing and wherever it lands, that's where I go.'

'So, what if you don't like the look of where the pin lands?'

'That is a bit like life in general, Ka-rra.' Kara loved the way he rolled his r's when saying her name. 'There are no second chances in this game called life.' He was a geek in romantic clothing, she decided. The handsome Spaniard then continued, 'I am so happy the pin fell here. It is a beautiful place, with a beautiful hostess.'

Hurriedly converting a weird little whimpering sound into a cough, she stood up.

'You go now?' Angel questioned.

'Yes, I must get back to work.'

'And maybe we could have a little drink later? We shall discuss *your* travels. *Si*?'

Kara just nodded and smiled, suddenly feeling that her world was very small.

'I think I will take a boat trip,' Angel decided.

'Good idea. Have fun,' Kara replied as coolly as she could. '*Hasta luego*, Ka-rra.'

'You didn't tell me Enrique Iglesias was coming to stay. Got a gig at the Ferryboat, has he?' Billy appeared by Kara's side as she started to make her way back up Ferry Lane towards the market. Kara laughed as he continued, 'I need to up my game with men like him sleeping in your bedroom. So, I was wondering—'

Kara's phone rang. 'Shit, it's Twisty,' she said. 'I'd better take it.' The call was swift and to the point. She ended it then turned to Billy and said, 'You know sometimes you think people may change, well . . . Sorry, Billy, what were you saying?'

Billy smiled resignedly. 'It was nothing. Go on, get going, sweet cheeks. You look stressed.'

The young man walked back down towards the ferry quay and sighed. Maybe being saved by the bell was a good thing. There was no rush. His heart had waited this long, it would just have to carry on being patient and trust that none of these fly-by-night guests would come along and steal hers.

Chapter 27

'Dad?' Kara answered her mobile as she arrived back at the outside stall. Lydia was handing a bunch of long-stemmed red roses to a tall, distinguished-looking gentleman wearing a three-piece suit. There was a queue three-people deep, all holding various blooms and waiting to be served. Lydia glared at Kara, who continued to converse with her father as she rushed around behind the table to help.

'You OK, Dad?' she asked. It was highly unusual for Joe to call her during working hours, especially on a market day when he knew she would be busy.

'I need to talk to you about your grandad,' Joe said, and Kara's heart sank. 'It's not urgent, so don't worry.'

But Kara knew that it was. 'Give me a sec and I'll call you right back,' she promised.

Kara quickly cleared the queue then restocked the metal buckets that were emptying fast on this busy Friday. Star believed that angels – and not only the flesh and blood ones that walked amongst us – were always looking out for everyone, and at that moment Kara truly hoped her friend was right.

'Kara.' Lydia came outside from the shop to the stall. 'I need a favour. I want you to go over to Crowsbridge Hall, pronto. Somebody's knocked the reception display over and ruined it, and it's their Summer Ball tonight. They have a

141

photographer coming in an hour to get pre-shots, so they want it redone as soon as possible. Here –' The woman thrust a massive, loosely tied flower display at Kara. '– add some of these to it. That should cover any damage.'

'What are you doing to me, wearing those tight jeans?' Billy greeted Kara at the front of the ferry as she pulled her handbrake up in the van then climbed out ready to go and see her dad, who was cleaning the front screen of the *Happy Hart*. 'No joke, you have the peachiest bum in Hartmouth.'

'And you obviously have the research figures to prove this fact.' Oblivious to the true feelings that were running around the ferryman's head, Kara just felt thankful that since The Kiss there had been no awkwardness between them. In her mind now, too, the pair of them were so much better as flirty friends. 'I need to speak to Dad; do you mind doing the tug?'

'Anything for you, Kerry Moon, you know that. Where are you off to anyway?'

'Bloody Crowsbridge Hall, they need their reception display redone.'

'Shit. I can't jump ship on a market day or I'd have come with you again.'

'No, you're fine. I doubt if little Miss Penhaligon will be around. With a grand ball up there tonight, she'll be having her hair done or something. And anyway, I'm over all that now,' she lied. 'But thank you.'

Billy changed places with Joe, who immediately joined his daughter.

'Get in the van, Dad, it's too windy out here,' Kara said, so they got in and sat next to each other, as if they were upstairs at the front of a double-decker bus but facing out onto a busy waterway rather than a road. 'Your hair looks so much smarter, now it's shorter,' she told him.

'Yes, 'bout time I started looking after myself, don't you think? Pearl did it.' He smiled at just the mention of her name. 'She's a woman of many talents.'

'So it seems.'

Joe turned to her. 'You don't mind, do you? About me and her?'

'Mind? I helped set you up, remember? And Dad – it's so good to see a smile on your face every day. I think she's lovely.'

'You do, really?'

'I mean, I've only met her the once, but yes. Please just enjoy yourself. Have some fun for once.'

A smiling Joe Moon put a hand on his daughter's knee. 'And how are you, my treasure?'

'I'm all good.' Kara gulped. 'You'd better tell me what's up with Grandad.'

'He'd just gone a bit forgetful. He put his phone in the fridge the other day and shut Bert in the shed. Luckily I heard the poor little fella barking like crazy before I left for the ferry yesterday morning.'

'It could just be old age. He is nearly eighty-four.'

'But he's always been so with it. I've never looked at him as an old man before.'

'Yeah, I know. I talk to him like a mate sometimes, not a grandad. He's so funny and wise.'

'He's a great man. Your Granny Annie, she was a wonderful woman, too. She was a good age when she went, but when she did go – God, that hurt. And I can't bear the thought of . . .'

'Aw, Dad.' Kara squeezed Joe's hand. 'Harry's not going anywhere yet.'

It was as if Pearl had opened up Joe's emotional floodgates. 'And I'm sorry your mum has been so useless for you. I didn't pick wisely, did I? All that auburn hair and big green eyes. I should have looked behind the scenes. A fine example of beauty being only skin deep, that one.' He then looked to his daughter. 'Thank goodness you inherited more than just her looks.'

'You must have had some happy times?'

Joe Moon just sighed. 'A few. I feel I've failed with Jen, too. I'd love to see more of her. I do try. I know we both work such long hours, but it saddens me that she hardly ever returns my calls.'

Kara didn't dare respond that if you really wanted to contact someone then you would make the time to do so.

'Dad, you haven't failed at all. And maybe now you can take some time off? Daz and Billy have proved them-selves capable on a Sunday, so maybe let go of the reins a bit. Daz is only part-time at Dillon's. Maybe he could take on extra crossings? I'm sure Pearl would like to see more of you. Have a weekend away even, work around her shifts.'

Crowsbridge Quay was now in full view. Five cars were already waiting in line. Ferry Lane market day was always a busy one. Billy began to expertly turn the tug to line up the ferry ready for disembarkation.

'Don't worry about Grandad,' Kara consoled her father. 'Maybe keep an eye on him this week. And if he gets worse, then let's suggest he sees the doctor.'

'He's always said that dementia would be his worst nightmare. He's been so with it all his life.'

'Maybe he'd had an extra cider or something? Was the phone and Bert incident the same night?'

Joe laughed. 'Actually, yes. I didn't think of that. It was Sunday night, when we had the wonderful lunch that Pearl cooked.'

Kara giggled. 'See? He was tucking into the red wine then. He was probably just drunk.'

'What am I like?' Joe managed a smile. 'I feel better already. I've turned into an emotional wreck about everything, all of a sudden.'

'You're an amazing dad, that's what you are.' Kara kissed him on the forehead. 'Right, you and me better get working. Have you got lunch?'

'Pearl has made me – well, me *and* our Billy here – a pasty for every day of the week.' Joe patted his tummy.

'Well, they do say the way to a man's heart is through his stomach, and by the sound of it, I think she's on the way there already.'

'Steady on, daughter, I've only just met her!'

'Unlike this ferry of yours, love doesn't have a strict timetable, Dad.'

Joe Moon shook his head at his daughter, smiled and got out of the van. At the same time, Billy came over and opened the ferry float's metal gates in front of the Passion Flowers van. He leaned down to speak.

'Gutted I'm not coming with you; I might have got another kiss.' He blew her one through the window. 'Be strong, Kerry Moon. You're worth ten of her.'

145

Kara was surprised to see one of the Dillons' fruit and vegetable vans in the car park of Crowsbridge Hall. She then giggled to herself as she saw a red-faced Darren looking left and then right as he ran down the steps of the lodge where Miss Fancy Pants Penhaligon lived. As he approached his van, she tooted her horn loudly. Realising he couldn't escape, his face was a picture as he came over to greet her.

'Oh er, hi, Kara. Um. Just delivering some aubergines and um . . .'

'Some of those cucumbers maybe you were on about earlier?' Kara teased.

'Yeah, right. I'd better get back over; it's market day and all that. See you later.' He turned to hotfoot it away from her.

'Daz, wait a sec!' she called. He turned back around. Kara glanced at his earlobe, then reached into her jeans pocket and held out her palm with the tiny diamond ear stud resting on it. 'I found this.'

'Oh.' She could see the usually tough London lad was cringing inwardly.

'Yes, I found it upstairs in the corridor of Lydia's place. No idea how it could have got there, have you?'

'I can explain.'

'Darren, it's none of my business. In fact, just look at what you're doing as a public service to the community. Well, to me anyway.' Looking pointedly from his groin and then back up to his face, she added drily, 'But earring aside, the way you're going, you want to be careful nothing else falls off.'

Chapter 28

Kara sat awkwardly opposite the delectable specimen of a man that was Angel Perez. Big Frank gave her a cheeky wink as he came over with the Frank's menu.

'Beer? Gin?'

'I'll just have a cup of tea, please, Frank.'

'Me too, please,' Angel said. 'A lovely British cuppa.' He put on a terrible accentuated English accent, which caused them all to laugh.

'On my little trips, I try to do everything the traditional way,' he explained in his normal voice.

'In that case, we should have a cream tea too, then.'

'Oh no.' Angel pulled a face. 'I wish to have my tea black.'

Kara laughed and pointed to the scones that were behind the glass counter. 'They're called scones, I'm not sure if you have them in Spain. We serve them with proper Cornish clotted cream and jam, and eat them washed down with a cup of tea. It's called a Cream Tea, and it's such a treat.'

'Looks amazing, let's do it.'

'It's nearly dinnertime, though.'

'So . . . who says we have to follow the rules, Kara? I am on my mini-break.' He ordered a Cream Tea for each for them, and Frank went off to prepare them. 'Passion Flowers,' Angel said in his gorgeous Spanish accent. 'I like that name.'

He checked out her work T-shirt, then looked right at her. 'We all need passion in our lives, don't we?'

Kara found his intensity a bit overwhelming so was relieved when he changed track to say, 'Do you like the sound of the game I play?'

'Your travel game, you mean?'

'*Si, Si.* You should try it maybe. Do you have a boyfriend or are you alone?'

'I've just split with my boyfriend and being honest with you, Angel, I've only ever been abroad once.'

'How old are you?'

'Thirty-three.'

'Ah, I see.' He looked taken aback. 'But there is so much world out there.'

'I know,' Kara replied quietly.

Big Frank returned with two pots of tea and four large scones that were heavily laden not only with fresh cream and jam, but with tiny sweet strawberries amongst the layers.

'*Muy bueno!*' Angel became animated. 'Cream tea, you say? Wow!'

'Yes, and in Cornwall we put the jam on first as you can see. In Devon, the next county up, they put the cream on first.'

'Interesting. Why is this?' Angel dragged his finger through the thick clotted cream and licked it. He closed his eyes and said, 'Delicious.'

'I actually don't know, but apparently our lovely Queen likes it the Cornish way.' Kara lifted her teapot lid and began to stir the fragrant leaves inside. 'So that's good enough for me.'

'So why no travel, Kara? I can see this is a beautiful place, but so is Barcelona, where I live, and I still like to escape it.'

Kara felt tears suddenly hit the back of her eyes. The intuitive Spaniard noticed and busied himself stirring and pouring his tea. He then put his hand on top of hers.

'I loved somebody once,' he said. 'Too much. It was hard when she left.'

Kara loved his emotional honesty. 'My relationship was over way before I kicked him out,' she admitted.

'Give yourself the time you need to heal,' Angel advised her, 'and be kind to yourself. You will feel good again one day. That's how that heartbreaking business works.'

As Kara said, 'I really am over him,' a vision of her mother packing her bag in their hotel room and walking out of it suddenly overtook her thoughts. With Jago gone, there was now space for pain of a different sort.

'Good.' Angel nodded wisely. 'Because your heart won't let in anybody else until you are over him. It's a very clever thing, the heart.' He took a sip of hot black tea. 'Before I leave tomorrow, I must take a photo of you and James Bond *and* your grumpy little tortoise. I have a travel wall. Gabriella laughs at it.'

'Gabriella?'

'My fiancée.'

'She doesn't mind you coming on your travels then?'

'Why would she? We holiday together, but this is my little peace once or sometimes twice a year. Always maintain your individuality, Kara. When I travel alone I get to meet lovely new people like you. It makes for a more interesting life for us as a couple. Saying that, the wedding is in the autumn and we want at least three little *niños*, so she might not be quite so flexible after they come.' Angel started to go through the photos on his phone. 'Here she is, *mi vida*, my life.'

Kara was just stating how lovely Gabriella looked when

the phone rang in her bag. She glanced at the screen. 'Oh, it's my grandad. That's strange. Do you mind if I quickly take this?'

'Of course.' Angel licked his lips and took a big bite of his cream-and-jam-laden scone.

It took a second for Kara to realise who the calm female voice at the end of the phone belonged to.

'Pearl?'

'Yes, Kerry darling, it's me, Pearl. Harry has had an accident. Can you find your dad and tell him to come straight to Accident and Emergency at Penrigan General? I'm with your grandfather now.'

Chapter 29

Grandad Harry opened his eyes and reached out his pink, fat-fingered hand to Kara, who was sitting on a chair next to his bed in the A&E cubicle. His right eye was red and swollen, the lid beginning to close over completely. He had a stinging graze on his cheek, and his white beard had bits of dirt and leaf in it. He was still wearing his orange bucket hat.

'Grandad,' Kara said tenderly. 'What have you been up to?'

'I knew those bloody chickens would be the death of me.' He managed a smile, then grimaced in pain.

'Don't talk if it hurts,' Kara told him.

'That lovely nurse just gave me some powerful painkillers,' the old fella rambled on. 'She looked just like Joe's Pearl. It was uncanny. I'll be right as rain in a minute.'

'It *was* Pearl, Grandad. Are you hurting anywhere else, other than your face?'

'Just my arm. I've had an X-ray as they thought it could be broken, but it's nothing, just a sprain. Us Moons are made of strong stuff, you know.'

'I bet you're in shock too, though, so you have to listen to the doctors, Grandad. You hear me? Pearl says you came off your trike?'

'Yes.' Harry shifted and groaned, before continuing. 'I blame Henrietta. I was just putting some more cider vinegar in their water pot for the pair of them and she decided to make a run for it. I saw her heading out of the side gate onto the road, so hobbled my way down the garden, attached Bert to the trike and off we went in hot pursuit.' He sniggered feebly.

Kara couldn't help but laugh too. 'Grandad!'

'So, Bert then spots that dratted hen running into the gap in the hedge to the duck pond and decides to career through, taking me and the trike over with him. I haven't seen the little blighter move so fast in ten years.'

Kara helped him sit up and take a drink from the plastic cup on the side.

'Phew, that's better. Is your dad here?' Harry asked.

'Yes, he's here. Just went to get you a cup of tea. You scared the life out of both of us.'

'I'm sorry, my beauty.' He squeezed her hand again and rested his head back on the pillow. 'I'm tired, Kerry Anne.'

'I bet you are. I'll leave you to rest and see what the doctors say about you coming home.'

'I want to come home tonight.' Harry sighed. 'But don't go for a minute, duck. I want you here.' Kara could tell the old man's painkillers were kicking in as his hand became relaxed on hers. He murmured, 'You've given up too much already for this family.'

'What are you saying, Grandad? I'm all right.'

'You should have gone to that flower college; you didn't need to look after your dad.'

'I wanted to,' Kara said, and it was the truth.

'You're a good girl, you are.' Harry shut his eyes. 'I want you to promise me something.'

'Go on.' Kara felt a kind of fear go through her that she had never experienced before. 'Promise me that from now on, you will open your mind and follow your heart.'

She tutted. 'Why are you talking like this?'

Harry's voice was getting weaker. 'I want you to be happy and live your life to the full.'

'I will.'

'And make sure your dad is happy, too. That Pearl is a good woman. She's what this family, and especially your father, has needed for a long, long time. I reckon my Annie sent her along to Bee Cottage, you know. She saw.'

'Shush now, Grandad. Try and get some sleep.'

'You promise me?' the old man insisted with as much strength as he could muster. 'Say it!'

'I promise you.' Kara stood up and softly kissed his forehead.

'Bloody hell.' Kara put her hand to her heart. 'You terrified me.' She turned the van's engine off. 'Don't be knocking on my window like that when's it's dark. I thought you were Jago.'

'I'm sorry.' Billy held the door open for her as she got out. She noticed that there were lights on up in the flat. Angel must still be awake. Saying that, it was only nine thirty.

'What are you doing, lurking around here at this time of night, anyway?

'I er, just had a pint at the Ferryboat and saw you pull in.' Billy would never admit that he'd been waiting outside for the past two hours for her to come back from the hospital. 'How's Harry?'

'They've kept him in for the night for observation. He's a tough old boy despite his cuts, bruises and a sprained wrist.'

'What happened?'

Kara couldn't help but smile. 'The silly old sod was chasing a chicken on his trike and Bert pulled it over.'

'I shouldn't laugh, but . . .' Billy did so.

'I know. Trust Grandad. He's eighty-three going on twenty-three, always has been.'

'So, he's going to be OK?'

'Yes. We just need to make sure he rests. This has scared the life out of me.'

'And your dad, I bet.'

'Yes. I just dropped him home.'

'Well, if there's anything I can do.'

'Thanks, Billy, that's really kind.'

'Actually, Kerry, I was thinking that—'

'*Hola*, Kara!' Just then, Angel appeared at the front door.

Billy finished the sentence in his head . . . *it's time we went on that date.*

'I thought I saw the Passion Flowers van and wondered if you'd like to go for a drink at the pub with me?' Angel asked.

Feeling guilty at leaving her guest to pick up the bill in Frank's earlier, Kara reluctantly agreed.

'Billy, meet Angel, he's staying at mine tonight.'

'All right, mate?' Billy held out his hand.

'Please, come with us,' Angel addressed the young Londoner.

But Billy, taking in the Spaniard's height and brooding good looks, replied, 'Nah. You're fine. I need to be up early tomorrow.'

'That's never stopped you before.' Kara smiled at him. 'I just cut you short, sorry. What were you going to say?'

'It doesn't matter now. Have fun!' Billy winked at Kara, then with a pained expression, slowly made his way up Ferry Lane deep in thought.

Chapter 30

'Good morning. You're up early.' Kara poked her head in from the balcony door where she was watering the two pots of variegated pansies and pink geraniums that she had planted up last week. Considering their fairly late night at the Ferryboat, Angel looked fresh as a daisy. Kara put down the watering can and came back inside.

'My train leaves Crowsbridge at nine thirty, so I need to get going.' He then noticed that her eyes were red from crying. '*Mi querida*, are you OK?' He walked over and put his arms around her. 'You need a hug. We all need a hug sometimes.' The handsome Spaniard's big bear hug made her feel so loved that she burst into tears again.

'Oh, no, no, no, sweet lady. You sit on the terrace; I bring us coffee.'

'I'm supposed to be the host here,' Kara resisted.

'Go – sit.' He came back after a few minutes with two cups of coffee. 'I put sugar in even if you don't take it,' he informed her with a smile.

They sat next to each other on the bench. It was a glorious June day. Joe waved up frantically from the ferry, Billy just nodded his head and carried on loading cars on for the first morning shuttle.

'Is it your grandfather? I thought he was going to get better.'

'He is fine, thanks. Dad has already texted me. And he's coming home from hospital today. It's nothing, honestly.'

'You ladies, it's always fine or nothing, when really it's not fine and it is everything.'

Kara laughed. 'You're far too smart in this relationship business.'

'No, the reason is I come from a family of females.'

'It's just I have this dreadful fear about Grandad Harry leaving us. All these feelings have brought up a lot of other stuff, too. Stuff I don't really want to talk about right now.'

'OK.' Angel took a sip of his coffee. They sat in silence, apart from the cawing of seagulls and the watery creaks and clanks coming from the estuary below. Kara felt as if she had known Angel for much longer than a day. She was comfortable with him by her side.

She started to talk. 'Jago – that was my ex – our relationship hadn't been right for a long time. I found out he was cheating, so I made him go. But even though I know he wasn't right for me, I kind of miss him.'

'How long were you with him?'

'Eight years.' Kara gulped. That was longer than many marriages these days.

'You tell me you are thirty-three, so that is nearly half of your adult life you spend with this man. A long time. You have every reason to miss him.'

'When you put it like that, I suppose you're right.' Kara was surprisingly enjoying the alien taste of sweet, milky coffee.

'A man never knows how to say goodbye; a woman never knows when to say it, that's the problem.'

Kara smiled. 'God, that's so bloody true.'

'But like I said yesterday, give yourself some time. The

mind as well as the body needs rest.' He gestured at the Passion Flowers logo on her T-shirt. 'Your subconscious mind grows either flowers or weeds in the garden of your life.'

'That's very deep.'

'If we take the time to look inside, then we are all very deep, Kara.' He stood up. 'But now, I must shower and pack.'

Twenty minutes later, Angel appeared from the bedroom smelling as good as he looked.

'It has been a complete pleasure meeting you, Kara,' he said and kissed her hand. 'Thank you so much for my stay. My pin definitely knew where to fall this time.'

'Sorry I deserted you yesterday.'

Angel tutted. 'Family is where life begins and where love never ends.'

Kara was struck. 'My grandad says that!'

'That is not brain science. He is a lucky man, your grandad, I can feel the love all around him.'

Kara took a deep breath. 'What if he dies?'

Angel did not flinch or look away. 'He will die. We will all die. But to live on in the hearts we leave behind is to remain alive. My mother said that to me when my father died three years ago.'

Kara began to well up. 'He must have been young.' Angel took a breath to keep himself together and nodded as Kara said sincerely, 'You are a special person, Angel.'

'No, I'm not. Nobody is special, Kara, we are all just the same.' Angel picked up his overnight bag. '*Hasta luego*, and thank you again.'

'I don't know what that means. *Adios*, *hola* and *gracias* are my limits from school days.'

'It means see you later, or until we meet again.'

Kara opened the apartment door and James Bond rushed

past the pair of them to start noisily crunching his biscuits in the kitchen.

She ran downstairs to open the front door and stood watching as Angel strode off towards the ferry. Lifting her hand to wave goodbye to her handsome guest, she called after him, '*Hasta luego*, Angel.'

Chapter 31

The twin brothers Billy and Darren Dillon hurried as one down the black metal steps of their Ferry Lane apartment and on to the marketplace.

'Gone now, has he, your Spanish matador?' Billy said casually to Kara, who was out at the front of Passion Flowers across the lane, washing down the top of the glass door, which a seagull had splattered on earlier that morning.

'Anyone would think you were jealous, bruv,' Darren chipped in. Then: 'How's old Harry doing? Good, I hope.'

'Yes, thanks. He seems to be doing all right. Dad picked him up from the hospital last night. I'm going round to see him later.'

'Tell Joe that if he needs me to do any more shifts – you know, on the ferry – if he wants some time with his dad, I'm happy to do it,' Daz offered, much to Billy's surprise. 'Other than today, that is, because I've got to help Mum and Dad on the stall.'

'I appreciate that. Thanks so much, Daz.'

'No, *thank you.*' He winked knowingly at Kara and put his finger to the glinting diamond stud, now back in its rightful place.

'Nice bloke, was he?' Billy enquired. 'He seemed polite enough.'

'Yes, he's lovely. He sticks a pin in a map and travels

somewhere different every year. And his fiancée encourages it. He's given me my faith back in men, to be honest.'

She tried to ignore Billy's palpable relief at the Spaniard's engaged status. 'Quite the little business you've got going now.'

'Yeah, a guy from Australia of all places has just booked, too. He's going for a job at Crowsbridge Hall and said my place was the cheapest in the area.'

'You should do a price comparison then, Kar.' Star had come outside to check how her window display was looking.

'Yes, there's nothing cheap about our Kerry Moon.' Billy smiled at her. 'Funny how it's all single geezers though.'

'No, it's not,' Star piped up. 'They see the view of course, but Kara's hostess picture we put on the site is hot, hot, hot!'

'Stop it,' Kara warned her. Then, 'Now go to work, all of you. I've got seagull shit to clean up.'

The boys headed off down to the ferry quay, but Star stayed outside.

'Billy is so smitten,' she said.

'He's not,' Kara scoffed. 'He's just being nice. And the last thing I want is a man at the moment.'

'That's what I thought,' Star replied wistfully.

'I forgot about you and Jack. Has he been in touch since . . . you know?'

'I wish. I think he's such a loyal guy that he wouldn't start texting me behind his girlfriend's back.'

'Steren Bligh, get real! Loyal? You slept together! How can that be him doing the right thing by her? Have *you* tried to get in touch with *him*?'

'Just the one message and I heard nothing back. It's crazy, but I felt like we had a real connection.'

'I hate to put it to you, and I know I'm not the guru on all things relationship, but I think it was probably just a one-night stand.' The ever-buoyant Star looked very deflated as Kara added, 'I'm sorry, mate. Didn't mean to hurt your feelings. I know you both liked each other.'

'Yeah, I'm sorry too. I finally meet a man I really fancy, who I clicked with on an emotional and physical level, and not only does he live over three thousand miles away, he's also not single.' She paused and looked hopeful. 'You did say that he said his mind had been clouded or something though?'

'Oh yes, I forgot about that.'

'Kara? Kara!' Lydia Twist's dulcet cries could be heard from inside the shop. 'The Hartmouth Bay Hotel want their restaurant flowers early today; they have a women's charity brunch and need everything in place before ten. Chop, chop.'

'I'd better get in there.' Kara put her arm round her friend's shoulder. 'Try not to overthink it. Jack said he had to get back for personal reasons. Anything could have happened.'

Chapter 32

Pearl was humming along to Elvis's 'Love Me Tender' when Kara pushed open the front door to Bee Cottage. She was sitting at the kitchen table shelling fresh peas from the garden into a colander. On seeing Kara, she stopped what she was doing and turned Radio 2 down. 'Aw, here she is.'

'Something smells fishy.' Kara peered into the oven.

'It's a special dish for your grandad's homecoming. He was going on about Stargazy Pie the other day, so I looked it up. It's a funny old recipe.' Pearl pointed to a photograph of some pilchards with their heads on. 'These have to stick out of the top of it.'

Kara smiled. 'The times he's mentioned that bloody pie to me too and the story of Tom Bawcock, which I still have not paid any attention to. Bless him.'

'Bless him, indeed.' Pearl gave Kara a conspiratorial smile. 'Maybe we should let him tell us the story at dinnertime.'

There was something about Pearl that made her so easy to love.

'Did you have a good day, sweet child?'

'It was OK. Tiring as usual, but nothing to a shift on A&E, I should imagine, so I'm not complaining. Is Grandad in bed?'

Pearl's laughter was loud. 'I can't believe you asked that!

Of course he's not. He's gone up the garden with your dad to make sure those chickens don't escape again.'

'I don't know why I asked that either.' Kara grinned. 'Someone found Henrietta, then?'

'Yes, the vicar found her digging up his prized carrots in his allotment, so he wasn't best pleased.' Pearl put down a bulging green pea pod. 'What do you want to drink, love? There's white wine, or some of that tasty cloudy lemonade I got from the market in the fridge.'

Kara let out a deep relaxing sigh. It was Pearl's ability to make a house a home and a kitchen a sanctuary that had been missing here for so long. Her dad and grandad did their best, but there was something about a woman's touch and presence that made it feel complete.

'Lovely, thanks so much.' Kara went to the fridge to take out the lemonade.

'Get the wine out as well for me, will you, dear? I'm off tomorrow so can afford to give myself a drop.' Pearl wiped her hands on a tea towel and poured herself a glass of wine. Kara noticed that her hand was slightly trembling, as she did so. She also noticed her taking a huge intake of breath as if to brace herself for what she was going to say next.

'I'm not here to ever take the place of your mother, you know that, don't you?' she said.

'There was never really a place to take,' Kara replied, feeling herself well up.

Pearl's speech accelerated. 'And as for your dad, he will always be there for you. And so will I, if you ever want to chat with me about anything. I'm a good listener, Kara.'

Kara could sense how awkward and nervous this lovely woman had been when opening up this obviously pre-planned conversation.

'I've honestly never seen my dad this happy,' she said. 'And it's all due to you. Thank you, Pearl, from all of us.'

'Really?' Pearl wiped her eyes. Then she laughed a bit shakily, saying, 'He just needed a decent meal, that's all.'

Kara was amused. 'No, he needed a decent woman and that's what you are – a very decent and good woman. In the short time we've known you, you've filled this house with much-needed love and laughter.'

'Thank you for accepting me so readily.' Pearl felt very emotional. 'I haven't smiled like this for a very long time, either.'

They took a moment before Kara said in a different, lighter tone, 'I know what I meant to ask: do you have children of your own?' Then on seeing Pearl's stricken face, she wanted to run out of the door and up the garden.

'I'll say it really quickly, it's easier that way. I've told your dad, of course.'

'You don't have to tell me anything if you don't want to.' Kara took a big drink from her cold lemonade.

Pearl patted the seat next to her at the kitchen table. 'I want to tell you, dear. What I'm going to say doesn't define me, but if I'm going to be around for a long time, which I hope I am, I want you to understand.' She took a mouthful of wine. 'My Don and I were very happily married. We struggled to have a baby for years, and when I got to forty, we'd given up all hope and then all of a sudden, there she was. Our Alesha. Our miracle. Our own little bundle of pure joy.'

Kara remained quiet and focused on what Pearl was telling her.

'We were so excited about her first birthday. Had planned to go over to St Lucia to show her off to my family, but sadly that wasn't to be.' The pain now etched on Pearl's face made Kara take a very deep breath so as not to burst into tears herself. 'SIDS, we call it in the business. Sudden Infant Death Syndrome.'

'Oh, Pearl. I'm so sorry.'

'And that was that. Our beautiful little girl was with us for what seemed like minutes. The grief of losing a baby tore me apart. Tore both of us apart. But we clung together like sailors in a storm; it made us all the stronger as a couple.'

'That is the saddest story I've ever heard.'

Pearl shook her head and said mournfully, 'No, the saddest thing was that when Don retired from his job as a postman and I had just two years to go at the hospital, he was taken too.' Harry had already told Kara this, but she just let Pearl carry on talking. 'We had planned to do all the things we had talked about during our married life. And then some bloody little wanker in a stolen car snuffed out my Don on a pedestrian crossing.' Her face contorted. 'We had so many hopes and dreams.'

Kara now had tears running down her face. 'Oh, Pearl.' She put her arm around the woman's wide shoulders.

'I don't know how I've actually put one foot in front of each other since.' Pearl sniffed then stood up. 'But – no more tears. Just like I won't replace your mother, your dad will never replace my Don. But I know he would have wanted me to be happy. And your dad is a good man too, Kara. I know it sounds silly, but Ireany my sister said to me, "When you know, you know." And I did about my Don, and as soon as I saw your father in that car park, with his handsome rugged face, scruffy white hair and skinny little body, I knew he was right for me. I think we rescued each other.'

Kara blew her nose. 'I think you did too, and I'm so pleased that you did. You are so welcome in our lives, Pearl.'

Completely oblivious to this grand outpouring of emotion, Joe Moon appeared through the back door into the kitchen, saying comfortably, 'I thought I heard your voice, Kerry love. Your grandad said to pop up to the shed when you get here. He's sat in his chair. You'll never guess what! He only went and WhatsApped Jen – and she answered! We've just had a long chat. She looked so well. Showed us round a new posh flat she's got in London and she's got a new man too. If you hurry, she may still be on to him.'

Kara made her way slowly up the garden.

Harry saw her and called out, 'You've just missed our Jenifer. I tried to stall her, but she had to go.'

'It's fine, Grandad. Dad says she's doing well.'

'Yes, she looked a picture. New flat, new boyfriend. She seemed as content as we'll ever see her, I think. Still a snooty cow, mind,' he grinned. 'But I'm happy. I've seen all of you today now.'

Harry was sitting back comfortably in his threadbare armchair. Bert was sleeping soundly curled up on his lap; irregular little snores were coming out of the little terrier.

'What did she say about your eye?'

Harry was now sporting a proper shiner, red and purple, and his eyelid had closed right over.

'She asked me how many rounds I'd done and with whom.'

'It looks awful. Does it hurt?'

'No. Pearl has kept me dosed up on painkillers, and even my arm is feeling better today.'

'Your beard is all clean and trimmed too,' Kara noted.

'She did that an' all. I've never been looked after so well.' Harry paused. 'Get her to move in, won't you, Kerry duck.

Tell your dad I think she's wonderful, and that he'll be more than happy with her.'

Hearing his words, Kara felt a frisson of the same fear she had felt in the hospital. She pulled herself together. 'You can tell him yourself.' She cast around for a change of subject. 'It's good you found Henny the runaway hen.'

Harry chuckled the deep laugh that Kara had grown up hearing and knew so well. 'Your dad was just telling me that I should have seen the vicar's face. He was trying to remain all godly and charming, but underneath he was about to explode with rage. Turns out those carrots of his she dug up and pecked were for the Hartmouth Summer Show.' He laughed heartily again, his tummy moving up and down as he did so, Bert moving with him, not even batting a doggy eyelid.

As Kara joined in with his mirth, the words, 'I love you, Grandad, so much,' came out of her mouth.

'I love you too, darling. And don't forget what I said about you following your heart and dreams too, eh?' Tears started to form in Kara's eyes. For at that moment, she knew. They both knew.

'Me and Annie, we didn't go many places, we found our contentment here in Hartmouth and with each other. We didn't need anything or anywhere else. The sea, the estuary, the beaches and fields in this green and pleasant land, just perfect. That's like a line from "Jerusalem" – my favourite hymn, that is. But you go wherever you need to now, my beautiful girl.' The old man was so very tired.

'That's so lovely, but stop being weird now, Grandad, please.'

'You won't forget that every flower is a soul blossoming in nature, will you?'

Kara took a deep breath. 'Of course not. I love it that Granny Annie is the rose called Agatha Christie, keeping an eye on us all on the back wall.'

Harry nodded, suddenly breathless. With the last of his strength, he managed, 'I've left my stick down in the porch. Your dad helped me up here, so Kerry, love, do you mind getting it for me?'

Kara put the stick down on the floor of the old shed, removed her grandad's old orange bucket hat and kissed him lovingly on the forehead. She then sat on her faded red chair opposite him and pretended for one or two minutes more that he was just sleeping. It was only when she leaned forward to lift Bert carefully from the old man's lap that grief hit her like a bolt of lightning. Letting out a long deep wail, the wail that only the death of a loved one brings, she shouted out for her father. For not only had Grandad Harry gone to join Granny Annie in the stars, but his trusty old Jack Russell had gone with him on that last journey to be with his beloved owners.

Chapter 33

'Are you sure you want to be entertaining a B&B guest tonight when it's your grandad's funeral tomorrow?' Star asked Kara with concern as they sat eating ice creams in cornets outside Frank's.

'It's just for one night. He's getting to me late and he's got an early interview the next day over at Crowsbridge Hall. So, it'll be no bother. It's an easy sixty quid.'

'OK, as long as you're not taking on too much.'

'I'm fine, I promise. The bed's made up already and he can go to Frank's for breakfast. I'm not going to get involved this time. I'll give him his key and that's it.'

'How's he getting across to the Hall, then? I thought your dad was closing the ferry.'

'Just in the afternoon whilst the funeral's on. Grandad had friends in Crowsbridge who will want to come over and it's not fair to make them drive all the way round the coast road. Darren and Billy want to pay their respects too, so they will work before and after the church service.'

'How are you feeling, anyway?'

'Strangely OK, to be honest. It's only been a few days, so it's just like he's on holiday and I haven't had a chance to miss him yet. I do go to the cottage and keep expecting him to walk into the kitchen and make me laugh, though.'

'I used to love seeing him pedalling so slowly up to Duck

Pond Park, with poor old Bert trying to be patient. Such a character.' Star smiled.

'They both were.' Kara brushed away a tear. 'The sweetest thing is that the little fellow died on his lap. It was as if he waited for his master to go.'

'Their spirits will be together for ever now,' Star said wistfully.

'It's hit Dad hard. But Pearl is supporting him through it all.'

'They're still going strong, then?'

'Very much so. It feels like months they've been together, rather than weeks. I think she will move in now. Grandad wanted that to happen, gave his blessing. What with him sorting out the Internet dating too for Dad . . .' Kara paused. 'It was as if he knew he didn't have too long left.' Kara's voice cracked.

Star hugged her. 'Well, they do say some people have a sixth sense about it. Are you all right with it, if Pearl does move in to Bee Cottage?'

'Yes. I want her to. She's given me more affection in the brief time I've known her than I ever remember my mother showing in thirteen years.'

Star ran her tongue around her dripping ice cream. 'Well, that can only be a good thing, can't it?'

'She's also said she's happy to take control of the *Harry's Honeysuckle Honey* production line, and due to her love of cooking, there are always scraps for the chickens. So, they will be looked after too. Everyone's a winner. Even Dad is finally putting on much-needed weight. Poor Dad, though.'

'He'll be fine. You and he just need to do the grieving, as we all do when we lose someone we love. You can always talk to me about it, mate. Nothing fazes me. I quite enjoy a good old death talk.'

'What are you like?' Kara's ice cream dripped on to her cut-off jeans. 'Bugger! I just put these on.'

Star wiped her hands on a napkin, put some sun cream on her nose and tipped her head back to the sun. 'Flaming July soon.'

'Flaming freckles and pink skin for me then.'

'Oh, Kar, you wouldn't be you without your freckles.'

'Anyway, I'd better get going.' Kara stood up. 'Any word from Jack?'

'Jack who?' Star shrugged. 'I was being ridiculous. I'm just a bit annoyed now that I put out like that, and I didn't even know him.'

'What does that Rumi poem say, now? Something about meeting dark thoughts and shame at the door, laughing and inviting them in. It's good advice. Let it go, mate. I bet he won't be thinking what you're thinking. Blokes never are.'

'You're probably right.' Star stood up.

But Kara hadn't finished. 'And what is it that you always say to me? "People come into our lives for a reason, season or a lifetime." Maybe you don't yet know the reason why you met him, that's all.'

Chapter 34

With Kara wanting to practise her eulogy for Grandad Harry's funeral the next day, she had given Star's daughter a fiver for meeting her Aussie B&B guest, Brice, outside Passion Flowers and walking him down to Ferry View Apartments.

Kara checked her watch. Brice had emailed her and said that he was getting the last coach from London Victoria to Penrigan; if it was running on time, they should be here any minute. She turned on the radio just in time for the local weather reporter to give his spiel.

'The first electric storm of late spring is brewing and should be hitting the south-west coast around midnight. This will mean a sticky evening for most of us, making way for the last day of June to be bright sunshine with a light easterly breeze. So, batten down the hatches, all you seafarers out there, it's going to be a rough one.'

Being fond of a violent storm and glad that it was going to be fine tomorrow, Kara said, 'Good,' out loud. She then bent down to top up James Bond's biscuits and check that Sid Vicious' water temperature was OK. Finishing off making her cup of tea, she went out on to the balcony, sat down and started to reread the words she had written for Harry's send-off. Tears were running down her face as she got to the end of it. Boy, it was sad, but oh so relevant for her dear, wonderful grandfather. She just hoped she could get through reading it and honouring his memory without breaking down.

Another half hour passed, and Kara began to get slightly worried as to where her guest was, but Skye obviously wasn't sitting waiting or the usually impatient teenager would have contacted her. Kara was just going to text to check the young girl was OK, when the buzzer went off and a distinct Australian accent said through the intercom, 'Let's crack open a cold one, Mrs Moon, your Antipodean guest has landed.'

Kara quickly checked the back window and saw Skye hurrying back up the hill, then she opened the door to a loud and obviously tipsy young man wearing long beige shorts and a bright blue Rip Curl branded T-shirt. His curly blond hair was tied back surfer-style in a ponytail. He was around twenty-one, Kara reckoned, and stood at a gangly six-foot-two.

'If I'd have known how many blinking fields there were around here, I'd have just brought my tent. Hi, Mrs Moon.' He put his rucksack down on the floor and held out his hand to her. 'I'm Brice, Brice Jones. But most people call me Jonesy.'

'Hi, and welcome to Ferry Lane Apartments. I'm Kara. And still very much a Miss.'

'Play your cards right then, lady, and who knows?' Brice winked at her and she couldn't help but smile. His devil-may-care attitude reminded her in many ways of Billy, whom she realised she hadn't spoken to properly in a while.

'Was the coach late?' she asked.

'Er, yeah. Something like that. Fancy a drink?' He pulled four cans of chilled lager from his rucksack.

'Let's get you settled first. I'm going to my grandad's funeral tomorrow so I can't go to bed too late. I'm doing a reading.'

'Aw. I'm sorry to hear that, Kiri.'

'Kara.'

'I promise I won't keep you up – unless you want me to, hey. Maybe a drink is the answer. Have ya got any Coke? I've a small bottle of spiced rum in here too.'

'Jonesy, Jonesy, Jonesy. My Grandad Harry was just so lovely; I miss him so much already,' Kara slurred. 'I'm a bit worried about James Bond though. This storm is crazy.'

Brice screwed his face up. 'James Bond?' he said aloud. His hostess must be far drunker than he thought she was.

The empty bottle of rum on the table was being used by Brice as a goalpost alongside a can of lager to flick peanuts through. The wind now whistling across the estuary at a rate of knots was causing torrents of rain to sporadically smash against the balcony doors and bay window. Huge flashes of silent but jaw-dropping electric sheet lightning were flashing around the sea and right across to Crowsbridge in rave-dance-type fashion.

'He'd be proud of the send-off you're giving him this minute. So let's drink to him again.' Brice lifted his glass in the air and shouted above the elements, 'To Grandad Harry!' And then mimicking Kara's Cornish twang, 'Who was so luverly.' Another gigantic spike of lightning lit up the whole room and an immediate rolling boom of thunder shook the apartment.

'Grandad Harry,' Kara repeated, face shiny with sweat, her head wobbling slightly. Then CRASH – another booming thunderbolt, which sounded like it was now right above them.

'Wow! I think your grandad heard us. I bloody love a good storm.' Brice drained his glass of the sweet rum and Coke. 'I must pee.' He clumsily got up from the table, knocking over Kara's empty glass as he did so.

'And I must go to bed. I must. Jonesy, I must,' Kara sang out after him. Her head was floppy and beginning to hurt. 'I don't get drunk much lately.'

There was the sound of a toilet flushing and Brice reappeared at the table holding Sid aloft, index finger and thumb to the side of his shell. 'This little fucker just tried to bite me. Come on, let's see if he can run through the goalposts. Time him – go on, time him – and then whoever guesses nearest out of three wins . . . I don't know what we'll win, but it'll be a laugh.'

There was another explosion of thunder, then a scream as Sid sank the sharp edge of his mouth into Brice's cheek, followed by a crunch as the drunk man dropped the little terrapin on to the floor. Then as if in slow motion a bedraggled James Bond tore into the living room, spotted Sid under the table, picked him up in his mouth, then hurtled back down the stairs and out through the cat flap into the darkness of the wild stormy night.

'Shit!' Suddenly realising the enormity of the situation and ignoring both Brice's whimpers of pain and the dangers of a Force 8 gale, Kara pulled on her plimsolls and headed out of the door and down the stairs in pursuit of the kidnapper and his victim.

'James Bond, James Bond, where are you?' Kara shouted into the air as she headed along the estuary wall. A powerful gust of wind blew her hair right over her face, covering her in sea spray and almost taking her off her feet. She had quite often seen her naughty moggy hanging around near Frank's bins. There were steps there that went down to a covered area, and she was sure that was where he did most of his mousing.

'James Bond, please, *please* don't kill Sid,' Kara bleated, now feeling decidedly sick as a fork of lightning lit up the whole road and enabled her to see a flash of black and white heading towards Frank's and down the steps just as she had predicted. She began to run as fast as her drunk legs would allow, sheets of rain and sea spray stinging her face as the vile weather hit her full on. Her hair quickly turned into rats' tails, clinging to her soaking-wet T-shirt.

'Got you, you little devil.' Frank's security lighting flashed on for her to see her disobedient moggy sheltering in the corner, still holding the writhing little terrapin in his jaws. But this cat was up for a game of cat and turtle, and as he fled from his hiding place, he rushed past his mistress who, on trying to grab him, lost her already shaky footing and flew down the five very slippery steps to land in a heap at the bottom.

With the rain bashing down on her, her left foot full of pain, and her mind full of anguish, Kara Moon began to howl.

'Kerry? Kerry? Oh my God.' Billy jumped down the steps in one go, took off his jacket and placed it over the shivering woman. 'Up you come now.' He gently lifted her off the chilly concrete ground.

'My foot. I've hurt my foot,' she wept, then *whoosh*, she turned her head and projectile vomited, splashing Billy's trainers and the bottom of his joggers as she did so.

'I'm so sorry,' she wailed. 'I'm drunk, Dilly Billon. Dilly Dillon. Drunk.' She then let out a moaning sound and laughed. 'All those D's, Dillon, Drunk – Double D's like my big wobbly tits.'

Billy couldn't help but smile at the new drunk character revealing itself from behind his sweet amour. Avoiding the pool of sick and with the rain beating down on him too, he sat next to her on the bottom step. 'Yes. You're drunk, really drunk, but it's OK. I'm here now. Let's get you home to bed.'

'I don't want to go to bed.' She burst into tears. 'I don't want to go to bed because when I wake up, we have to say goodbye to Grandad Harry, and I don't want to do that.' She groaned again.

Billy bit his lip and pulled her close to him. She was soaking wet and shaking, and she smelled of vomit. 'I know, Doll, I know. But you need to get some sleep, you really do, or you will feel awful tomorrow. Come on, let's get out of here.'

Kara's head lolled as she kept up her soulful lament. 'And I'm sad. I'm sad because nobody wants me. My mum didn't want me. Even Jago didn't want me. What's wrong with me, Billy?'

'Oh Kerry, there's nothing wrong with you. They have the problem, your mum and Jago, it's not you.' He took in her anguished face and soulful green eyes. 'If you could only see what I see, you'd never be sad again. You are SO beautiful.'

'I'm not, I'm fat and freckly and ginger.'

'No! You're curvaceous, sun-kissed and gorgeous,' Billy shouted above the elements, rain dripping from every feature of his face.

But the troubled girl's ears remained shut. 'And I don't want to be on my own forever. Jago said that I was useless, that without him, I would be nothing. Maybe he's right.'

'Jago is a cunt,' Billy said under his breath.

'Ah! You said the C word, I'm telling.' Kara, in her now childlike state, suddenly smirked, then burst into tears again. 'My head is spinning, and my foot really does hurt.'

Guiding her to the small undercover area, Billy managed to sit her on an empty crate. 'Which foot is it?' Kara pointed down to her left one. Ignoring the stench of sick that was coming from her garbling mouth, he carefully eased off her sopping wet plimsoll and sock. Her left little toe was already colouring up red and stuck out at a slight angle. It was quite possibly broken. With the alcohol acting as an anaesthetic, he pushed it gently back into its rightful place, ripped a piece from her sock and tied it to the toe next door.

'And I think Sid Vicious is dead,' she suddenly announced loudly and with a huge blubbering sigh, Kerensa Anne Moon then flopped her head on to the young man's strong shoulder and promptly fell asleep.

Chapter 35

'*And did those feet in ancient time, walk upon England's mountains green . . .*' The rousing words of William Blake's
'Jerusalem' reverberated around the carved stone structure
of the seventeenth-century Hartmouth Church. A magnificent feat of religious architecture, it perched high on
Hartmouth Hill above rolling fields descending to the cliff
side, and looked out over the estuary mouth. Weather-
battered gravestones sat at angles in the churchyard, revealing
the heritage of centuries of Hartmouth fishermen, market
and townsfolk.

Kara, dressed in her one and only pair of black trousers
and non-matching black suit jacket, sat in the front pew with
her father, her face a deathly pale. Her untamed auburn
curls were tied back in their customary ponytail, looking like
a fox's fluffy brush. Pearl sat with Kara's older sister Jenifer,
who with her perfectly cut blond bob, neat little figure and
tight Victoria Beckham dress looked like she'd just stepped
off a London Fashion Week catwalk, rather than the two
fifteen ferry from Crowsbridge. In true Jen style, she had
arrived at the last minute, for which Kara was grateful, since
it meant she didn't have to try and converse with her before
the proceedings.

Walk upon England's mountains green? No chance of
that today, Kara thought. She would be lucky to make it up

to the lectern with her broken toe. What's more, she had never felt this hung-over in her entire life. Blacking out was another first and she was still reliving the horrifying moment of waking up next to Brice, with no recollection of how or why, with her toes tied together with a piece of old sock and her hair looking like she had been plugged into an electric socket. Even more distressing was when Billy, who for some reason had her flat keys, walked in to see her walking out of her bedroom in just a T-shirt and knickers, closely followed by Brice in his boxer shorts as he made his way to the toilet. Billy had given her a look she had never seen the likes of before. He'd thrown the flat keys on the table and slammed back down the stairs. Grandad Harry had been so right in his mantra of, 'When the drink's in, the wit's out.' The whole night had been a complete and utter disaster.

In order to keep her focus on getting through the next thirty minutes alive, and to try to remember what on earth had happened last night, she started to practise the deep breathing she had learned at the one and only yoga class she had ever attended with Star at the church hall three years ago. At the same time, she was aware of being in the midst of the amazing architecture and jaw-dropping stained-glass windows throughout the ancient building. Albeit not one for religion of any kind, she even found herself saying a prayer for Sid Vicious, willing a miracle that he be alive and well and walking on water in his tank when she returned home. She grimaced as she let out a little burp and tasted sick in her mouth.

On Kara's arrival at Bee Cottage that morning, Pearl had immediately spotted her hung-over state and limping gait. Helping her to take two paracetamol with a pint of water, she cleaned and bandaged her bruised little toe and offered to read the eulogy for Kara if she felt too ill when the time came. Kara was grateful for the offer, but had explained that she must get up and do her own personal reading or she would for evermore feel guilty for failing her grandfather.

Now, feeling rougher by the minute, she continued to mumble incoherently the words of 'Jerusalem', wondering why on earth hymns or songs of any kind were chosen for funerals as everybody was far too upset to sing them with conviction or without blubbering.

'You look ghastly,' Jen whispered to her, as the hymn ended, and the vicar took to his godly stage.

'Thanks for that, sis.'

A slight respite from hating herself came when Kara noticed how beautiful the two floral pedestals placed either side of the altar looked, now that they were in situ. Lydia had again proved her lack of compassion by moaning how much extra work they had due to Grandad Harry's funeral. In fact, when she had uttered that comment, Kara actually couldn't speak for three hours, so shocked was she. So, taking it upon herself to make Harry and her dad proud of her with the church displays, and with no expense spared, she made the most of her personal discount and chose every one of her grandad's favourite flowers. Kara had of course at the last minute slipped in a couple of the Agatha Christie roses from Bee Cottage, plus a miniature rock crystal (a stone of Moon and Mercury) in the shape of a bumble bee that Star had given her as a gift.

It had taken two days for Kara and Joe to put together the heart-felt eulogy that Pearl was now coming to the end of reading with such warmth and conviction.

'And that is why dear Harry Isaiah Moon, husband, father, grandfather, beekeeper, gardener, fisherman, chicken owner, friend and damn right decent man of the Hartmouth community, will be so sorely missed. May he rest in peace now beside his beloved wife Annie and their doting four-legged friend, Bert.'

Joe, with tears streaming down his face, gently poked Kara to let her know it was her turn to get up. Pearl gave her hand a squeeze as she sat back down and whispered, 'Take it slow, you'll be fine, child.'

Kara limped to the lectern and looked out over the sea of faces in this beautiful building. She checked where Billy was for reassurance, but with a stony face, he carried on looking right over her head. Big Frank, who was rushing off straight after her poem to do the final preparation for the wake, put a thumb up to her and winked. She felt sick, she felt shaky, she felt ashamed at her actions, whatever they had been, from the night before, but above all, she felt sad.

Taking a huge deep breath, she shut her eyes momentarily to level herself and a vision of Grandad Harry formed in her mind. There he was, sitting opposite her in his threadbare green chair and he was speaking to her. 'You've got this, kid. Imagine they've got no clothes on.' The exact words he had said to her when she'd played the Angel Gabriel in the school nativity play when she was just ten years old.

She sniffed back a tear, took another deep breath and began to read, slowly and clearly, the poignant words that she had so carefully penned with love.

'You said that every flower is a soul blossoming in nature. I truly believe that.' Kara's voice wobbled. 'A great soul like yours would never disappear, so from now on, every bold-coloured flower with a sturdy stem and soft petals I come across, I will think of you. My Grandad Harry.'

Kara paused, tears falling down her face. Joe looked intently at her, willing her to carry on.

'Your existence will never be forgotten,' she resumed. 'You touched the hearts and souls of not just me and our family, but everyone you met. With that sharp wit and those twinkling light blue eyes of yours, nobody could resist you. Just the fact that you did exist, brought me here. And for that reason in your honour and memory I intend *to be*, and *be better*. With your guiding light within me, how could I not?' She cleared her throat and said more strongly, 'We will miss you, but we will never forget you, not today, not tomorrow, not ever.'

And as she hobbled back to her seat, Kara Moon was determined that she would honour that promise in the future. And knowing that such a special man as Harry Moon would live on forever through her, she felt not only proud, but immensely lucky.

Chapter 36

'Welcome, I'm so sorry. Welcome, my condolences.' The mourners filed into Frank's as his partner Monique greeted them one by one in her sexy French accent. Thankfully the weather report had been right, and the wild storm of the night before had made way to a beautiful first day of July. Which was lucky, considering there must have been at least a hundred people in the church, who were now able to sit outside.

Young Skye had been commandeered to run the ice-cream stall and one of her friends was there to help wash up and clear tables. Joe had instructed Big Frank to offer teas and coffees, his discreet alcoholic beverages and platters of mixed sandwiches. Those present could order anything they wanted, and the grieving ferryman would settle at the end.

At fifty-nine, Monique Dubois was ten years older than her partner. But you wouldn't have known it. She was Priscilla to Frank's Elvis. An ex-Moulin Rouge performer, half French, half English and with the enviably lithe figure of a dancer, she was always immaculately dressed and never went anywhere without her bright red lipstick. Her platinum-blond shoulder-length hair was always tonged perfectly into a 1950s siren look. Today she was wearing a chic black jumpsuit and had somehow managed to tie the stripy Frank's-branded apron in a way that only a Frenchwoman could make look stylish.

'*Oh là là! Mon bijou.*' Monique kissed Kara cheek-to-cheek three times. 'Bless you all. How sad it is, losing your wonderful Harry. And when I saw *you* last night, Kara,' she put her hand to her chest, 'I was out of my mind wiz worry.'

'Saw me?'

'Yes, the security we have here, you know what he's like.' She pointed to Frank. 'I think an ex-bad boy is the worst. We even have a camera watching our cameras.' She smiled. 'They all flash straight to his phone. We live too far away to get to you last night, so Frank he didn't want to worry your dad, last night of all nights, so he says that Billy will come. He knew Billy would come.' She patted Kara affectionately on the cheek. 'We all love you, Kara.'

Frank caught sight of her red hair in his eyeline and came over to say, 'You were grand, there, Kara Moon. Quite the poet, yourself.' He then tipped his head towards his partner. 'She only comes out for weddings, funerals and bar mitzvahs, this one.' Monique blew him a kiss, then made her way into the crowd with a large tray of egg and cress sandwiches. Frank then added, 'You need coffee and bacon, don't you?' Kara nodded. 'I'll make you a sarnie and tip you the wink.' He went back to pouring coffees from the machine.

Kara went outside to get some fresh air. She clocked Jen leaning on the wall looking out over the water. Seagulls were circling noisily overhead, ready to swoop down on their prey of crumbs, or if they were lucky a whole ice cream. A group of this size would surely provide a memorable feast for a greedy flock.

In trepidation, Kara approached her elder sister who greeted her with, 'I think Dad must have invited anyone Grandad ever shook hands with.'

Kara was upset. 'Can't you ever be nice? Harry was simply well liked and loved by many.'

'Whatever. But funerals attract a plague of bloody locusts when there's free food on offer.'

'How are you anyway, Jen? Dad tells me you've got a new man and you're happy with him.'

'Yeah. Markus. He's great.'

'Is that it? "Great"?'

'Yes, what more can I say? Dad told me you finally saw sense and got rid of that good-for-nothing parasite you were living with. I could have told you the day you shacked up with him that he was going to do the dirty on you.' Kara held back tears as her sister continued nastily, 'Great you're doing the B&B now though – you can vicariously live through all your guests, seeing as you've never stepped out of this dead-beat place.'

'I love it here.'

'You know no different, that's why.'

'I've started to save.' Kara couldn't bear the way her sister made her revert back to the thirteen-year-old schoolgirl she had been when their mother had abandoned her. Like Jen, their mother must have despised her.

'That's something, I suppose. Gives you a chance not to waste any more of your life looking at the same view every – single – day.'

'Well, now Dad has Pearl, I feel that I can move on.'

'Move on?' her sister sneered. 'You're thirty-three, for God's sake, and not anyone's keeper.'

'You wouldn't understand,' Kara said quietly.

'There's talk of the new woman moving in, I hear. How long's she known him? Ten bloody minutes!' Jen's voice turned spiteful. She lit a cigarette. 'Probably realised Grandad was going to croak and is after his money. Ruddy gold-digger.'

Kara felt anger rising within her. If she hadn't felt so ill, she would have let rip. Instead she said, 'Can't you just be happy for him? She's worth ten of Mum.'

'In your opinion, Kara.'

'Have you seen her? Mum, I mean.'

'Yes. I had to fly over to Spain in March, where she met me. We message each other a lot.'

'You do?' Kara's voice tailed off. 'She doesn't even have my number.'

Jen suddenly softened. 'She does ask after you.'

'She does? Why's she not here today then?'

'You probably don't remember but there was no love lost between her and Grandad Harry or Granny Annie. She was always looked on as an outsider. You know what this place is like. Marry *out* at your peril!' Jen made a funny face. Kara realised that despite how much her sister looked like their dad with her blond hair, pretty blue eyes and high cheek-bones, she definitely had the personality of their mother, Doryty. In fact, Kara found it hard to believe that they had come out of the same pod.

'I can give you Mum's number if you want,' Jen said airily. 'Or actually, I'd better check with her first.'

Kara, still holding on to her anger and tears with all her might, said slowly and with venom behind her voice, 'Do you have to be such a bitch?'

At that moment, Joe Moon appeared and put his arms around them both.

'My girls. So lovely to have you together.'

Together? Kara thought. She had never felt further apart. Saved by a shout from Frank with her bacon sandwich, she put her head down, made her excuses and disappeared into the back kitchen to try and appease her still evident hangover and regain a modicum of calm before venturing outside of this sanctuary. She didn't notice Billy following her in.

'You'll be getting a reputation as a right slut, if you carry on as you are,' he said.

'You what?' Kara wiped the ketchup dripping from her mouth with the back of her hand. 'Say that again.' Her face had gone as red as her hair. Anger and grief were obviously a potent combination.

But Billy, still full of righteous fury himself, was undeterred. 'It wouldn't surprise me if you slept with the cave man and Enrique bloody Iglesias, too! Sweet little Kara, my arse!'

Kara shook her head in disbelief. 'I haven't slept with anyone for . . . let me see, probably two years now, because even my boyfriend didn't fancy me if you really want to know the truth!'

But Billy wasn't listening. 'I got out of bed at gone midnight to help you last night. You were in a right state. I took you inside. I even got you into bed safely and you still,' Billy blew out loudly, 'and you *still* managed, blind puking drunk, to go into his bedroom and spend the night with him!'

'No, no. You've got it all wrong.'

'I saw you this morning with my own eyes!'

'I don't need this. What's wrong with you? I've just buried my grandad. My sister is here, the sister who needs to check with my mother first before she gives me her phone number! So fuck off, Billy Dillon, and give me a fucking break!' Kara burst into tears.

The distressed lad automatically went to hug her, but Kara pushed him violently away. 'And I'm not sure why you're so bothered about my bloody business, because that's exactly what it is: *my* business. Let people talk. They're probably all gossiping about me and Jago's indiscretions anyway.'

'Oh, Kerry, I'm so sorry.' Billy ran his hands through his floppy fringe. 'I'm bothered because, because Kerry, I—'

Monique appeared in the back kitchen carrying two empty platters. '*Bonjour*, the handsome William Dillon. How are you?'

'Sorry, Monique, I've got to go. We have a crossing at four.' Billy ran out of the café and down towards the ferry, where he bumped straight into Brice, who was just coming out of Kara's flat.

'Hey – Billy, isn't it? Can you tell my lovely hostess I've left her keys on the table? And can you also thank her for a mad night. I'm still wasted, man.'

Billy felt his right hand forming into a fist as the Australian continued, 'Your face this morning, mate. I wasn't making a play for your girl, honest. Something like four a.m. I hear her clattering about, then the toilet flushing. Next thing, she gets into bed right beside me and falls fast asleep, snoring right in me ear. I knew it was her grandad's funeral today, so I didn't have the heart to wake her. You're a lucky man, there.' Brice chuckled. 'Woo! She's a fox.'

Chapter 37

Kara was limping around the apartment cleaning up from the carnage of the night before the funeral when the door buzzer went. She wiped her hands down the side of her already dirty shorts and pressed the intercom.

'Moo Moo, it's me.' On hearing the voice of her cheating ex, she froze for a second, then demanded, 'What do you want?'

'I've come to get Sid Vicious.'

Kara let go of the button. 'Fuck!' she hissed, then to Jago: 'You'd better come up.'

'What do you mean, he's dead?' Jago peered into the empty tank.

'I woke up one morning and there he was under his heat lamp like this?' She stuck out her tongue, tipped her head to the right and put her hands up to resemble the reptile's little feet.

'I didn't expect you to be able to look after him properly.' Kara wasn't sure if what she was feeling was guilt or anger as her ex continued nastily, 'James Bond still alive, is he?'

As if on cue the black-and-white cat shot into the kitchen

with something in his mouth. Something which looked very much like the shell of a painted terrapin. Kara tried to shut the door of the kitchen on him, but it was too late, Jago had noticed.

Cornering James Bond, the John Lennon lookalike grabbed the empty shell and lifted it up in the air. 'My Sid. You murdered my Sid.'

'Face it, he never did have much chance of a happy ending with a name like that, did he?' Kara tried not to laugh at the absurdity of the whole situation.

'This isn't a laughing matter. That bloody cat killed my terrapin, didn't he?' Jago gently put the remains into the empty tank. 'The little bastard.'

'Certainly not. He must have just dug him up. I buried him on the beach, so he could swim to a watery heaven,' Kara lied, her shoulders shaking again. 'Maybe you can use him as an ashtray or something now.' Her hysterics suddenly turned into a torrent of tears.

'You're a crazy bitch, you are.'

'A crazy bitch? That's nice. You turned me this way, so just fuck off, Jago Ellis, and make sure you take that bloody tank with you too.'

He wasn't used to this new strong character. 'Do you not want to know where I'm living?'

'I actually don't give a shit.'

'Your language! What's happened to you? I've got a job and everything now too.'

'Well, I guess you kind of had to, now you're off *my* payroll!'

'Don't be like that, Kar, I miss you.'

'No, you don't, Jago.'

His voice softened. 'I really do and I'm so sorry to hear

about Grandad Harry, too. Look, I didn't appreciate you. I know that now. I just want you to listen to this song.'

Predicting what was coming, Kara sniffed loudly. 'I don't care if I never listen to another bloody Beatles song again.'

'No one can say that and mean it. And it's just John Lennon, nobody else, singing this masterpiece.' Jago pressed a button on his phone and the haunting melody of 'Woman' started to fill Number One, Ferry View Apartments. When it came to the bit about being in her debt forever, Jago looked right at Kara and sang the words out loud.

She wished he wasn't doing this. This was all she had ever hoped for, every time he had been mean to her. An apology, a declaration of love. A pain hit the bottom of her stomach as if all the butterflies of hope that had once lived in there had suddenly died. She had loved this man so much, had given him so many chances. Had helped him so many times in order to try and get him on his feet. The face of her grandad flashed in front of her again. She stood tall and spoke slowly and deliberately.

'You should have thought about that when you were shagging Lady frigging Penhaligon behind my back. And for the record, I know for a fact that if she says you're the *only* man in her life, she's lying.' She looked at him contemptuously. 'You two really do deserve each other.'

Jago was now slightly startled at Kara's continuing vitriolic reaction, but if he was honest, it also turned him on a bit. Where had the feisty part of this sexy redhead been hiding all these years? And as for Rachel, he really couldn't care less if he was her only one or not. His fling with the heiress had been nice while it lasted and now it was over. He was missing sex though, and it annoyed him that he hadn't found a replacement before Rachel had given him his marching orders.

'I know you'll be back, Moo Moo. You won't be able to cope without me.'

'Just go!' Kara screamed, thrusting the tank into his arms.

Kara sat on her sagging sofa and stared at the empty space where the deceased terrapin had once lived. Poor Sid, he hadn't deserved to meet his end in such a terrifying and cruel way. If she had been sober there was no way it would have happened, and for that she did feel bloody guilty. If she was honest with herself, she had come to love the little fella and his quirky ways. Although in his case, his bite had been worse than his bark!

James Bond was now sitting on her lap purring with not a care in the world. She stroked him from his head to the tip of his tail, tears of loss falling on to his shiny black fur. 'Oh, James Bond. Why is life so hard sometimes?'

Grandad Harry, Jago and Sid Vicious had all gone; some leaving bigger holes in her heart than others. Holes that needed to be filled, but at this moment, with what or whom, she wasn't quite sure.

Chapter 38

'Kara? Are you OK, honey?' The voice at the end of the phone sounded concerned.

'Star, is that you? Shit, what time is it?' Kara replied groggily. She had awoken from a nightmare where she was blindfolded and tied to a chair in a dingy room and Jago was telling her that now they were married, she would be under his control for ever.

'It's nine a.m., that's why I'm ringing. Twisty just came to me and asked if I knew where you were.'

Kara groaned. 'I've been so knackered since the funeral and after getting drunk like that, I must have just crashed out without setting my alarm. I still feel a bit rough, to be honest. And my toe is so sore.' James Bond was snoring quietly at her feet. His crazy exploits had worn him out too.

'Look, as long as I've known you, you've never ever taken a sickie. I'm going to tell Lydia that you're not well. Have a day in bed, just take it easy. Even the Ice Queen can't dare judge you on this one.'

'I don't know. I—'

'Do it. I'm insisting. Skye is only in college this morning. I can offer her services in Passion Flowers later, if needs be.'

'OK,' Kara replied resignedly

'Do you need anything?'

'No. I've got a bit of food in. I'll be fine.'

'OK. Well, I'm just a phone call away. Please just chill, Kar. It's been a stressful few weeks for you. In fact, maybe it's time you started to think about taking some holiday. Even if it's a staycation, it will do you good.'

Knowing that her friend wouldn't be able to settle without knowing Lydia's reaction, Star texted back immediately with: *She was actually quite human. Asked if you could text her later and let her know if you'd be in tomorrow x*

Kara opened her bedroom window wide, got back into bed, laid her head down on her pillow and pulled the covers up over her. A gentle summer breeze filled the room. She sighed and let her body relax. Star was right. The stress of Jago leaving and her grandad dying had taken more out of her than she had realised. Plus, getting everything ready for the Airbnb guests and making sure they were all OK had also been stressful in its own way. Brice had sent the nicest email on his return. He hadn't got the job at Crowsbridge Hall, probably not helped by him stinking of alcohol and being unable to string a coherent sentence together, but coming to Hartmouth, he wrote, was meant to be. Being by the sea had made him realise how much he was missing Australia, so he was now contemplating leaving his bar job in London and looking for a job back home on the East Coast. He also confusingly said that he had bumped into 'her boyfriend' and had set things right by telling him that he hadn't made a dishonest woman out of her.

There was something rather lovely and naughty about being off on a weekday. Making a noise of complete contentment, Kara stretched her legs out, much to the annoyance of her moody moggy, at her daring to encroach on his own relaxation space. 'Go and make me a cup of tea, James

Bond,' she said aloud, then laughed. She had been missing out on the basic fundamentals of being in a relationship for far too long. Couldn't even remember the last time anyone had waited on her or even when exactly she had last had intimacy of any kind. The closest to that being the wonderful warm hug from the gorgeous Angel – oh, and *that* kiss with Billy. She sighed. The Billy she had so obviously misjudged, considering the rude and offensive idiot he had turned into after her grandfather's funeral. The Billy who had made her so awash with anger, she thought she might literally explode. It made her so sad to think that someone she had felt she could trust with her life, could suddenly behave so insensitively – and on one of the worst days in her whole life, too.

She fell back into a deep sleep and was just having a wonderful dream about her favourite James Bond actor Daniel Craig pulling up to Hartmouth Quay in a speedboat and whisking her out through the estuary mouth to a remote island, when she was awoken by a man's voice coming from outside. Feeling a little discombobulated for being woken up with a start for the second time this morning, she slowly sat up, swung her legs over the side of the bed and stumbled outside onto the balcony wearing only a red T-shirt, which just about covered her bottom. Her long auburn hair looked as if three seagulls had been nesting in the back of it.

Bleary-eyed, she glanced down to the street below.

'Kerensa, Kerensa, wherefore art thou, Kerensa?'

Putting her hand to her face, she yawned. 'Not again. What are you doing?'

Billy could sense the annoyance in her voice, but he was undeterred. 'I'm coming up.'

Grumbling to herself, Kara went and released the door for him, then realising her state of undress, got back into bed and pulled the duvet right up to her neck.

'Where are ya?' Billy dashed through the front door.

'In my bedroom.'

He pretended to cover his eyes as he walked in, then placed the most beautiful bunch of flowers she had ever received on the bed next to her. All of her favourites were staring back at her: pale pink roses, freesias, gerberas and every colour of sweet peas. Sticking out of the top was a heart-shaped card saying simply, *I'm sorry x*

'I'm mortified at the way I reacted at Harry's funeral,' he said. 'I was totally out of order. It wasn't the time or place to be such a dick. I was so selfish.'

'It wasn't and you were.' Kara remained stony-faced and then moaned.

'What's up?' Billy said immediately. 'Star told Daz you weren't feeling so well. Can I get you anything?'

'Could you make me a cup of tea, please?'

'Coming up. I'll put these in the sink for now too.'

'Thank you so much for these,' Kara said, breathing in the scent of her beautiful bouquet. 'How did you know what flowers to pick?'

'You'd be surprised how much I know about you, Kerry Moon.' He winked at her, thinking he would be eternally grateful to Star for writing down a long list of flowers for him, some he hadn't even heard of. 'Right, let me get this tea for madam. White, one sugar, isn't it?'

'This is getting freaky now. If you say you know my shoe size, I may faint.'

Kara sat up in bed on his return and carefully reached for her steaming mug of tea. Aware of her messy hair and her white face, even paler than usual, she said, 'Sorry I look such a mess.'

Sitting at the end of the bed, Billy's face opened into a grin. 'I always did have quite a thing for Medusa.'

Kara managed a smile back. 'I still hate you, but thanks for the tea. It means a lot.'

'It's a cup of tea, Kerry. And made, in this instance, with pure love.'

Tutting, Kara shook her head at him. 'You are such a sod.' She took a sip of the hot tea. 'So, did you tell Twisty the flowers were for me? Was she coping OK?'

'Being honest, I asked Skye to sort it. I'm literally on a quick break from the ferry, so I just ran up and back to collect them. I had to see you.'

'I didn't sleep with Brice, Billy,' Kara blurted out. 'Not that I should have to answer to you after the way you talked to me at Frank's.'

'I know you didn't. Hence me feeling even more of a prick for being so bloody awful to you.'

'Ah, I get it now. I wondered what he was on about when he said he had seen my boyfriend.'

'Would that be such a bad thing then?' Billy asked quietly. 'Me, being your boyfriend, I mean.'

'Oh, Billy.' Her face was pained as she thought back to the feelings The Kiss had evoked in her in the car park at Crowsbridge Hall.

He lay down next to her on top of the covers, first removing the flowers. 'Come here, you.' He pulled her towards him.

'My breath smells, I look awful.'

'As if I care about that!' Billy hugged her tighter, causing Kara to make a little squeak. It felt as if he was going to squeeze every bit of air out of her, but it made her feel oh so warm inside. 'I've never been in love, Kara, but I've never felt this way about anyone else before. You are such a special person. I just wish you could believe it yourself. And you can deny it as much as you want, but I know you care about me too. That kiss at Crowsbridge Hall told me everything I needed to know.'

Kara shook herself free. 'All I can say is, our kisses must be talking different languages.'

Billy got off the bed. 'Not every man is going to hurt you, Kerry. So please don't discard "us" without a thought.'

'But you're so much younger than me, and you're so handsome and loads of girls want you and—'

'Kerry. It's the heart that decides. It's only when the bloody head gets involved that there's a problem.'

'But I want children.' The words rushed out of her without warning.

'Wow, it's a bit early in our relationship to be asking me for those.' Billy made light of it, causing Kara to laugh.

'Grandad Harry said that age is just a number.'

'And look how much sense he talked. If you listened to him and your heart, maybe we should just give it a go and see what happens?'

Kara sat right up in bed. 'I think you're great, Billy, you know I do, but—'

Suddenly, there was a sharp knock at the flat door. 'Oh God,' she panicked, 'only Jago knows the downstairs code.'

'Stay there. I'll get it.' Billy jumped up.

'Oh, so she's got *another* fella in here. That's a surprise – not,' Cora Blunt, the skinny, pinch-faced neighbour from Number Five, Ferry View Apartments said meanly. 'I thought Kara might be ill or goodness knows what as her van is outside. Anyhow, this was sticking the wrong side out of the door.'

Billy thanked Cora and handed Kara a yellow envelope, sealed with a glittery sticker of an aeroplane.

'What's this?' She ripped open the envelope. A postcard with the Statue of Liberty on the front flew out, along with a piece of paper. Billy handed her the postcard, which she began to read aloud.

> 'The world is your oyster,
> Kara Moon is your name,
> The stars and stripes are calling,
> It's time for you again.
> Come bite on the Big Apple
> For all of it is free.
> The trip of a lifetime,
> Embrace it, please, with glee.'

So engrossed was Kara in reading the letter that had come with it, she didn't even notice Billy making his way silently out of the bedroom and down the apartment steps.

Chapter 39

Kara puffed loudly as she power-walked around the perimeter path of Duck Pond Park. She was thankful to be feeling so much better on her official Sunday day off, and also that Star had agreed to join her before she started work. Kara was even happier that her badly bruised toe had stopped hurting.

'So, who do you think it's from then?' Star was puffing too. 'Bloody hell, I'm unfit. Here, let's sit on the bench.'

They sat down facing the calming view of the duck pond, taking in its luscious greenery and variety of contented-looking ducks and their respective ducklings.

'Have you got the postcard with you?' she went on.

Kara handed the postcard and flight details to her friend.

'A paid trip to New York – it's like a dream,' Star said wistfully.

'Look, Star, it wasn't you, was it?' fretted Kara. 'Just tell me, then you can explain why and where I have to exactly go and—'

'Kar, I'd love to be able to offer such a grandiose gesture, and if it was me, I'd obviously be coming with you in search of the only man who has floated my boat in a long time.' She paused. 'Hey! Maybe it was from Jack? That when he said his head was muddled, it was about you!'

'No. Of course not.' Kara didn't dare mention that the

very same thought had fleetingly crossed her mind. 'Anyway, I can't go. The flight leaves in ten days' time. I can't travel on my own, and I have work, *and* I've got Airbnb bookings – and what about James Bond? Oh, and there's the small issue of spending money.'

'Well, you won't have to worry about Sid, at least.' Star expected her friend to lighten up at this and giggle, but she didn't.

'Oh don't. I still feel so bad about him.'

'Kara, listen to me. You must go.'

'Lydia probably won't let me. Three weeks is a long time to be away by any boss's standards, I should imagine.'

'The uptight cow won't be able to stop you. The flight is booked, and she won't burn her bridges. She needs you, Kar. You know that. She'll manage. But if you are going to do it, you'd better tell her soon.'

Drifting on the calm water of the pond, two swans appeared in front of them, gracefully swimming along together with their heads held high. Star put her hand gently on her friend's leg. 'Stop a second and look. This is amazing. It's definitely a sign.'

Kara said, 'Is it? Really?'

'Yes, hear me out on this one. I love swans so much. They are a strong spiritual indicator. And if they appear in your life it means that there is a very fortuitous period ahead of you. The angels will protect you and you don't have to worry. It is time to leave the past behind you and to start a new phase in your life.'

'Are you just making this up because of what's going on?'

'No!' Star was indignant. 'You know how much I believe in all this stuff.'

'My head feels like it's going to explode.'

'All the more reason to take a step back from real life then.'

'I'm so confused, mate, about so many things.'

'Tell me, darling girl.' Star took a contented breath; she loved being surrounded by trees and water. 'What's troubling you so greatly?'

'Billy really likes me, and I do have feelings for him too, but it's as if I'm subconsciously pushing him away. I can't seem to form any constructive thoughts at the moment.'

Her friend replied wisely, 'There's been a lot of change in your life. And if you're feeling like this, maybe it *is* time to start a new phase, be brave, feel the fear and step out of your comfort zone.'

'Oh, I don't know. Even the idea of going on a long-haul flight on my own to a country I know nothing about terrifies me.'

'I understand that, but it's not like they don't speak the same language over there, is it?'

'I guess so.'

'And as for Billy, he's not going anywhere. You're just out of an eight-year relationship. You need some time to simply be, and find out what it is you really want for yourself, now, you really do.'

'It's a massive decision.' Kara sighed deeply.

'Yes, it is. But look, Kar, somebody – whoever it may be – is giving you this gift, this opportunity. I can't make your mind up for you, but I suggest you think strongly about it.'

At that moment, one of the swans looked towards them, raised its beautiful long neck and body up out of the water and shook its wings furiously.

'See?' Star said knowingly. 'I told you it was a sign.'

Chapter 40

Kara yawned loudly as she approached the market, her flowery umbrella shielding her from this morning's sharp summer showers. Charlie Dillon was just opening up. 'Thank Gawd it's not a market day in this weather.' He held his hand out to the rain.

Kara yawned again, then apologised. 'Sorry, Charlie.'

'Burning the candle at both ends again, were you, Kara Moon? Don't tell the missus you've got another Spanish *señor* in there, or she'll be all for getting out her castanets and moving in with you.' He winked.

Kara was hunting for the shop keys in her bag when Billy came flying down the outside stairs and set off down the hill to the ferry, his hoody just allowing his boyish face to show as he blew a kiss back at Kara and shouted, 'Nice arse, love!' Then, laughing, he announced, 'Have a good one, Kerry Moon.'

Only Billy Dillon could get away with saying that in front of all and sundry.

Kara shook her head and, happy that she hadn't upset him since he had declared his feelings for her and walked out of the apartment without a word, let out a huge sigh of relief.

Kara unlocked the door to Passion Flowers and went inside. She stopped for a moment to breathe in the heady smell of the shop's interior, then wedged open the door to bring fresh air and lightness into the familiar Monday-morning dankness. She dabbed at the soil of a few potted plants to see if they needed watering, then started to write a list for the flower-market order. It would be nice to have time off from that chore, she thought. Not having to get out of bed at an ungodly hour for a change.

Last night, she had managed a maximum of two hours' sleep. She had tossed and turned, her mind busy with weighing up the advantages of taking the opportunity being handed to her versus dealing with her fear of going abroad alone and leaving behind everything that was familiar and safe, albeit for just a short time.

Kara asked Star to message Jack, thinking that if she could at least meet up with him, maybe she wouldn't feel quite so alone, and he could show her around. Of course, Star had been delighted at the excuse to be in touch with him, but he hadn't responded to her, nor had he read the emails that Kara had sent him through the Airbnb site.

When she was awoken at six thirty a.m. by James Bond shaking rainwater all over her face, she still hadn't made a decision about whether to stay or go.

Lydia came through the back door and, rather like James Bond, she shook her umbrella over the potted plants.

'The company van is filthy, Kara,' she said irritably. *And good morning to you too,* Kara thought. 'Could you wash it tonight, please? It's not a very good advert for the business, now, is it?'

'Yes, of course. Good weekend, Lydia?' Kara replied brightly through gritted teeth, her reasons for getting on a flight to America increasing by the minute.

Her boss merely grunted and went straight into her little office, just as the shop bell went and in breezed Cora Blunt.

'Hi, Cora.' Kara greeted her nosy neighbour as politely as she could manage.

'No more guests this week, then?' the woman asked snidely. 'Bloody noise you were making the other night. Australian, wasn't he? I dare say that letter was from him, eh?' She drew herself up. 'And Jago's mother told me what happened to her son's tortoise. You should be reported to the RSPCA, you should.'

Kara could sense that Lydia had stopped whatever she was doing in the office and had her ear to the door.

'Terrapin,' Kara corrected politely. 'And it was nothing more than a terrible accident. Cora, how can I help you? Did you want something?' Kara finished the sentence in her head. *Or did you just come in here to be a complete and utter bitch?*

'Just some spray carnations, if you have them, please. They're cheap, aren't they? Pink. Mrs Carney's dog died yesterday. They thought it was just a bit of a cough but turns out the poor thing had flu. Who knew dogs could even get flu?' Without taking a breath, the pinch-faced woman carried on. 'And I suppose you're wondering how I know your ex-mother-in-law – well, not quite mother-in-law, but you know what I mean.' Kara wasn't wondering at all, but knew she was going to be told. 'My sister works with her as a cleaner up at Crowsbridge Hall, you see. Pops round hers for a cuppa, sometimes. She says your Jago was having it away with that Lady Penhaligon. Is that why he left you, Kara? Money talks, doesn't it?'

Tired and now pushed to her limit, Kara bashed her hand down on the table. She spoke slowly and deliberately. 'That . . . is . . . enough.' She could sense the glee of the spiteful woman who had just achieved her goal.

Lydia came round to the front with a static smile. 'Call for you in the office, Kara.'

Kara marched through to the back, only to realise there was no phone call. She leaned against the wall and took a deep breath, trying to still her shaking hands.

Taking the cellophane off the carnations, Lydia wrapped them quickly in brown paper as Cora Blunt went on, very full of herself, 'I was just telling that young woman the facts. If she'd have stayed to listen, I could have told her that Jago wasn't seeing that Lady Penhaligon any more.' She lowered her voice. 'Rumour has it that Rachel is having it away with that scallywag Darren Dillon from the fruit and veg stall. Dirty little tart!'

Lydia made a funny gurgling noise in her throat.

'Are you feeling all right, dear?' Cora Blunt offered.

'That'll be nine pounds eighty-five, please,' the florist almost spat.

'For a bunch of spray cars?'

'Yes, you heard me,' Lydia replied curtly.

'Well, you can keep them, and I won't be coming in here again, with prices like that!'

Lydia slammed the door behind the malicious woman.

Kara came back out to the counter to apologise. 'Sorry, Lydia, she pushed me too far.' But Lydia was quite clearly too full of her own pain to have any consideration for Kara's.

'I don't care who she is,' she said tightly, 'but if you *ever* talk to a customer like that again, you're fired!'

'You *what*?' Kara could feel her own anger rising again. 'You heard what she said to me.'

'Yes, but the customer is always right.'

A destructive wave of unstoppable anger took over any sense or kindness. 'I hate to say it, Lydia, but in the case of

Darren shagging dear darling Lady Penhaligon, then yes, *that* customer was right! And you don't have to fire me,' she raged, 'because I quit!'

'What did you say?'

'You heard me, Lydia, I quit!'

Her boss reared up, and like a cobra, she struck. 'I don't need you, anyway. You've been next to useless lately, what with mooning about over your ex-boyfriend, your dodgy toe, your ruddy grandfather – and having to take time out for those bloody B&B guests of yours. So, it's good riddance.'

'So at long, long last we agree on something!' Kara spat, tears of years of frustration now flowing down her cheeks.

'Yes, we do!' Lydia hollered.

Kara forcefully threw her bunch of shop keys to the floor and shouted back, 'And you can wash your shitty van yourself, too.'

Chapter 41

'Is that you, Dad?'

'Yes, let me up, love. I've got that suitcase you wanted to borrow.' Joe Moon had only ever been in Kara's flat once, the day he helped move her in. It had always been a 'thing' that she would visit Bee Cottage, rather than him coming here. He would never say it out loud, but she knew it was because he had had no time for Jago, not even at the start of their relationship.

She heaved the old black suitcase onto the bed, causing James Bond to jump up and start prowling and sniffing around with a look of distaste; it was as if he knew it was going to be taking his mistress away with it soon.

'Thanks for that. Can't believe I don't even own one. Have you got time for a coffee?'

'Yes, that would be lovely. I finish early on a Wednesday now, too. Darren's doing a good job and it keeps my Pearl happy.'

'*Your* Pearl, eh.' Kara dug her dad gently in the ribs and was pleased to feel that his once sinewy frame was filling out.

'Are you honestly OK about me and her – Pearl, I mean?'

'Dad! Of course. Stop asking me. I love her, and to see you so happy, I can't describe how that makes me feel.'

'It's just that I want to talk to you about something and I want to be sure . . .'

'If you're not about to tell me she's moving in with you imminently, then Grandad Harry will be haunting us both forever more.' Kara grinned.

'You mean that?'

'Yes! With bells on. I think she's amazing. It's right. It's the right thing to do.'

'That was easy. I'm not sure if our Jen would feel the same, though.'

'Oh, Dad. I don't think Jen feels anything – well not where her family are concerned, anyway. And even if she does, you should ignore her. This is your time.'

'I'm so blessed to have you, Kerry Anne. How are you doing, anyway? This is all a bit exciting, you going to New York and all. I was so worried that because of what happened in Spain . . . well, it might have put you off going away ever again.'

'No, Dad. It wasn't that,' Kara replied quietly.

A brief silence, then, 'So Star is looking after the flat for you?'

'Yes, and James Bond and the Airbnb clients. I'm not sure how she'll cope with it all as well as with her work, but she seems to think it will be fine.'

'And what about a passport. Have you managed to sort that already?'

'It sounds sad, I know, but I always kept an up-to-date passport in the hope that one day I would be able to pluck up the courage to go abroad again.' She found herself unable to meet his eye.

'That's my girl.' Joe didn't let the immense sadness he felt at her comment show. 'And I can't believe you told old Twisty to stick it!'

'I can't, either. Oh, Dad, am I mad doing this? I haven't even got a job to come back to now.'

'No. You *have* to do this. How long are you going to be away for?'

'The note that came with the postcard said I had to take three weeks off. All other information, including my return plane ticket I will receive when I'm in New York, apparently.'

'Er, yes, that's a point. Pearl said that I should write down where you're staying, so we know exactly where you are.'

'That's the thing – I don't even know that yet, either!'

'Bloody hell, this is a proper adventure, isn't it?'

'It's mental! I'm to look out for a taxi driver with a name board when I arrive at the airport in New York, who I assume will be taking me to where I'll be staying.' Kara's voice went childlike. 'Oh, Dad, what have I done? I've left my job to go on some hare-brained journey. You do know something, don't you? Tell me, please.'

Joe wouldn't catch her eye. Instead, he picked up her Puffin savings jar from the side and shook it. 'Doesn't sound like that's going to get you very far.'

'It's fine. I've saved the Airbnb money, and when I come back if I have to work in a supermarket, I will. I'm free from being bullied and I've got the new Airbnb bookings to get me though for now, so I will manage.'

'That's the spirit, my girl, and you know your old dad will always help you get by, if needs be.' He reached into the pocket of his trousers and handed her an open envelope.

'What!' Kara's mouth dropped to the floor as she quickly fingered the flat notes. 'There must be at least a thousand pounds here!'

'Two, to be exact. You can't be going all that way and not enjoy yourself properly.'

'But Dad—!'

'No buts. It was your Grandad's wish. He wanted you to

have this, plus this letter. He wrote one to our Jen, too. I gave it to her the day of the funeral.'

'Oh, bless him.'

'Yes, he'd showed me the drawer I needed to open the day he died, and never before. The letters and cash were in there. Not sure what else is in your letter, but it feels lumpy.' He handed the crumpled cream envelope to her. 'I'll let you open it in peace. Almost broke my heart for the second time in a week, reading the one he left me,' Kara's dad said gruffly. 'He was a great person, wasn't he, my father? Made me the man I am today.'

Kara nodded. 'He did a bloody good job of it, too.' She kissed Joe on the cheek. 'I love you so much. We just need to get on with living, that's what Grandad would have wanted, wouldn't he?'

'I love you too, darling, and yes, he would. So, don't you be looking back now. Go on this adventure. Enjoy every minute and forget about your old dad for a while. I'm more than fine.' He put his hand on her shoulder as if about to say something else, but emotion had closed his throat. He moved outside to look over at the ferry, which was just approaching from its last journey of the evening across from Crowsbridge Quay. 'I could get quite used to commanding ship from here, while holding a cold beer.' He smiled. 'Those Dillon boys are good lads. I'll go down and close up the ferry for them.'

It felt as if Kara had only just said goodbye to her father when the buzzer went again. It was Billy. He walked through the lounge and straight out on to the balcony. She followed him out, saying, 'You all right? You look stressed.' He had his back to the sea and held the railings behind him with both hands. More handsome than ever, he said nothing, just took in the face he loved looking at and gave her the smile that made Kara feel a bit funny inside.

'Sorry about my dramatics recently,' he told her. 'My mum always said that wearing my heart on my sleeve would get me in all sorts of bother.'

Kara replied cheekily, 'I'd rather it was there than hidden up your "aris", like Jago's was.'

'Kerensa Moon!' Billy laughed. 'I'm so proud of you walking out on Twisty, you know.'

Kara sighed. 'I feel guilty – and sorry for her, in a way.'

'Who – Old Twisty Knickers? Well, don't. You do know our Daz has been giving her one, don't you?'

'I wasn't sure if you knew.' Kara bit her lip. 'It was the only thing that seemed to put a smile on her face. And with some misguided loyalty to her, I felt it wasn't my business to let you know.'

'We're twins, Kerry, I know when Daz needs to take a shit.'

Kara wrinkled her nose. 'You're vile. Anyway, have you come to serenade me goodbye? I was hoping for at least one more sonnet before you left.'

'I'm not a performing seal, you know.' This made Kara laugh again. 'More importantly, have you got any beer?'

Kara shuddered. 'No. After the other night I've made sure there's only soft drinks in this fridge. I've got Diet Coke.'

'That'll do.'

They sat drinking straight from cans outside. The July sun was about to go down; a glorious sunset waiting in the wings ready to explode onto the horizon of the currently calm English Channel. James Bond appeared and stretched himself full length in front of them both. Billy bent down to stroke him.

'So, I have come to say goodbye obviously, but also to run something by you.'

Hoping he wasn't going to get all emotional on her again, Kara gulped. 'Go on.'

'Star and I had a chat and thought it might be easier if I moved in here to help with the Airbnb bookings you have over the next couple of weeks, and also be on hand for this little man. We don't want him bringing in any more turtles, now do we?' He sat up straight on the bench.

'You'll be moving out when I come back though – right?' Kara's face was deadpan.

'No. My grand plan is that once I'm in here, you have to stay with me forever and have my babies. All ten of them.'

'What are you like! But if you're cool with staying here, then of course I'd feel far happier. I just didn't want to put anyone out.' Kara felt a rush of relief. 'And it puts less pressure on Star, as she has enough to do. Especially now Skye seems to be in full teenager rampage mode.'

'Good.' Billy crushed the now empty can in his hand.

Kara couldn't understand why she suddenly felt tears forming. Billy, of course, noticed immediately. 'Oi, girl, you're not missing me already, are you?'

'It's just you're so bloody kind. I have amazing friends and Billy, I'm sorry that—'

He put his finger to her lips. 'You never have to apologise or explain to me. Concentrate on you and your adventure from now on, OK?'

'No, I want to say something.' She cleared her throat. 'I don't know what I'm feeling, to be honest. I'm scared about going away and not really sure what I want. I just would rather be going away with an empty heart, I know that.'

Billy pulled her into him and gave her one of his massive

hugs. 'You, missus, will never have an empty heart as you are so loved, by so many people.'

She looked up into the handsome man's deep violet eyes. Then, without thought, she put her mouth to his, pulling away at lightning speed as soon as her lips touched his. She then walked through to the kitchen and, becoming all brusque and businesslike, said, 'Here you go, keys and codes. Star has another set. Can you manage between you, with giving keys to the guests? There's only two booked in anyway, so hopefully no bother. And I will have my mobile with me.'

Mirroring her determined disregard for what had just happened, Billy answered, 'Don't worry, we've got this.' He put the keys in his pocket. 'OK, I'm starving, and you have packing to do.' He reached inside his rucksack and handed her something folded inside a grey paper bag. 'I didn't have the chance to wrap it properly.' He squeezed her shoulder. 'Have the time of your life, Kerry Moon. Don't even think of this place. Me and James Bond will be waiting for you when you come home. That's if you decide to come home. You might run off with a handsome stranger.'

As Billy disappeared down the stairs, Kara sat on her saggy sofa and opened up the paper bag. James Bond came in, had a sniff, then went off to noisily eat his crunchies in the kitchen. Inside was a small brown book, the hard cover of which had definitely seen better days. Kara put her hand to her heart as she whispered its title aloud, *'Vintage Tattoo Designs,'* then turned to the page where Billy had placed an old ferry ticket as a marker.

She let out a little squeaking sound as looking back at her was a page of the most beautiful templates of rose designs, and at the bottom in Billy's scribbled handwriting, the words, *Do it . . . for you X*

Chapter 42

If it hadn't been stressful enough for Kara having to navigate the whole airport experience from Heathrow by herself, she had also ended up sitting on the very back row of the plane, knee to knee with an overweight, self-confessed Ohio snoring champion. To top this off, she had dropped yoghurt down her jeans and was now confronted on arrival in JFK airport by a stony-faced New York official with a huge handlebar moustache, asking her a question to which she had no idea how to answer.

'Sorry. What did you say?' she stuttered, stalling for time.

The man repeated, 'I said, what exactly is the reason for your visit to New York City?'

'I, er, I want to see where er, Carrie Bradshaw lived.' Why on earth had she said that? She had only ever watched two episodes of *Sex and the City* in her entire life, and those had been on this very flight.

The man's face remained unchanged. 'Where are you staying?'

'This is going to sound really crazy, but I don't know . . . yet. A taxi driver is going to be waiting for me in Arrivals and he is going to take me to where I am staying, I think.'

The man handed back her passport, then discreetly nodded to his colleague behind her. Startled to feel a hand on her shoulder, Kara turned around to be confronted by a tower of a uniformed woman, with broad shoulders, a tight grey bun, a shelf of a bosom and a face devoid of both make-up and emotion.

'Follow me, please, ma'am.'

The blood drained from Kara's face as she did as she was told, her breathing all of a sudden irregular.

'Sit.'

Kara clumsily plonked herself down opposite the woman in the small room she now found herself in. Her palms were sweating profusely. There was nothing in it aside from them, a table and the two chairs they were sitting on.

'Open your hand luggage, please.'

Kara did so, shaking like a leaf. The official then picked out the cream envelope, which Joe had given his daughter before she left, and held it up to the light.

She had been so busy getting herself and everything ready back home in Hartmouth that she had forgotten all about it, had thrown it in her bag as she went to leave for the airport and had planned to read it on the plane, when she had time to properly concentrate. However, she had been so fearful of getting up and taking her handbag from the overhead locker, in case she made everything fall out, that instead she had just sat and fiddled with the entertainment system and eaten and drunk everything that had been presented to her, to make the time pass.

'What's in here, then?' the big-bosomed one demanded.

'It's a letter from my Grandad Harry. He died very recently. I haven't had a chance to read it yet.'

The woman ignored the lonely tear that was now running down Kara's cheek, saying, 'It feels like more than a letter to me.'

What Kara lacked in Carrie Bradshaw knowledge, she

made up for in airport customs-type programmes and she suddenly felt sick. With her grandad being such a character, she wasn't sure what on earth he might have left her. Confident that it at least wouldn't be Class A drugs, Kara obeyed the woman's request for her to open the slightly bulky envelope.

Kara smiled as she saw her grandad's familiar handwriting on two sheets of the old Basildon Bond notepaper he had kept in his shed and on which he used to write his many To Do lists. The handlebar-moustached man now reappeared with her suitcase, which he placed in the corner of the room, and stood next to it. Kara's face dropped further; they certainly weren't mucking about here.

'This is clear,' he informed his colleague, who was now holding up a small plastic bag which looked to be full of seeds of some sort.

'And what's this?' the woman asked, her expression forbidding.

'My grandad was a keen gardener,' Kara said nervously. 'They must be – I mean they *are* – seeds.'

'Why would you bring seeds to America? You do realise that failure to declare prohibited agriculture items can incur a civil penalty of up to one thousand dollars for non-commercial quantities?'

'I didn't know, honestly.' Kara began to panic, wishing she was sitting looking out to sea with James Bond on her lap, rather than at this steely-eyed woman in front of her. 'I have never travelled on my own before. They won't harm anyone, I'm sure.'

'Yeah, yeah. Do you think we've not heard this a million times before? We need to get them checked out.' The stern one looked to the man for affirmation. He nodded.

'If they are prohibited, we will confiscate them and fine you. And then CBP agriculture specialists will dispose of them for us. Do you understand?'

The man took the small bag of seeds from the woman.

But Kara had to know what her dear grandad had left for her; she couldn't allow them to take something that he so wanted her to have, away to be destroyed.

'Can't I just read the letter first?' she begged. 'It'll say what they are, I'm sure. They're for the garden, that's all.' Her voice quietened. 'My grandad was so special to me.' Kara went to take the letter from the table. The woman put her hand on hers to stop her, then sensing the genuine distress of the innocent-looking redhead in front of her, she relented.

'I'll read it,' she said in her slow New York drawl, then began to decipher the scribbled words.

'*My darling Kerensa Anne.* Kerensa? Interesting name you have here,' the woman commented.

'Get on with it,' Moustache Man said gruffly, now resting his backside on Kara's case. The woman began reading as fast as her voice would allow her to.

'*My darling Kerensa Anne, second granddaughter, chief of shed meetings and taker of my heart. You're reading this because I've decided it was time for me to go up and see your Granny Annie. I don't want you to be sad. I want you to remember the fun times we had together. I'm still in that heart of yours, loving you and guiding you. You said yourself you were glad to be part of me and that is exactly what I am, part of you. Think of me through good and bad times and I will always be there. Be honest, Kerry duck, in whatever you do. And always let your heart decide.*'

The female airport official sniffed. Even Handlebar-Moustache Man, realising that this would be too much of a ruse to get a few old seeds through their customs net, had a quiver to his lip. Scary Woman carried on:

'I'm hoping you set yourself free now. Free from the responsibility of your father; he has Pearl to look out for him now.

'Who's Pearl? What a great name too!'
'Gibson!' Moustached Man said sternly. 'Just read the goddamn letter.'
'OK. OK I'm doing it.'
Kara felt inclined to smile at the woman's sudden attachment to the situation.

'I know I said it to your face, but I will say it again. Promise me that from now on you will open your mind and follow your heart. Travel. (The few quid I've left you will help with that.) And let a man complement your life, not take it over. I believe it's all written anyway; you are too good and kind not to find happiness and I can already sense that you will make a great mother. And about your sister – well, what can I say? You don't have to be beholden to her with anything, either. There's no rule book with families. She loves you in her own way, I'm sure. As did your mother, who, although I'm not excusing her, deep down had her own problems, if we cared to look inside. I won't go on as we were lucky, me and you. Just like me and my Annie, we said everything to each other that was needed whilst I was alive. We had no secrets. Just shared a big bundle of joyous love. And for that reason, I

now come to my little gift to you. This is my first ever secret between us, because I'm not telling you what they are, you will have to wait and see for yourself.'

Kara let out a cross between a laugh and a cry. It seemed funny hearing her grandad's voice through that of a feisty New Yorker – and how amused would he have been to hear this story. That in the exact moment she needed him to say what the seeds were, he had done the complete opposite. If she did have grandchildren of her own, this story could be related and laughed upon for years. Suddenly, seeing the funny side of the whole situation, Kara no longer felt afraid.

The female official, having grown up in the Bronx and not used to such sugary emotion, seemed hungry to carry on reading. 'Let me finish, girl, before you come out with dramatics,' she warned Kara, concealing her own emotions.

'All you need to know is that you are to plant the seeds from this little packet, so that the plants they produce grow up and entwine the Agatha Christie rose. Never forget that every soul is a flower blossoming in nature, and when the seeds have done their thing and each time you go to Bee Cottage, you will be reminded of us both. Me and your Granny Annie wrapped around each other in total harmony; just how we lived our lives.

Life is so short, my darling Kerry. We are only here for a long weekend, so you might as well enjoy it. Keep Laughing and Bee happy!

It's been a blast! All my love, Grandad Harry X.'

There was a silence. Fearing that if she started crying, she might never stop, Kara somehow kept herself under control.

The woman got up, turned away, sniffed loudly and cleared her throat. The man came to the table and picked up the little packet of seeds.

'A fine tale, well done,' he said. 'But I still have to take these, it's the law.' He took a while to check the zip was secure on her case, before wheeling it to her and saying, 'It could take hours to get the seeds verified and it looks like you could do with some rest. We have your number; I will be in touch with regards to any penalty and confiscation.'

The female official looked at her colleague quizzically. It wasn't like Dick Gallardo to let anyone go without proof of contraband.

Kara, now feeling a mixture of intense relief and deep sorrow, mixed with jet lag, stood up. 'I didn't know,' was all she could muster.

'We're just doing our job,' the man replied, unapologetically.

Chapter 43

Kara awoke to the antithesis of a peaceful Cornish estuary town. Sirens screamed up from the busy street below, a sound both alien yet also so familiar to her, from all the American gangster films that Jago used to watch in the flat.

So tired was she when she had arrived last night that she hadn't even remembered opening the window to the bijou room in which she now found herself. Without even peering down at the sidewalk five floors below, she closed the window to shut out the noise then lay back on the bed. She immediately felt far too warm. Looking around her, she was relieved to see controls for an air-conditioning unit above the window, and she cranked it up until she felt as if she was in a refrigerator.

What she did remember from last night was her journey to this modern apartment building, which she knew was close to Central Park. The yellow cab, so familiar to her from countless TV shows and films, was much smaller inside than she had imagined. It was as if her knees were actually touching the driver's cabin in front. The seat was a lot harder, too. She had never seen so much traffic moving at speed in her whole life, and she realised that the saying 'the streets of New York never slept' was no lie. Her senses had been overloaded with the lights, skyscrapers, traffic noise and many sirens. She had gazed out of the window the whole way here, like an intrigued child, taking in every sight, sound, smell and sensation. In fact, from the minute she had stepped off the plane it was as if she was on some kind of American movie set.

It was a shock, and it brought home to her how small her life was. That all she really knew was her little estuary town in Cornwall and the surrounding areas. Apart from the distant memory of her holiday in Majorca, when her mother had upped and left, but she didn't like to count that. She hadn't even been to London. Maybe when she got back, she should make the effort to visit Jen, if only to be shown around the capital city. She'd made it to Truro, Cornwall's capital city, once, but that was as a kid and her mum had been more interested in clothes shopping than anything else.

It had been such a relief after her stressful episode with the authorities to see a friendly-looking Hispanic man patiently waiting for her with a name board at the airport; he not only dropped her right outside the apartment block in the Upper West Side of Manhattan but had given her a yellow envelope containing keys and instructions on how to get in, and another for her to open at her leisure.

The journey had been mysteriously paid for upfront, with the driver giving nothing away other than his name was Luis. Pearl, who had once visited New York with her husband on a Christmas trip, had told Kara that tipping was part of the culture here, so she should have some small notes and coins handy at all times. Realising just how long Luis had been waiting for her at the airport, she generously gave him a twenty-dollar bill. Delighted, he told her that his number was on the envelope: if she needed to travel anywhere else during her stay, she should get in touch as he would be able to take her. He also advised that she must be sure to read everything that was in the envelopes.

Kara checked her watch: 8 a.m., which meant it was around lunchtime at home. No wonder she felt so hungry, but it was good that she had got off to sleep so easily. She must text her dad the address as she had promised. The last thing she wanted to do was worry him.

Her room was small, but very clean. It resembled a hotel room, but it was a serviced apartment, she guessed. There was a small kitchenette with a shiny quartz worktop on which sat a couple of bone-china mugs painted with colourful images of burlesque dancers, plus a posh red SMEG kettle. A small fridge sat below, and there was a sofa in the other corner of the room and a flat-screen TV on the wall. A few tourist pamphlets lay on the mirrored bedside table. A wooden door led to a bathroom, which housed a beige-tiled walk-in shower, a toilet and a handbasin. A Hollywood-style lighted vanity mirror was fixed above the basin and when Kara walked back through to the bedroom, she noticed the same favourite black-and-white print of Audrey Hepburn in *Breakfast at Tiffany's* that hung above the jukebox at Frank's, but here hung over the bed. Seeing this made her realise just how far she was from home and a feeling of panic shot through her.

Being in New York all alone, and not knowing what on earth she was doing here, really was a little bit scary. What a shame Jack had turned out not to be the man either she or Star had thought he was. If he had bothered to answer his phone or emails, she could have met up with him and he could have given her a proper show-round. It upset her to think that she was such a poor judge of character. He had seemed so nice, had even given her the beautiful earrings she was wearing now, with the note *No more 'I wish'* on them. She smiled to herself. Ironically, it was that note that had helped her make the decision to come away. She thought back to Star's theory, that throughout life, you would encounter a variety of people; some for a reason, some for a season and some for a lifetime. Maybe the reason for meeting Jack was not about Star at all but was for him to give *her* that message. Life and its inconsistent coincidences hurt her head sometimes.

Star had obviously encouraged Jack to buy the earrings. A nice gesture from him, but also Star's opportunity to give out more messages from her beloved guardian angels. As usual, Kara had kept the little Crystal Meaning card that Star always provided. She reached for her bag and found it tucked into a pocket of her purse. The card read: *This stone can beautifully guide you in the quest for emotional happiness and help you move forward after a period of doubt.* She really did have the best of friends.

Leaning over, she filled the kettle and flicked it on. She then went to the yellow envelopes that Luis the taxi driver had given her. The first had his number and the address of this apartment scribbled on the front, and contained the instructions for getting into the apartment block and where to leave the keys on her departure. In just three days' time! She had thought she was here for three weeks! Kara had hunted for a return ticket last night, but found nothing. Hadn't the original note said it would be here, though? This was all getting a bit too weird. But to be fair, so far it had been wonderfully organised. Maybe she just needed to trust it.

The second envelope had proved more fruitful. It contained another postcard, this time with a picture taken from the Strawberry Fields memorial in Central Park. Kara remembered Jago telling her that Strawberry Fields was designed as a garden of peace in honour of John Lennon. Apparently when his Liverpudlian hero had lived in the nearby Dakota Apartments, before he was shot down far too soon, it was his favourite area in the park. The postcard showed a black-and-white mosaic with the word *Imagine*. Kara strained her eyes to read and remind herself what the squeezed-in, typed font on the back said.

MONDAY
This is your trip of a lifetime,
Kara Moon, embrace it with glee.
Sing Strawberry Fields forever
And start to enjoy being free.
Turn left out of the apartment, then cross the street. Just imagine all the fun you're going to have from now on!

TUESDAY
Today is the day
To mix work with play,
To follow your passion,
Which is flowers, you say?
Luis, your driver, will be waiting outside the apartment block at 10 a.m.

WEDNESDAY
Today is the day
You must open your mind,
For by visiting this store
A new you, you may find.
Luis, your driver, will be waiting outside the apartment block at 10 a.m.

THURSDAY
Be ready for 7.
What's come through the door?
Another adventure.
Yes, there will be more.
Luis, your driver, will be waiting outside the apartment block at 7.30 a.m.

Kara was truly perplexed now, but also slightly relieved that there was a chance that whatever was coming through the door on Thursday would give her details of her next destination, at least! Who on earth could have done all of this for her, with such care and attention to detail? Mixing work with play tomorrow – what was that all about? And Wednesday, it looked like she was going shopping. Whoever it was who had arranged this didn't know her that well then; she really wasn't much of a fan of clothes shopping, especially for herself. Her phone buzzed with a text. It was her dad. Joe had written: *Just let me know you got there OK, darling, and where you are exactly.* She smiled. If it had been her dad who had arranged this, surely he would have needed some help to go to these lengths of pretence. She reached for the envelope on which Luis had scribbled down the address of the apartment block and messaged her dad back, assuring him she was fine, then set the bath running. It was a bigger tub than hers at home and she was under no time constraints to get out of the door today so was looking forward to a long soak.

Whilst the water slowly filled the deep tub, Kara switched on the TV to see a huge weather map of America and heard a report saying they were having a mini-heatwave in New York City. Thankful she had brought some shorts with her, she pulled the old black suitcase up on to the bed. On undoing the zip, she was startled by something flying out onto the bed. Seeing what was before her eyes, a warm fuzzy feeling enveloped her. She picked up the completely intact little plastic packet of seeds and held them to her chest.

And as she made herself a cup of tea and took it through to the bathroom, back at the airport Dick Gallardo was finishing his nightshift, feeling good that for once in his life, he had followed *his* heart.

Chapter 44

The John Lennon memorial was strangely quiet when Kara arrived and took a seat on the bench there. She was glad she had brought the postcard with her as it was now acting as a fan in the 30-degree heat. She had dithered about getting her legs out in her shorts, but it was too hot for jeans and she didn't own a summer dress. She had always envied how sylph-like and beautiful Star looked in her trademark floral numbers, but remembering how her mother had always made comments about long dresses not suiting Kara's shape (even before she had developed boobs), she would never wear one.

When a scruffy guy with dreadlocks and a guitar sitting opposite the famous mosaic started singing 'Imagine' in a soulful voice, Kara took a breath. She knew every word, every moment of this song and had to confess that she did love it. Could Jago have masterminded such a romantic event as this? She dismissed that thought immediately. He was far too selfish. He had always wanted to come here, though, and one of her dearest dreams had been to save up enough money to surprise him with a trip, but with the blue pot being constantly emptied by him, it had always stayed as just that: a dream. She hadn't ever thought that maybe he would bring her here one day. God, their relationship had been so fucked up. Or maybe she shouldn't be blaming the relationship or him, but should take responsibility for her own choices.

Jago Ellis had been her first true love, so she really had no yardstick of what this relationship lark was all about. Apart from the way that he had made her feel the minute that he had nonchalantly walked into Passion Flowers and asked her what flowers she thought a woman might like to receive on a first date. Fancying him straight away and wanting to impress him with her arranging skills, she had thoughtfully made up a beautiful bouquet, even popping daffodils into the bunch, as they represented new beginnings. He had collected them and then left the shop – only to come straight back in, hand her the bouquet and ask her meet him in the Ferryboat on the Saturday night for a date. It had been love at first sight for her then, she was blinded by it, and before she knew it, she had dived into the relationship head first. It had felt like a kind of natural progression for Jago to move in to Number One, Ferry View with her within just a few short months, and the rest was history. But when his true colours had started to show, she still sat it out, constantly hoping that the man holding that original bunch of first-date flowers would reappear, but he never did. She should have ended it years ago; she had chosen not to. Unprompted, tears of loss and regret for all the wasted years started to trickle down her cheeks. How could you miss someone who treated you so appallingly?

She eventually recovered and started to put her hair, which was hanging damply around her shoulders and making her feel even hotter, up into its customary messy bun.

When the musician stopped singing, he said, 'Tears, lady? And no wonder. That's the finest song any man on this planet has ever written, you hear me?'

His Deep South accent had a pronounced lilt at the end. Putting his guitar down next to him, he looked to his left, then his right, then began foraging around in his battered brown guitar case on the ground. From amongst the notes and coins, he fished out a huge joint. Lighting it, he inhaled deeply and blew marijuana-scented smoke up into the sky.

'Ain't no man worth splashing those cheeks with no salty water, I tell ya,' he said, offering her the spliff. 'You wanna puff on this, honey?'

'I'm not with him any more,' Kara mumbled. 'And, er, no thank you.'

'Then Jeez Louise, why them waterworks?' The musician looked her up and down. 'Is it them thighs o' yourn?' His laugh was deep and appreciative. 'I mean, us men, we *love* seein' a woman with a layer of fat on her enough to get a seal through the winter, but you, you ladies, you just don't see that, now do ya?' Grimacing at this analogy, Kara went to speak, but he put his hand up to stop her. 'All I see is a mighty fine-looking woman.'

Kara couldn't help but smile as the now obviously stoned musician continued, 'But if you do get that urge to sort yourself out, I hear there's a doc in the Hamptons who'll nip you, tuck you – and, I've heard, fuck you – for an extra fifty thousand bucks, if you so fancy.'

Now laughing, Kara reached in her purse for a ten-dollar bill and handed it to him. 'Thank you so much for cheering me up.'

'Even I cost more'n that, English lady.' The guy revealed a lop-sided grin, sniffed the money, then threw it in the guitar case. His voice dropped an octave. 'But thank you kindly, ma'am.'

As Kara stood up, the man gestured to her to wait. 'Don't

compromise yourself, lady. Remember this: you're all you've got.' Kara stared at him, feeling surprisingly moved. Her emotions seemed to be going on a trip all of their own today. The man carried on to his one-woman audience: 'You're all you've got,' he repeated. 'Janis Joplin, she say that. She left us too early, just like John Winston Lennon here did too.'

A group of tourists now entered the gated area. Back in performance mode, and ready to play for his public, the guy picked up his guitar, winked at Kara and began to sing 'Imagine' again.

Chapter 45

'Kara Moon? I'm Dahlia Gage. I love your name, by the way – I've never met a Moon before.'

Dahlia wore large, dark glasses that took up most of her small round face. Her hair was black, straight and cut sharply at shoulder length, and she was tall and willowy, like a catwalk model. She held out her hand tentatively to Kara, who took it and shook it politely. Luis had driven the half-hour journey across the city at speed – well, as fast as he could considering the amount of morning traffic in New York – so it was nice to be in the presence of such a calming influence, within an even more serene backdrop.

In the cab, Kara had begun to realise that being abroad wasn't as scary as the actual thought of doing it. Yes, granted, she had been blessed to have Luis to drive her around, but everyone else she had encountered so far had seemed so friendly. It helped that they talked the same language, of course, but she hadn't found anything too difficult yet – apart from thinking she was going to be done for importing bio-hazardous goods into the USA.

'Dahlia is quite a name too,' she responded, 'and quite apt for working here.'

'Yeah, my mum's called Rose and she wanted to keep the flower name theme running,' Dahlia told her, 'so my sister is called Heather.'

'Dare I ask if you have any brothers?'

Dahlia smirked. 'Thankfully for them no, but she had earmarked the name Bud, just in case a boy did come along.'

They both laughed.

Where are you from?'

'I have a Dutch father and my mum is English. I grew up in Cambridge in the UK. That accounts for my mixed-up accent.'

'Ah, I did wonder what the accent was. I'm from Cornwall.'

'How lucky are you? I've surfed down there before – stunning beaches.'

'Yes, it is a gorgeous place to live.'

'So, Kara Moon, we had better get moving. The official bit I have to say, is "Welcome to the New York Botanical Gardens." I'm your guide for the next couple of hours, and as it's just the two of us, we may finish a bit sooner. You are booked on to the Orchid Trail. And if you love flowers, you'll be so happy here.'

Kara smiled; she liked Dahlia already. 'I literally am so excited. It's like my birthday and Christmas coming all at once. At home, I work in a florist's called Passion Flowers and, well, I just love anything flower-related!'

'I'm so pleased. It's always nice to share the beauty that this place holds. I can feel that positive energy coming from you already. Before we get too excited, if I can just ask that we follow the marked path at all times and that you don't touch anything.'

'Of course.' Kara was already looking in awe at the impressive Victorian-style domed conservatory building.

'What you are looking at is the Enid A. Haupt Conservatory,' Dahlia informed her, starting the tour. 'Born in Chicago in 1906, Enid has been described as one of the greatest patrons that American horticulture has ever known. We are just going to be in here today. But so you know for future reference, the gardens were established in 1891 and are located on a two hundred and fifty acre site that contains a landscape with over one million living plants.'

'Wow!' Kara suddenly thought how much her grandad would have loved to hear all about this.

'I know – amazing, huh? That's also around the same number of people who visit the gardens annually. It's a horticulturist's dream.'

Kara felt as if she was in heaven as they started to walk past an amazing mirrored cascading fountain through to the exhibits. Some of the orchids were so massive that you had to stretch your neck to see the top. The colours, displays and scents were just everything that Kara loved. Every turn and corner revealed a different colour theme and a new perfume, all so beautifully set out that she was in complete awe.

'What's this one?' she asked.

'Describe it to me,' Dahlia requested.

'It's like a massive white star,' Kara replied, wondering why on earth the guide didn't just take those massive dark glasses off so she could see it for herself.

'That's an easy one. It's Angraecum sesquipedale, also called the Christmas Orchid, Darwin's Orchid, King of the Angraecums, or the Star of Bethlehem Orchid. It is a native of Madagascar. Charles Darwin predicted the existence of a moth whose proboscis could reach the bottom of its nectary, namely the Hawk Moth, which was discovered in 1903 – or if you want to get fancy, its official name is *Xanthopan morganii praedicta.*'

'That makes it even more special – as is your memory, Dahlia, it's photographic!'

Kara sat down opposite Dahlia in the onsite café, placing two iced teas down in front of them.

'How much do I owe you?' the guide asked.

'Nothing at all. I'm just blown away by your knowledge and by this wonderful place.

'I'm glad, and thank you.' Dahlia was thoughtful for a moment. 'Wasn't it Mark Twain who said that kindness was the language that the deaf can hear and the blind can see?' The guide smiled her wide smile. It took a second for Kara to digest this quote, then to realise how dumb she had been. So enthralled had she been with the exhibits and so involved in the easy-flowing conversation that had occurred between the guide and herself that she hadn't even realised that Dahlia was blind.

As if she knew what Kara was thinking, Dahlia took off her glasses to reveal a deep red scar that travelled from the side of her left eye down her cheek, stopping at the top of her neck. Her right eye was flickering, her left eye was glass, the iris of which was a bright peacock blue.

'Car accident,' she explained succinctly. 'I was lucky to survive it. I kept my life but lost my sight. I usually have the scar on show in my personal world, but I do get that it may make people feel slightly uncomfortable, so I wear the big glasses here. No one even notices the scar then. I like it when people don't realise I can't see. It's a bit of a game.' The woman laughed.

'But how do you get around without a stick or anything?'

'The scent of the flowers and the ruts in the path.'

'Unbelievable. You're so brave.'

'No, I'm not. I just adapt. Every time we change the exhibition in here, I relearn it.'

Kara looked at her again, thinking that Dahlia must be in her late thirties. She also noticed her wedding ring.

'You're married?'

'Yes, to Duncan. I've been with him ten years now, and he's a good man. He was studying medicine at Cambridge when we met. We have a gorgeous little boy, too. Oliver.'

'How old is he?'

'He's nine now.' Dahlia smiled at the thought of her beloved only son. 'So, how would I describe *you*, Kara Moon?'

'Unruly red hair, freckles, round face, big boobs, fat thighs and a round bottom, to be exact.'

Dahlia tutted. 'That's your description, not mine. In my opinion, no beauty shines brighter than that of a good heart. Are *you* married?'

Kara sighed. 'Just freshly out of an eight-year emotionally abusive and controlling relationship.'

'I don't like to hear that.' Dahlia shook her head.

'It's the first time I've said it out loud, so that's progress. But there is a guy at home who adores me. I think I'm too old for him and worried he may get bored. He can get anyone he wants because he's so handsome, whereas I'm a bit awkward with my body and what's more, I want kids.'

'People should fall in love with their eyes closed, if you ask me,' Dahlia said casually, shaking the ice around her tall glass. 'And listen to actions, not words. That's the important bit.'

Kara looked at the woman sitting with her, so brave, so clever, whose beauty shone above and beyond her scars, and she suddenly felt a peace that she hadn't experienced before.

Dahlia leaned forward and wiped the tear from Kara's cheek. 'I knew you were crying, but please don't. You have the world at your feet, Kara, from what you've told me. You obviously have a gift with flowers yourself, and if it helps, you've won me over, that's for sure – fat bottom or not.' They both laughed and Dahlia went on, 'Looks are not what maketh a woman. My mum always used to say that to me, before I was going off anywhere. She also used to say, "Celebrate yourself." I think that is what you must do from now on, Kara Moon. *Celebrate yourself.*' She checked her braille smartwatch. 'OK. Time to go. Your taxi will be waiting.'

'One sec, I just want to google the meaning of your name. I'm so into all this stuff.' Kara reached in her bag for her phone. It connected instantly to the Wi-Fi. 'The Victorians loved it . . . OK. Here we go. When given as a gift, the dahlia flower expresses sentiments of dignity and elegance. It is also the symbol of a commitment and bond that lasts forever. The dahlia flower is still used today in gardens and flower arrangements to celebrate love and marriage.'

'Can we keep in touch?' was Dahlia's instant reply.

'I'd like that a lot.' Kara reached over to her new friend's hand and squeezed it. 'And thank you. Thank you again so much. I've had the most remarkable time.'

Chapter 46

'Oof! I do love a curvy girl to play with. And that hair!' the personal shopper gushed on sight of a nervous Kara entering the swish private area within the Saks Fifth Avenue department store. 'And I say that from the heart, you gorgeous creature.' His voice lowered. 'I mean, how can one actually *dress* a stick insect? Oh yes, those women can wear everything off the catwalk, but who wants to be like them, so joylessly thin? Pushing lettuce around a plate, pretending it's a fillet steak – and how could anyone in their right mind turn down an apple pie with cream!'

He held out his hand to Kara who, smiling secretly to herself, noticed that the smartly suited man in front of her didn't have an ounce of fat on his own short, toned body. With his perfect smile and styled black hair, he reminded her of a gay version of Billy.

She suppressed a yawn. Yesterday had been a wonderful but tiring day as, not content with just the botanical gardens, Kara had insisted Luis drive her around, like a 'proper tourist'. He had taken her to the Empire State Building – just for a look as she didn't fancy traipsing up it – followed by McDonalds in Times Square and then on to a boat trip past the Statue of Liberty and Ellis Island.

'Kara Moon, isn't it?' the man said, ushering her to a plush velvet chair. 'What a beautiful name you have too. I'm

Philippe, your personal shopper or, as I prefer to call myself, your fairy godmother for the day. If you don't leave here feeling like a superstar and looking like a goddess, you can sue me.' He blew Kara a kiss. 'Now let's get going, shall we? Methinks a little bit of champagne is in order before I start to wind my tape measure around your lusciousness!'

Even before a single sip of alcohol, the savvy stylist had worked his magic on Kara. The way they discussed her body shape and likes and dislikes hadn't made her cringe one bit. And she was surprised to realise that she already possessed quite a good knowledge of what colours suited her. She just hadn't been bold enough to try them back at home. The bright pink Passion Flowers uniform couldn't have been further away from her new colour chart.

In less than no time, Philippe's assistant arrived, pushing a crowded clothes rail. On it was a selection of dresses, tops, trousers, jackets, and along the bottom shelf, a range of handbags, boots, shoes and even hats. Taking a deep breath, Kara entered the changing room as instructed and removed her top clothes. Thank goodness she had put on matching underwear today!

'Are you ready to be transformed, you delectable specimen?' Philippe said as he directed through the changing-room curtain.

Kara suddenly realised that Philippe hadn't uttered the 'G' word once. In fact, she thought, he had been nothing but complimentary about all of her – but then again, that was his job.

Ginger, ginger, ginger. Oh, how she was bored of that horrible word. Her hair was a rich, dark auburn. As she looked at herself in the long mirror, her mind lied to her as usual and instead of focusing on her natural womanly beauty, her beautiful emerald-green eyes fixated on a round, plain pale face set within a sea of freckles, a mass of red frizz on her head, and her body supported by a big, round bottom and hefty thighs.

'OK, my lady. No more mirrors for now. Get your robe on, because I have decided to take you to the VIP dressing room at the back,' Philippe announced.

Kara made herself decent and came out smiling. This lovely man's enthusiasm was warming her heart and suddenly she was enjoying herself hugely.

And then the real fun started. The VIP changing room was so spacious and comfortable that she was put immediately at ease. As the outfits started coming at her thick and fast, she felt as if she was on the set of *Pretty Woman*. Every time she opened the white and gold door and posed in a different outfit, Philippe would pounce: he would twirl her around, tweak at her and pull her in, with her hair enduring the same process. As he worked, he would hum and mutter to himself, then nod and frown at each part of the process. It was when he smiled and called his assistant in to see his final choice that she knew he was satisfied.

'Now, Amy, please take this lady into the finishing room. I want hair, make-up and ooh yes – these earrings and hat for sure.' He handed the young woman the accessories with the command: 'You have half an hour. Right now, I need caff*eine* and a *preen* myself after all that. No looking in mirrors until she's done, honey, remember.' Then he turned to Kara. 'You were a magnificent muse, darling. See you very soon.'

Kara meekly followed Amy off to the finishing room. The soothing sensation of somebody applying her make-up and styling her hair was strangely hypnotic, and when Philippe reappeared with another glass of champagne for her, she felt more relaxed than she had in a very long time.

The sweet man put his hand to his chest. 'Oh my, Amy, you've done a marvellous job, and Kara – what can I say? You are a *vision*. A transformation has taken place.'

Kara laughed. 'I love you, Philippe! And that's not even the champagne talking.'

Philippe himself felt warm inside and quite emotional as he wheeled the full-length mirror from the corner of the room and put his hand on the edge of the red velvet throw that was covering it.

'Are you ready for this, beautiful lady?'

And, as the covering dropped to the floor, so did Kara's mouth. Letting out a funny little gasping sound, she took in her new look. For years she had thought a long dress wouldn't suit her, but it turned out she couldn't have been more wrong. Her boobs brought it up enough to show her cinched-in waist, and her height made it a perfect length. Combined with the flat designer sandals and a sun hat with a floral ribbon to bring out the green in the dress, and the ornate silver earrings, she for once liked what she could see looking back at her. Apart from her red nose, that was; she had put sunblock on everything but the tip of it, so it seemed. No amount of foundation would cover it, so she would just have to embrace looking like Rudolph the Red-Nosed Reindeer until it settled down. At least it matched her hair!

Her make-up brought out her beautiful features and her

hair cascaded down her back in big, smooth waves. Yes, the woman she could see was no longer that freckled, frumpy ginger-haired girl, but Kerensa Anne Moon, red-headed goddess. Tears filled her eyes. Philippe was already dabbing at his. The assistant had a big grin on her face.

'Thank you,' Kara whispered as she tried hard not to ruin her make-up by crying. 'Both of you.'

'Do you believe it yourself, now – just how beautiful you really are?' At times like this, Philippe felt on top of the world. It gave him so much joy to help others make the very best of themselves. He knew it was important, on so many levels.

Kara nodded. 'I feel like Cinderella about to go to the ball.'

And as she started to dance around in front of the mirror in delight, she realised that not only had she met her real-life fairy godmother, she had also found her self-esteem. And from now on, she was going to do all she could to celebrate herself!

Chapter 47

'Hang on a minute, let me stand on the bed. Is that better? And what are you doing up this late, anyway?' Kara lifted her arm to try and guarantee a phone connection.

'Skye's on college holidays. She's been out until now, and I woke up to her being sick. I tell her not to drink spirits, but does she listen to her mama.'

'Like we never did it as teenagers.' Kara smiled. It was lovely to see and hear Star. 'I didn't think a video call would work. WhatsApp is brilliant, isn't it? It's definitely free when you're abroad, right?'

'Yes, deffo. So, how are you doing?'

'I'm fine. I'm enjoying myself.'

'And is that a dress you are wearing, Kara Moon? I don't know, you've only been gone what seems like minutes and you're already a changed woman. You look amazing!'

'I feel like a changed woman.' Kara was animated. 'You'll never guess where I went yesterday. I went to Saks Fifth Avenue, you know, the famous department store here.'

Star sounded a bit grumpy. 'Yes, of course I've heard of it. We may live in the deepest, darkest depths of England, but I do know what's where in the world.'

'Well, I hadn't. Anyway, you know I've never been one for clothes, but whoever has organised this arranged for me to meet with a personal shopper . . . and get this, had sent them one thousand pounds for me to spend.'

'Shut the front door!'

Kara proceeded to tell her all about her amazing experiences, and her voice was hoarse by the time she got to the end. 'So when I left, I literally did feel like a million dollars! Loaded with a plethora of different-sized Saks bags, I stomped along the street shaking my hair around like I was in some kind of Hollywood movie.'

'Look at you with the American lingo already, we call it a film back in our world, lady.'

Kara laughed. 'Don't worry. I promise you, my Cornish accent *will* be staying.'

'So what did you get?' Star asked hungrily.

'I got a couple of dresses, some designer jeans and I've always wanted a crisp smart white shirt, so got one of those. I even got a new hat and some nice trainers, flip-flops, flat sandals, a top to go with my khaki shorts, a bag and a pair of boots for the winter. Philippe said that I was to spend the whole thousand pounds on myself, so I did.'

'SO jealous, but good for you,' Star said. 'Shame we're not the same size, I'd be borrowing it all. Like Skye does with all my stuff. Little Madam! Show me what you are wearing, right now. I can't see it properly.'

Kara moved her phone up and down her body so that Star could get a good look.

'Being taught how to wear things in the right way and learning what suited me made me realise I like the comfort of a dress, especially when it's so hot. It looks OK, doesn't it?'

'You look bloody stunning, Kar. That style is perfect for those tits of yours and I have to say that green really does suit you. I love those gold gladiator sandals too. Very posh.'

'Well, I'm off again on an unknown adventure today, so I thought I'd better make an effort and also put on flats as I'm assuming that I could be walking around an airport.'

'Oh yeah, you sent me a photo of the postcard. Has something come through the door yet? It's just so exciting, Kar.'

'I know. Nothing as yet through the door. I just can't stop wondering who's behind it all. I've been going through everyone. You don't think it was Jago, do you?'

Star made a disbelieving sound. 'I doubt it.'

'Billy, then? It definitely wasn't you, was it? And I'm sure Dad couldn't have done all this by himself.'

'Kara, just enjoy this, embrace it, and I'm sure whoever is doing it will reveal themselves eventually.'

'But—' Kara butted in.

'Please, just get on with it. You'll be home in no time and wishing you were still away, I bet you. So, what else have you been doing, then, aside shopping like a celebrity?'

'What haven't I been doing, more like. So, on Tuesday, I went to the New York Botanical Gardens to an Orchid Trail there. Star, it was SO amazing. I had the most inspiring guide, called Dahlia. It was just breathtaking, the whole thing. Just the smell of all the flowers alone will remain etched in my memory forever. I really want to keep in touch with Dahlia too, she's lovely. You'd like her, I think. She's blind, but nothing stops her. That made me feel even more inclined to do more with my life, too.'

'Wow! Bloody great name she has, as well,' Star commented, knowing that this trip could have gone two ways and feeling happy that her friend was sounding so full of it. 'Aw, and of course, that makes sense of the note you got about flowers being your passion! Go on.'

'Yes! There's just so much to tell and I need to finish packing, but briefly I went to Central Park on my first day and then chilled in a wonderful eatery called Tavern on the Green, which you've probably heard of already. Again, I hadn't.'

'I have heard of that, actually, as I've been slightly obsessed with finding out more about New York since Jack went back there and was reading about that area just last night.'

'Anyway,' Kara went on, 'I had a delicious steak sandwich there and then I was knackered so I came back to my room, watched some crap TV and went to bed early. It was my wonderful flower experience on Tuesday, followed by some proper touristy stuff, which I won't waste our call with now. Today was the shopping trip and *then* – get me – as I had an hour to wait for Luis to come and get me, I sat in another restaurant on my own. I've never done that at home, well apart from Frank's but that doesn't count as he's like family. It's hard to explain but it's so good to feel a bit, well, a bit anonymous for once. You know what Hartmouth is like, with everyone knowing your business.' Kara burst out, 'I feel so free, Star. I haven't had a holiday for so long. I can't believe that I haven't done it before. I'm having a great time.'

'It's all good – you so deserve it. So just carry on carrying on, girl. And make sure you take some photos.'

'You know I'm not a big photo taker. I don't like to see myself in them, anyway.'

'Well, force yourself. By the way, I saw Billy today,' Star went on, and Kara's stomach flipped. 'James Bond is fine, and your first Airbnb guest is arriving tonight. Billy is all set.'

'Did Billy say anything else?'

'No, he was rushing, he'd just left his ferry hoody at his flat and unlike you bathing in sunshine, we've got a rainy week here. Anyway, have you been to the Dakota building and stalked Jack for me yet?'

'I hate to say it, Star, but that could have been a lie, too. I mean, have you seen the place? I read up about it. You'd have to have some money and be someone special to live there, and Jack didn't strike me as being super-rich. What's more, his girlfriend is an out-of-work actress.'

'Oh, OK. I did message him one more time, but that's it now.' Star sounded deflated. 'I need to try and forget about him.'

'Yes, I think you do. Have you seen Twisty?' Their last dreadful encounter still haunted Kara.

'She's actually shut the shop until further notice.' Star immediately wished she hadn't let this bit of news out, as despite Kara having quitted her job there, Star knew that this would bother her.

'What?' Kara couldn't believe her ears.

'It's not your fault, Kar. She just . . .' The phone line started to go a bit funny. 'It's not your worry now. Look, I'd better go before I lose you.' Star added cheerily, 'Catch up soon. Carry on enjoying!'

'Love you,' Kara replied. But it was too late, the phone had gone dead. Why on earth had Lydia shut the shop? In all the years she had known her, the woman had never once done that. Whenever she went on holiday, she would get someone in to help her, but never would she have closed Passion Flowers.

Pushing this thought to the back of her mind, Kara checked her watch: 6.50 a.m. She picked up the postcard with the Strawberry Fields image on it to double-check her instructions for today. Just as she was looking down to the sidewalk below there was the sound of something being pushed noisily under the door. She gasped, ran quickly to the door and opened it. Then, peering down the corridor, she did a double take, for there in full view was a very familiar-looking short, bearded man pressing frantically for the lift.

Leaving the door ajar, Kara started to walk towards him at speed. 'Jack? Jack, is that you?'

The man swore under his breath and turned to her. 'Kara? What on earth are you doing here?' He had a black eye and his right arm was in a blue plaster cast, cradled in a white sling. Shocked at both the sight of him and his injuries, Kara was suddenly rendered mute. The lift doors opened, and he rushed inside. Sticking one foot out to stop it moving for a second, he shouted, 'I can't hang around, but please tell Star that I'm so sorry.'

Chapter 48

Kara was more than relieved when the captain announced that they were about to begin their descent into Brisbane airport. It was hard to believe that just a week ago she was in an estuary town in the depths of Cornwall, never having really travelled before in her life, and now here she was, over on the other side of the world. When she had got in the taxi outside the New York apartment where Luis had been waiting for her, she looked again at the new postcard with a kangaroo on the front, and again at her fresh instructions, and could scarcely believe that her next destination would be Australia.

She realised now why people moaned about long-haul flights and why James Bond howled every time he was put in his cat basket when she took him to the vet's. It was uncomfortable not being able to sit and move and lie as you wanted to. She had been fine for the first few hours and had watched films that she'd always meant to watch. She'd even viewed a few more *Sex and the City* episodes, which had made her nod in agreement at the fancy four's observations on men and relationships in general. It was when she'd awoken after a fretful sleep and realised that she still had three hours to be stuck in the same position that she had almost gone stir crazy. Her hair was tangled, her body was smelly. Her teeth needed cleaning. Even her mood was uncomfortable. She had to keep telling herself that if she were to follow her urge to run up and down the middle of the plane screaming, she could well be arrested and deported back to England. Also, from now on, she thought, if anyone she met ever moaned about jet lag, she would be nodding in agreement at their blurry predicament rather than thinking they were making a complete fuss about nothing, as she always had in the past. In fact, if somebody asked her right now what day it was, let alone the time, she would have no clue.

She didn't want to appear ungrateful, but she couldn't help thinking that to have had somebody to share all these new experiences with would have made the trip even better. Still, she was thankful to be on the aisle seat this time so she could get up and down as she wished. She was also relieved to have spent the last leg of her journey with a Japanese couple who spoke no English, were quiet and polite and hadn't even got up for the toilet once.

As the plane taxied to its landing point, she reached for her handbag, this time stowed under the seat in front, and took out the new postcard. Whoever had arranged this trip for her had gone to such lengths to get it right. Her new thinking was that maybe it was down to her grandad. It was the sort of crazy thing Harry would think of doing. He had been insistent on getting the Internet up and Pearl had said that she had been to New York before, so she could have advised him on that part of the trip, at least.

Kara turned the postcard over.

SUNDAY

Metropolis to rainforest,
To Fraser Island you must go.
There is beauty in the world, Kara,
That everyone should know.

TUESDAY
Be ready for 11.
What's come through the door?
Time for a new adventure.
Yes, Kara, there is more.

In with the postcard were instructions for her onward travel from Queensland's Brisbane airport. There was to be another flight to a place called Hervey Bay, where she was to stay overnight and then travel the short distance by ferry to Fraser Island.

The natural beauty of the island took Kara's breath away. As she walked through the impressive rainforest, she found it hard to get her head around just how tall the pines were, with their massive three-metre girths. The forest guide informed the group that the trees could reach more than two hundred metres.

Just being in this awe-inspiring place, dwarfed by the forest, brought it home to her how many things there were that she didn't know about this glorious planet. Like Grandad Harry had said, life was short, so what on earth had she been doing wasting nearly a decade of it with Jago Ellis and working for someone who treated her like a skivvy?

How lucky all the noisy wildlife around her was, she mused, to be living in such a beautiful environment. On the way here, and for the first time ever, she had seen long expanses of bright white sand and clear blue water. Cornwall was jaw dropping and dramatic in its own way, but this was

Nature showing off to her exuberant best. A joy to every sense.

As she got back in the red 4x4 with her five travel companions from all corners of the world, she again felt the glorious sensation of being both happy and relaxed.

Sam, their chilled-out-almost-horizontal tour guide turned round from the passenger seat and faced them. He was uncannily like Brice, the Aussie guy who had stayed with her, Kara thought. Sam had the same blond hair, but straight not curly, and an almost identical full-lipped mouth. It would be wrong to typecast all Australians the same way, but the two she had met certainly wouldn't look out of place on the *Home and Away* credits.

'OK,' Sam announced. 'I should have done this first, sorry, but I want to tell you a bit more about this wonderful island. Hold on tight while I'm doing it though as we are heading for some dunes, people.'

Kara found the Australian accent sexy or maybe it was just because it was attached to the fit, tanned young man. She was also in a delirium of tiredness that she had not encountered before. It must be all the different time zones. Determined not to miss a second of this stunning landscape or the informative talk, she took a large glug from the water bottle provided and began to listen intently to Sam's off-pat brief.

The group had also been provided with a packed lunch. Kara hadn't had one of those since she went on school trips and was excited to see what culinary delights were in store for her. Probably far removed from the basic cheese and pickle sandwiches and packet of crisps her mother begrudgingly used to send her off with. Where she had enviously looked inside many of her fellow classmates' Tupperware containers, with their bounty of chicken and mayo sandwiches, countless sausage rolls and every chocolate bar you could wish for.

'So, we are now on our way to Indian Head,' Sam spouted as the driver beside him negotiated the sandy terrain, 'the most easterly point of the Island. Indian Head is known as a "coastal headland". For those of you who don't know already, coastal headlands are high, coastal landforms that are identified by steep drops in their cliffs, extreme breaking waves and rocky shores at their base. We quite often see schools of fish, turtles and whales here. What we do have to be careful of is sharks, so there's no going in the sea here. Only last week a spear diver was involved in a shark attack.'

There was a unified gasp from the travellers.

'Yeah, and if Jaws doesn't get you then the dingoes will,' Sam laughed.

'Are there really dingoes?' asked a bespectacled German.

'There sure are. The dingoes on Fraser Island are said to be the purest of breed on the east coast of Australia. It is estimated that there are twenty-five to thirty packs of dingoes that live on the island and that each pack has around three to twelve dingoes.'

'I don't think I'll be getting out, then,' Kara said, half to herself.

'I'll protect you.' Sam turned briefly and winked at her, and a tingle shot through her that took her back to The Kiss in the Crowsbridge Hall car park.

There was a collective 'Whoa!' as the 4x4 shot up in the air, then Sam called out, 'So, let's do this.' The handsome twenty-something looked down at the clipboard he was holding. 'Some more facts. Fraser Island is the largest sand island in the world. Its World Heritage listing ranks it with

Australia's Uluru, Kakadu and the Great Barrier Reef. It is part of Australia's natural and cultural heritage and is protected for all to appreciate and enjoy. And I, my friends, am one lucky man to be able to work here this season.'

He took a drink from his water bottle. 'Here is the only place in the world where tall rainforests like those you saw earlier are found miraculously growing on sand dunes at the elevations they reach. What's more, the island can also boast that the immense sand blows and cliffs of coloured sands are part of the longest and most complete age sequence of coastal dune systems in the world – and they are *still* evolving.'

There was a ripple of applause as he reached the end. Sam waved his clipboard in the air and said, 'OK, so Indian Head is next . . . Let's go!'

'So, everyone, before we step back out into the heat and climb this impressive headland, let me tell you a little bit about it.' Sam swept his blond hair out of his eyes and looked down at his clipboard.

Kara gazed out at the turquoise-blue sea and then up at the towering craggy natural landmark next to them. The beaches in Cornwall were beyond beautiful, but so much smaller, and most of them were a whole lot rockier. Here you could look to the left and right and see no ending. It was a surreal experience for her – as if her whole world at the moment was just sea, sky, sand – and Sam.

'Did you say climb?' she asked nervously, stopping the handsome guide in his tracks. 'I'm so knackered.'

'Yep. I will be leading you up to a viewing point where,

if we're lucky, we may spot whales and even a shark or two. One sec.' Sam cleared his throat. 'So, before I was so rudely interrupted by the tired traveller in the corner –' He winked at Kara while some other members of the group laughed and, feeling herself reddening, she looked away – 'Indian Head was named by Captain Cook in 1770 for the aboriginal people he saw assembled there. The term "Indian" was used at the time for the native people of many lands. But hey, that's enough of a history lesson. Let's go see some wildlife, if we can.'

As the group scrambled out of the 4x4, Kara stayed inside. Sam poked his head into her. 'You all right?' Kara shuffled about in her rucksack. 'Shit, I didn't upset you just then, did I? Sorry, I was only joking.'

'No, it's all right. It's just – I don't want to do the climb. I feel a bit scared. I've never done anything like it before and it looks SO steep and SO high.'

'Honestly, it's fine. There's a well-trodden path and we only go up some of the way.'

'I d-don't know,' Kara stuttered.

Sam signalled for the driver to start the ascent with the others. 'I'll follow you up in a minute, mate,' he called after him.

'I'll hold your hand or be right behind you, whatever you feel more comfortable with,' he told Kara. 'I promise you will be safe. You know, it's good to let go of our fears sometimes, try different things. And when you get up there, you'll just love it. Have you ever seen a shark before?'

'No, but I've dated one.'

They both laughed.

'Haven't we all, hey?' Sam said, then squeezing her knee, he asked gently, 'Ready?'

Chapter 49

Kara was now so completely exhausted after her busy day of sightseeing and exploring that before she took a quick nap, she set her alarm for fear of sleeping right on through the night. Bloody jet lag! She had no idea what time it was in New York or the UK and in fact no longer cared. It was 7 p.m. in Eastern Australia and that was all she needed to know. She had been reading that it was probably better to keep her sleep patterns in line with the country she was in, but tiredness had overcome her and she figured that as she was on holiday, she could do what she wanted, when she wanted. Oh, the freedom! She lay back on her pillow, letting out a big sigh as she did so, thinking back over her day.

She wished that she hadn't been such a baby and turned down Sam's kind offer to help her do the climb like everyone else. She could have gone up to the viewing place on the headland and enjoyed the 360-degree views that everyone was raving about after their descent. The worst thing about her not just letting go and doing it was that she had missed seeing the whales. She had always yearned to see whales in the wild. Instead, she had stayed sitting on the beach, wearing her huge sun hat and looking out at a flat ocean, just waiting for everyone else in the group to come down, full of the delights that they had all seen.

Sam had been the perfect gentleman throughout the day.

Detecting her nervousness at all things new, he had helped her on and off the truck and made sure she knew exactly what was going on. But why oh why had she not trusted him and let him guide her up Indian Head? Bless him, he had tried so hard to encourage her and, if she was honest, his gentle handling of her had heightened the obvious attraction that flowed between them. And just as Kara was slipping into sleep, a quiver of excitement went through her at the thought that Sam might be at the beach barbecue later.

All the other groups who were staying in the same hostel were invited to the beach barbecue that was taking place later that night. Kara drank from the water bottle next to her bed and stretched noisily, glad that she had been given a room on her own as she wasn't sure if the roughing-it kind of travelling was for her. The thought of waking up in a room full of strangers would be a step too far, so she was grateful to whoever had arranged this trip for having anticipated this. Thinking again who might have done this, she decided it would have to be someone who had money, as flights to America and Australia can't have come cheap.

Her train of thought was interrupted by a WhatsApp message. It was a photo from Star of James Bond sitting on the balcony of her flat with a Frank's coffee lid in his mouth and the words *All OK in Ferry Land* and a smiley face. Kara smiled.

Thinking of Star made Kara recall the weird encounter with Jack. It was surely too much of a coincidence that he should be staying in the same block as her – and why would it be him dropping the postcard off to her, anyway? If Star had set this thing up, which was doubtful as she definitely didn't have the financial resources, she wouldn't have lied to Kara about not being in contact with Jack. Kara could tell that her sadness about him not contacting her was genuine. In time, Kara would pass on what Jack had said, but not right now. She needed time to reply to Star properly. He had just said sorry and nothing more than that, so it wasn't as if he was wanting to see her again. And what on earth had happened to the poor guy? It looked like he had properly been in the wars.

It felt a bit weird receiving a message from home. She really did feel like she was a million miles from her own life and in a way, it was quite nice to forget about reality for a while. She made her mind up that she would carry on just messaging the bare minimum, which of course included updating her dad each time she arrived at a new destination, as he had asked her to. It was also unbelievable that after working so hard at Passion Flowers for so many years, and being programmed to get up early most days and just get on with the slog, how easily she had slipped into this doing nothing vibe. Unbelievable, but brilliant.

However, despite all that, she had been thinking about Billy a lot, and if she was honest was slightly disappointed that he hadn't messaged her once to see how she was getting on. But she was here to clear her mind, so maybe that was for the best. He obviously didn't care about her as much as he had professed to, and maybe her being out of sight and mind would encourage him to go off with someone else, anyway. She could then go home and concentrate on finding someone who was serious about settling down and having a family, and he could live his young life and not feel he had to be tied down. The last thing she would want to happen would be for them to have a meaningless fling and their friendship be ruined because of it.

Convincing herself of this scenario, Kara had a quick shower, then slung on a pair of khaki shorts, one of her new flowing white tops and the pair of flip-flops (known as 'thongs' in Australia, she had learned) that she had fortunately bought during her shopping spree. Too shattered to bother washing her hair, she scraped it up on top in a messy bun. For the very first time in her life, she also chose not to wear a bra. Closing the door of her room behind her, she headed for the beach, following the red glow of the campfire. As she drew nearer to the group, she could hear an old Counting Crows track drifting across the sand dunes and the gentle splashing of the waves on the shore.

'Hey, Kara.'

Straining her eyes in the moonlight to see who was greeting her, she was pleased to see it was Sam. 'Come and join us.'

The fringe of his sun-bleached hair flopped over one eye and he had a funny habit of flicking it back with his index finger. Kara had glanced more than once at him during the tour earlier. She loved the way the hairs on his brown muscular legs and strong-looking arms had turned completely fair in the sun. What was it with her attraction for these younger men?

The music was cranked up and the beer and wine were flowing. After a while, Sam passed her a joint. 'Er, no thank you,' she said.

'Go on, it will make you feel good, I promise.'

'I said no,' Kara replied far too grumpily, then stood up and wandered over to a secluded dune so that she could just lie and look at the stars and the full moon, which had laid its bright path across the sea. It made her think of her grandad. 'Granny Annie's pathway', he used to call it when the moon did that over to Crowsbridge Quay. Followed by, 'I know she's waiting for me at the end of it, but there's a few more years in this old codger yet.'

But sadly, time had run out. She tried to brush the thought of her darling grandad away, but too late, the grief monster combined with two large plastic glasses of white wine struck and a torrent of tears started to run down her face.

She was mid-sob when somebody flopped down next to her.

'Mind if I join you?' It was Sam. Then he noticed her tears. 'Jeez, Kara, I hope it wasn't me who upset you. I didn't mean to push anything on you, I just thought you might like it.' He dug out a screwed-up napkin from his pocket. 'Here, I've just wiped my mouth on it, but there's a clean bit, I'm sure.'

Kara blew her nose and again the drink took hold of her senses. 'Ignore me, I'm tired and my grandad died just before I came out here and I split from my boyfriend who was cheating on me and I quit my job of fifteen years and my mum left me and my dad when I was on holiday twenty years ago. She must have really hated me.'

'Shit, girl. I might have to do a bit of crying for you to get all that out.'

'Maybe I *should* have a toke on that joint.' Kara managed a little laugh. 'When I say it out loud it does sound pretty terrible. Being honest, I've never taken drugs before and I rarely drink, as when I do I blurt out my whole life story in ten seconds to complete strangers.'

'That's not a bad thing. Not to take drugs, I mean. But I'm gonna roll one anyway.'

They both lay looking up at the vast, glittering night sky.

Kara giggled. 'I feel like I'm floating.'

Sam laughed too. 'I told you you'd like it. Just relax and take in the stars and the sound of the ocean.' She felt his fingers gently wrapping around hers and didn't make any attempt to move them.

'I don't like losing control.'

'It's OK, you're safe with me,' Sam said gently, and meant it. 'Like you would have been earlier, if you'd have trusted yourself *and* those around you a little more.' He stroked her hair, then looked right into her watery green eyes. 'And it's all right to give a little sometimes. Be bold. Just be yourself and not conform to what you think others want you to be.'

'I never lost control when my mum was at home. I always had to have my wits about me. She would shout a lot, you see. Not at Jenifer though.'

'Jenifer?'

'My older sister. Mum loved her more.' Kara attempted to sing along to the Counting Crows track 'Mr Jones', which was drifting from the group who were now dancing and singing along around the campfire over the other side of the dune.

'This is such a tune.' Sam shut his eyes.

'I haven't heard this one before.' She had only recognised the other one that had been playing as it was on Jago's repertoire when he was obviously stoned. Kara started making up words to the lyrics then broke into more giggles. 'I should be a pop star, that's what I should be.'

'My last name *is* Jones,' Sam announced.

'Yeah, right – and I'm the Queen of Sheba.'

'You're the Queen of something, that's for sure. Sorry about your sister, by the way, that sucks. I have a younger brother. He's pretty cool, though. He had to do the late shift in the kitchen tonight, much to his annoyance.'

'Bet he's not cuter than you though,' Kara flirted, then shivered. 'I keep forgetting it's your winter here.'

'I'll warm you up.' Sam tugged her gently by the arm. 'Come on, let's dance!'

'I don't know, I'm a bit shy and I'm not very good and—'

Sam pulled her up towards him and performed some hilarious dance moves, pushing her arms up and down with his, causing Kara to laugh loudly. He then dipped her right back in a ballroom-type swoon and looked closely at the vivacious woman in his arms. The moonlight caught her pretty features. Her eyes were sparkling with life and as green as the sea. Her long curls flowed down to the sand like a wild red cape. Sam was all for natural beauty and Kara Moon was just that, a natural beauty. The hypnotic sound of the surf, music and laughter intensified his already hyped-up senses.

'Do you mind if I kiss you?'

Kara, now stoned and a little drunk, giggled again. Without waiting for a reply, the handsome Australian leaned down and kissed her. His lips were soft and warm. The thrill of his tongue gently exploring her mouth made her gasp. He broke away to ask if she was OK and a now fully relaxed Kara just nodded. Guiding her down to the sand, he put his hand up her top and began exploring her uncovered breasts. Her nipples were erect. Her breathing became faster. It had been such a long time since she had experienced physical contact of any kind that she squirmed at the feelings of pleasure that had been missing for so long in her life. When she put her hand down to caress him flesh to flesh, he frantically undid the zip to her shorts and slid two fingers inside of her. They writhed around on the sand, kissing, touching, and stroking.

'I'd love to fuck you,' Sam whispered.

'Do you have a condom?' Kara hadn't fully lost control.

Sam rummaged around in the pockets of his discarded shorts.

'Bollocks! No,' he replied, then continued to kiss her passionately.

'Keep doing what you're doing, then.' She moaned as he removed his fingers from within her and then, sliding down her body bit by bit, he arrived at her sweet wetness and began to pleasure her with his tongue.

'Mr Jones, you're a very naughty boy!' Kara panted, writhing in complete ecstasy. And then under the light of a magical starry sky, Kerensa Anne Moon celebrated herself by releasing years of pent-up sexual energy on the dunes of the biggest sand island in the world with a handsome Australian called Sam, to the tune of 'Good Time' by the Counting Crows.

Chapter 50

'Jonesy, what *are* you doing?'

Brice Jones put his fingers to his lips to shush his colleague as he pushed a yellow envelope under the door of Room 206.

On hearing voices outside her door, Kara awoke from her deep, dream-filled slumber and groaned. Her head was hurting. She reached for the bottle of water on the floor next to her and gulped it down thirstily. Memories of the evening before started to filter back in. Her clothes were strewn in a heap at the end of the bed. She was wearing just the knickers she had had on the night before. The tattoo book that Billy had given her was on the pillow next to her.

'Oh God,' she said aloud. 'What have I done?'

There was she, thinking that Billy would be the one going off with other women whilst she was away, but no, it had been Kara herself making out with a nigh-on complete stranger – and in the open air, what's more. There was sand in the bed – in fact, there was sand in every crevice of her body. Kara managed a laugh. Who'd have thought, she marvelled, that Kara Moon would have almost had sex on a beach. Being so far away from home had certainly made the 'out of sight out of mind' saying ring true with her. But no, Kara decided, it had been wonderful, just what she needed, and she wasn't going to let guilt overtake her. She had never promised Billy anything, in which case she hadn't been unfaithful, had she? But she had obviously been thinking of him last night for her to get the tattoo book out.

She started to get her stuff ready to go across to the communal shower and then noticed it – another yellow envelope on the floor by the door. Whoever had arranged this was bloody amazing with their attention to detail. And also, bloody generous. She had still only spent a handful of the Aussie dollars that she had changed at the airport, as on arrival here the receptionist had told her it had all been paid for upfront.

'I really like those redhead girls.' A smiley Sam sung the distorted lyric as he greeted Kara at the breakfast table. 'Great line, that.' He winked at her. 'It's from the song "Good Time" by the Counting Crows.'

'Great rhythm to that one too if I remember rightly.' Kara smiled back as the blond, handsome man came and sat opposite her, his twinkly grey eyes looking right into hers.

'I really enjoyed last night,' he said in a low voice.

'So did I.' Kara's face reddened. 'I'll never forget it.'

'Well, you say that now . . .' Sam grinned again, then added softly, 'It's OK to lose control now and again, isn't it?'

'Maybe it is,' Kara nodded, relieved to be seeing him before she left. She really couldn't have picked a better partner for her first ever one-night stand. 'I feel quite the slut.' But inside she was hoping that he wasn't actually judging her.

Sam shook his head. 'Quite the opposite. If we all took

sex as another thing that us humans love to do, like eating or drinking, for example, then people wouldn't get so hung up about it. Who says that there has to be an emotional connection to enjoy it?'

Kara was heartened by the wise words that were coming from such a young mouth.

'I say that if you're single and not hurting anybody, get shagging, girl. A fulfilling sex life that's true to who you are is essential for your health, I reckon.' Sam then jumped up. 'On that note, Kara Moon, it's been great to meet you. The four-by-four will be leaving for the ferry shortly so you better get packing.'

'How very official.'

'A man of many hats, I am.'

'That you are.' Kara stood up too.

'And Kara?'

'Yes?'

'Promise me one other thing.'

'What's that?'

'Keep dancing like nobody's watching. It suits you.'

Chapter 51

Kara had fallen asleep as soon as she got on the luxurious bus that was taking her to her next destination. Happy that nobody was sitting next to her, she woke up slowly, blinked and checked her watch. Feeling so much better than earlier, she made a little noise of contentment and then rummaged in her bag to check her most recent postcard and letter. The card showed an enormous sandcastle on a beautiful white sandy beach, with the words:

WEDNESDAY
Time for sweet reflection
To make this Antipodean trip complete.
At Noosa and its sands
Enjoy this calm retreat.

FRIDAY
Be packed for 10 o'clock.
What's come through the door?
It is the last adventure.
Yes, Kara, there's just one more.

She checked with a fellow traveller what time they would be arriving in Noosa, then googled where she was staying. Happy that she was to remain in Australia and that there was no long-haul flight in sight for at least the next three days, she hummed a little song. Kerensa Anne Moon was going to another beach!

Chapter 52

'How's our Kara Moon getting on, do you know?' Big Frank was clearing tables outside his café as Star sat and enjoyed an after-work gin cordial in the sunshine.

'She's bloody loving everything, by the sound of it.'

'That's grand. I just thought she might be a bit over-whelmed by it all. Did she say that the place she was staying in New York was OK for her?'

'Well, I didn't hear otherwise.'

'Good, good. I bet you miss her.' Frank went back inside with a full clattering tray of glasses.

As if Kara had heard him, a voice note came through on Star's WhatsApp.

'So, it's Monday morning, nine a.m., and I am lying on the whitest sands I've ever seen in a place called Noosa. The sky and sea are cornflower blue, and it's so peaceful here, and so laidback – you'd love it, Star. Hastings Street, where my Airbnb is, is full of cafés and bars, day spas and galleries. It's like a an up-market version of our market!'

Star spoke into her microphone quietly. 'Sounds amazing. How long are you there for?'

'My flight goes from Brisbane tomorrow. I've got SO much to tell you! Including some action of a sexual kind.'

'No!'

Star's phone rang. It was Kara. 'Rather than these bloody voice notes, I had to quickly call you.'

'It's so nice to hear you. Now spill the lot!'

'Well, one of the guides on Fraser Island. He was cute, and I even got a bit stoned. It was nice.'

'At last! A bit of *you* time.'

'It's good to have this headspace. To miss people. I think about Grandad all the time, too. I know it sounds weird, but I really do feel he is looking out for me. I don't miss work one bit. I so wish you were here with me.'

Star wished she was there too. It was a good two years since she'd had a proper holiday, Skye was becoming more and more unruly, and she still couldn't get Jack out of her mind.

'So, are you heading home tomorrow?'

'No, there's one more adventure. I don't know where yet, though. I'll have to wait for another yellow envelope. But what I do know is that when I find out who has arranged this for me – well, if it's a man I may just have to marry him!' Kara was suddenly animated. 'Oh my god, I have something so major to tell you. The thing is, I saw Jack.'

There was a gasp before Star replied weakly, 'Really?'

'Rather than send you messages that could get miscon-strued, I wanted to tell you properly, like this. So, I'm sorry it's taken me so long.'

'Just tell me.' Star sounded agitated.

'I was just about to leave the New York apartment. An envelope was pushed under the door, so I ran to see who was leaving it and there he was getting in the lift.'

'So, *he* left you the envelope?'

'I would be guessing if I say he did, but it does seem too much of a coincidence if it wasn't him.'

'And you know my thoughts on coincidences: signposts on the journey of our life, whispers from the universe etcetera, etcetera,' Star said, excitement in her voice now.

Kara, used to her friend's spiritual outpourings, just added, 'But listen to this, he had a broken arm and a black eye and as he disappeared in the lift, he shouted out to say sorry to you.'

'Oh my God! Maybe he had an accident, which would explain why he couldn't talk to me. Perhaps he was in hospital.'

'Have you heard from him at all?'

'No. I'm not going to lie, I used Skye's phone the other day just to see if he was avoiding me, and I found that the mobile number I have for him is now disconnected. There was no reply from his email either. Maybe now he's seen you, he'll get in touch. Why didn't you run after him?'

'I had to get to the airport and anyway, he quite clearly didn't want to speak to me. He couldn't get away quickly enough.'

'What should I do, Kar? I can't stop bloody thinking about him. This is so not like me.'

'Your old mate Blaise Pascal was right, wasn't he?'

They repeated together, 'The heart has its reasons which reason knows not,' then both laughed.

'I think you should listen to the advice that you give everyone else and let the universe work its magic on this one,' Kara went on. 'He obviously does care for you, to have said that. Be patient. He knows how to reach you.'

Star sighed and then changed the subject. 'In other news, James Bond is fine, Billy asks after you every time he sees me, and your new Airbnb guest is a woman. She's here doing some research for the Cornish Tourist Board, evidently.'

'Oh. I had assumed the name Robin was male. Is she pretty? I bet Billy loves that.'

'She's in her forties, I reckon, and umm, well she's not ugly and . . . Oh, talk of the devil.'

Joe had allowed Billy to finish early and the young man had spotted Star outside Frank's. Kara heard his familiar chirpy voice. With her heart obviously having its own reasons for not wanting to learn about him sharing her flat with another woman, she said abruptly, 'Oops, my battery's about to go,' and promptly hung up. Shocked at how fast her heart was beating and at the feelings that could only be described as jealousy running through her veins, Kara noisily shoved her sun lounger down into a flat position. If Billy Dillon dared to sleep with another woman, in HER flat, she wasn't quite sure how she would react. Frantically slathering herself with Factor 30, she lay back on her thick orange beach towel and putting her ear buds in, she found some calming music and allowed her mind to wander. Letting out a noisy breath, she pushed her thoughts away from Billy fraternising with another woman, to gifts. Hastings Street – she mustn't forget to go back there to one of the galleries she had browsed in earlier and buy the wonderful print of two swans gliding on a midnight lake; it would be a perfect gift for Star. A little swan necklace by the same artist should please Skye. Kara had already found a quirky Elvis in a bottle lamp for Joe and Pearl in a tourist shop in New York, and a rare vintage Broadway poster for Frank and Monique in a flea market that Luis had recommended to her on their way back from one of her excursions. As for Billy, she was sure she would know what to get him when she saw it. It would have to be something very special.

She yawned suddenly. She hadn't realised this travelling

lark would be so tiring. But then again, she hadn't expected to be waking up under the stars, then watching the sun come up over the sea with a man she had just met. It was as if she really had started living again and realised that life didn't have to be monotonous or unhappy; that we all have choices and, as Angel had said, it was good to be independent. You could have a relationship and a life outside it and that was a healthy way to be.

She thought back to her relationship with Jago. It had been such a dysfunctional coupling and now that she was out of it, she could see just how wrong everything had been. The awakening she had felt with Sam the night before had made that crystal clear. She and Jago had rarely made love in the last two years they were together, and before that it had been more out of habit than passion.

She thought about that wonderful kiss with Billy. Being with Sam had felt great – but That Kiss with Billy had made her feel warm right through from her head to her toes, as if there was a line of electricity connecting them, fizzing through her and creating a pulsating aura around her.

She had been surprised at how strong her feelings of jealousy had been, but if she was honest with herself, the thought of taking things further with Billy scared her. Maybe she was being ridiculous in her naivety. Granny Annie had told her that feelings always won over logic and if they didn't in the instance of love, then the outcome was always unrequited. And that there was nothing more painful than unrequited love. But what if he filled her empty heart, which she knew he was so capable of, then pulled the love plug and emptied it again? It would be devastating. And what if he was just after sex? Maybe that was his end goal. After all, he was young, and she was ready for more than a little dalliance. But then she recalled the lovely Dahlia's comment that listening to actions, not words, was the important bit in relationships.

It was Billy who had gone over to Crowsbridge Hall when she hadn't wanted to bump into her ex; it was Billy who helped her move furniture to get her room ready for her Airbnb guests; it was Billy who had come out in the middle of the night to rescue her from the storm, and put up with her vomiting; it was Billy who had stood with her in the back kitchen at Frank's and got so upset at the thought of her having been with Brice. And it was Billy who had given her the tattoo book, which now she thought about it was the sweetest, most thoughtful present she had ever received in her life. Maybe it was he who had arranged this trip for her? Thinking back on all the kind things he had done in the past, it could be. He really was a diamond of a man. But surely there was no way he could possibly afford it?

Kara's mind started to whir. She sat up with a start and reached for her mobile. Thinking of coincidences. New York and seeing Jack. 'Hmm.' She hurriedly scrolled through her photos to the one of Sam grinning from ear to ear at the sea's edge at sunrise. It started coming back to her. He had said his last name was Jones when the Counting Crows track was playing. She looked closely at him, then went to the Airbnb profile pic of Brice. Sam had also said that his brother was now working with him. Jonesy! Jones was a common surname – but surely not? This whole adventure was now becoming just a little bit too weird.

Her thoughts were interrupted by a family walking close to her sun lounger. Two young children, covered from head to toe in sun suits, ran screaming down to the water's edge, buckets and spades in hand as their weary mum and dad followed after with a blanket and umbrella. The grass wasn't always greener she realised, but having a family was important to her. A family that stayed together.

Pushing her erratic thoughts to the side, she shut her eyes again, breathed deeply and deliberately, and let the music overtake her. She knew she could only lie out for another hour due to her fair complexion, but the feeling of the sun on her body was so comforting. The warmth was a blanket of contentment, and she told herself to enjoy this present moment of happiness, and not worry or think too much about how she had got here.

As she began to relax, a vision of her grandad came into her mind. He was sitting opposite her in his shed, voicing the words that had been in his letter to her. *Be honest, Kerry, in whatever you do. And always let your heart decide.*

Feeling happier than she had done in years, and with a fleeting curiosity as to what Harry might have put in the letter he had written to her sister Jenifer, Kara drifted off into a blissful catnap.

Chapter 53

'Jen, darling, it's late. Are you coming to bed?'

The posh voice of Markus Hamilton filtered into his partner's fancy Putney home office; up on the twelfth floor, it offered an expansive view of the Thames.

'Ten minutes, I promise, sweetie,' she hiccupped.

Jenifer Moon had a final check down her email chain, then closed her computer.

'Good, good,' was her unemotional response to what she was reading. Far too much gin before bedtime was making her feel slightly maudlin. Sighing, she reached for the old cream envelope that was propped up on her desk and began to reread the letter inside. It already seemed an age since her grandfather had died, and since she had tearfully read his poignant words on that lonely train journey back to London after his funeral . . .

Dear Jenifer,

It's your old Grandad here. Well, I'm not really here now, hence you are reading this letter. Hopefully, me and your Granny Annie are catching up on Hartmouth Quay, eating pasties and drinking cider.

I hope the money will come in handy. Even though I guess it's a drop in the ocean for you, just promise

*me one thing – that you will spend it thoroughly
unwisely!*

Jen managed a smile.

*I'm not really sure what to say to you. I love you
because you are my granddaughter. I tried to keep in
touch the best I could. I know you were busy, and for
that I am glad. The fact that you are leading a life
that is full and involved can only be a good thing.
What I will say is that people can always find time for
others if they really want to. That must mean you
didn't always want to.*

*We missed you. Mainly at family parties, which I
know you found hard thinking of as such without your
mother there. But your dad and Kara and me became
our own happy little family, to which of course you
always had an open invitation.*

Tears pricked her eyes.

*I wish you happiness and love, Jen. 'Keep your heart
and your bowels open', my old dad used to say. I know
that will make you cringe: good – but I reckon you're
having a little laugh too.*

*Let it go. We all need to drop our guard sometimes.
See what's real. See what we really feel. See what others
really feel about us.*

Jen bit the side of her mouth, then checked the date on
the letter. He had written it the day before they had had
their very last conversation on a video call. The day before

he died. On reading this a second time, she was so pleased that he had been able to see her face and where she was living, plus to see Markus briefly and realise how happy she was.

But she squirmed on reading the next paragraph.

Pearl is a special person. She is not after your father's money; all she wants from him is love. I don't even have to speak to you to know you will be thinking this. Sometimes you have to trust in the greater good of people. Not everyone is out to get you or others. Most people in this world are inherently good.

Despite spending so little time with him, she was amazed at just how well her grandfather knew her. Her dad had sounded so upbeat when he had messaged her to say he had a new 'lady friend'. She had been so sure that Pearl was after her naive father's money, and on learning this, she now felt another huge pang of guilt.

And now to your sweet sister.

Jenifer put her hand to her chest.

I know that you being seven years older didn't make for your being close to Kara in any way. But she's a good girl, our Kerry. Did you realise that she was offered a place at Bishop Burton College to study Floristry and never took it? No, I didn't think so. She did it for your dad's sake: she didn't want him to be on his own. He grieved for the departure of that wanton wife of his for too many years. And yes, you can say that Kara is her

*own woman, that she should have just left your dad to
cope, which of course he would have done. But she didn't
have the strength within her to do it then.*

*Don't judge her for this, ever. It was her chosen path.
And maybe she needed her own branch to cling to in a
world of uncertainty. Her mother abandoning her like
that at thirteen affected her greatly.*

Jen sighed again deeply. She had had no idea that her sister
had been offered a college place. She had always assumed
that her ambition was limited, and rather despised her for
it. With her being away at university already, Jen also hadn't
really thought about the impact on a girl of thirteen, the age
Kara had been when her life was turned upside down by
their mother leaving.

She carried on reading.

*Be the big sister. Look out for each other. You never
know, there may come a time in your life when you need
her. And I can categorically say, with my hand on my
heart, that despite all, your little sister, who has the heart
of an ox, would never let* you *down.*

Be happy, be lucky, but most of all, BE KIND.

With love from your Grandad Harry X

'I'm ready for you, baby.' Markus Hamilton was standing in
the doorway, his huge erect penis a sight for sore eyes.

Jenifer Moon blinked away her tears and grinned. 'Well,
I'd best give you the time of your life, hadn't I, big boy?'

'Why's that? It's not my birthday.' The tall banker lifted her into a cradle position and kissed her lightly on the lips.

'Because I'm going home for a few days tomorrow, that's why.'

Home.

Chapter 54

Kara had been almost delirious with tiredness when she eventually got her head down in the beautifully kept, and spotlessly clean, family-run bed and breakfast in Las Ramblas in Barcelona. She made a mental note that when she did travel again, she would leave more time between mammoth long-haul flights. But she couldn't be ungrateful, for whoever had arranged this trip for her was opening up her world in a way she had never dreamed was possible.

On waking up, Kara saw that she had slept for an unheard of whole twelve hours. She had a long drink of bottled water, then realised she was ravenously hungry. Finding a packet of biscuits that she'd taken from the plane, she stuffed one in her mouth, then got up to fill and switch on the kettle that was in the corner of her room, next to a mug full of various drinks sachets. Her most recent postcard, which boasted a picture of the famous unfinished church La Sagrada Família, one of the Catalan architect Gaudi's most famous works, was propped up on the wall next to the television. Putting her cup of coffee on the bedside table, then stuffing in the remaining biscuit, she took the postcard, sat on the bed and began to read.

SUNDAY
This is Barcelona,
A diamond in the sun.

Free, you can enjoy it.
Spanish fun has begun.

MONDAY

Las Ramblas or the Port?
The cathedral or the beach?
Feel free to explore
The city's cultural treats.

TUESDAY

Time to relax
Or maybe explore,
Not forgetting a meeting,
A surprise for you in store.

WEDNESDAY

Goodbye, Barcelona,
Hear the castanets play.
Fly home from your adventure,
A new life is on its way.

'*Barcelona!*' Kara suddenly sang in full voice the word made famous by Freddie Mercury and operatic soprano Montserrat Caballé. A whole day to explore at her leisure. How marvellous! She messaged her dad her new address, gulped down the coffee, then realising it was too late now for breakfast, she took a long shower. Shoving the city guide and map she had found on her bedside table into her new bag, she headed squinty-eyed into the bright August sunshine. Then, remembering the trendy designer shades she had purchased in New York, she put them on and started to walk with purpose.

Six hours later and with aching feet, Kara made a noise of complete contentment as she cranked up the air conditioning in her whitewashed, picture-heavy bedroom and threw herself on to the freshly laundered duvet. So full was she from her late tapas lunch, that she had decided to have a rest before contemplating whether going out for dinner was even necessary. What a joyous day it had been, with a morning spent moseying around the various market stalls of Las Ramblas, then taking in a coffee and the most delicious custard patisserie outside a coffee house, all the while watching tourists and the mainly good-looking inhabitants of this beautiful city going about their business. She had then enjoyed a leisurely stroll from Catalunya Square right down to the Christopher Columbus Monument at the Port.

She found the whole concept of a beach being within a massive cosmopolitan city bizarre – which made her realise again just how small her life had been up to now. She had also been in awe at the sight of a cruise ship that had docked in the Port. Her mouth had dropped at the sheer size of it. It was like a hotel on the water. With the voice of Star in her head, she made sure to take loads of photos so that she would never forget this day.

Feeling thirsty, she had gone into one of the many port bars that looked over the water, ordered herself a small jug of sangria and then told the waiter to surprise her with his best array of tapas. She learnt that 'tapas' or 'tapeo' is a concept rooted in Spanish culture and read with interest from the translated menu that some people said that its origins dated back to medieval days, when taverns would serve a glass of wine covered with a piece of ham to avoid flies falling inside. Then she had gorged on *jamón ibérico de bellota* (acorn-fed Iberian ham), *patatas bravas* (fierce potatoes) and *buñuelos de bacalao* (salt cod fritters).

It really had been a day to remember. A day she had spent alone. Alone and happy in her thoughts. With barely an acknowledgement of home. Well, except perhaps wishing that somebody was with her to share the wonderful view from her restaurant viewpoint. Not just any somebody, but the handsome Billy Dillon. Who if she was honest, now that she had been away for over two weeks, was starting to fill her thoughts far more often than anyone else. Although of course, her dad, Star and James Bond did sometimes get the odd look in.

Leaning over, she reached for the roughly painted pale green shutters of her room's window and threw them open to reveal the pretty courtyard below. The sight of the beautiful purple bougainvillea creeping over the wall caused her to smile, as did the cooking smells drifting up from the street beyond. As the flat warm air hit her face, she realised that she should probably shut them again or the benefit of the cold air now rushing from the noisy white unit would be to no avail. Feeling too tired to bother, she was just drifting off into a glorious siesta when her phone beeped with a message. Expecting a reply from her dad, she thought she'd better look. Then, gasping with disbelief at the message before her, she sat up with a start. *Kara, it's your mother. Can you meet me in Cafè de L'Òpera on Las Ramblas, tomorrow at 16:30?*

Chapter 55

Sitting in front of Doryty Moon was like looking into a cracked mirror. In fact, their likeness was uncanny. Aside from a few wrinkles around the older woman's almond-shaped bright green eyes, the smooth forehead (from a dash of Botox, Kara assumed) and the perfectly dyed and shaped eyebrows, you could tell the mother-daughter relationship immediately. Doryty's thick auburn hair was loose and coif-fured. She was wearing an expensive pair of Prada sunglasses and a plain navy-blue shift that suited her top-heavy figure. She could easily have passed as ten years younger than her sixty-three years.

'I'm surprised you came,' Doryty said matter-of-factly as she stirred sugar into the coffees she had just ordered for them both. The heat of the sun had driven them inside the old café, with its beautiful traditional interior and smart uniformed waiters: a cool haven away from the hustle and bustle of the busy pavements of the popular district. 'Why *did* you come?'

Kara had in fact spent a sleepless night and wasted morning lying in her room, wondering whether to come or not. She had not called or messaged anyone at home to tell them or ask for their advice. Hadn't wanted her judgement clouded or to have any regrets. For she realised that the decision of whether to see her mother or not could be one that affected

303

her for the rest of her life. She had arrived at the conclusion that now she was an adult, she felt she deserved and wanted some answers as to why exactly the woman who had given birth to her, had walked out not only on her child, but also her husband almost twenty years ago to the day.

'I felt that you owed me some answers,' Kara replied quietly, then more directly, 'How did you know I was here, anyway?' Her shaking hand caused the saucer to clatter as she put her cup down.

'You look really well, darling. I'm pleased. This sun isn't much use for us carrot tops, though, is it?' She smiled, trying to defuse the tension that even the sharpest butcher's knife would have trouble cutting.

'You didn't answer my question.'

Doryty Moon thought for a moment. 'I'm surprised you even asked it.'

Knowing that she wouldn't get a straight answer from this difficult woman in front of her, Kara let it drop.

'How's Jesus?' So farcical did it sound saying these words, Kara couldn't help but smile.

'God. That was twenty years ago, darling. He's long gone. I'm actually living in Ibiza now, with Geraldo. He owns a chain of, umm, gentlemen's clubs. We have a wonderful life in a *huge* –' Doryty accentuated the word – 'villa, up in the hills. We also have a place here, just in case we fancy a city scene.' She took a sip of her cappuccino. 'I saw your sister in Madrid – did she say?'

'Yes, she told me at Grandad Harry's funeral.'

'How is your father? I can imagine he was devastated at losing the silly old fool.'

Kara went to say the word, 'Mum!' in anger but the word didn't sit well on her lips. The rational discussion that she had gone over and over in her mind for the last twenty-four hours was already taking a very different and ugly direction. Kara began to execute the breathing technique she had used so many times with Lydia Twist as Doryty spoke again.

'You look so grown up and beautiful – you were a spotty, pale little teenager last time I saw you. The Cornwall air obviously does have its uses, although I don't know how you cope with the boredom of it all down there. At least Jen had the sense to get away from it all.'

Kara felt tears pricking her eyes. How could this woman possibly be her mother? How could anyone actually get out of bed in the morning and be this unkind? Suddenly her grandad's words: *Be honest, Kerry, in whatever you do* entered her mind.

'Now you listen to me, *Mother*,' she hissed, venom now seemingly able to drive the M word with conviction. 'I don't actually know why you wanted to see me, you stupid, selfish, shallow woman. And if you haven't got one single good word to say about me, Dad or Grandad Harry, then I am getting up and walking out of this door. Have you not for *one minute* thought how you destroyed me by leaving me high and dry as a teenager? How you destroyed Dad, too? And as for sending one paltry birthday card a year, it would have been better if you had just disappeared totally for good. For one foolish moment I thought that you might be meeting me to say sorry. But do you know what? Even if you were to say sorry now, I wouldn't care. The damage has been done. I have learned that actions speak louder than words. I have also learned that love comes in many forms, and I don't think you've ever experienced even one form of it, because if you had, there is no way that you would have done what you did to our family.'

Yet more tears of years of frustration started to pour down Kara's cheeks. Doryty Moon's face remained unmoved, however, as her daughter continued.

'You married the most amazing man. He is kind, thoughtful and loving. Thank God I have him. He's met a lovely woman now and he is happy. Hopefully now he will see sense and divorce you to at last free himself from your evil web. And that's what I need to do now. Free myself.' She looked full into the woman's face. 'You haven't changed. Why the hell did you even ask to see me?'

Doryty Moon gulped, then making a funny noise with her throat, began to rush her words. 'I just wanted to let you know that I am here and if you do want to contact me for any reason, well, you know where I am. You have my number now. And . . .'

When her mother trailed off, Kara shook her head in disgust. 'You are unbelievable.' Her breath was now hitching slightly. 'But now you've started, *and* what?'

Aware of people now staring at her daughter's angry outburst, Doryty Moon signalled for the bill and replied quietly, 'Just think about it.'

Kara jumped up, grabbed her bag from the floor and spat, 'Goodbye, *Mother.*'

'Goodbye, darling. I . . . I love you.'

Kara then headed for the door, which one of the handsome waiters was already holding open for her.

Doryty Moon pushed away the bill, ordered a large brandy, then drank down half of it in one go. Her younger daughter was right, she *had* been the most terrible mother. Even now, when she had been given the perfect chance to be kind and make amends, she hadn't taken it. Or had she? For what she had really come to tell Kara was something that she and only one other person in the whole world knew. And weirdly, being faced with her daughter, who appeared so beautiful and together, had cemented her decision that the only right thing to do with this secret, the secret she had been uncomfortably harbouring for the past thirty-three years, was to take it to the grave with her.

It didn't matter who Kara's real father was. It was obvious that Joe Moon loved his second daughter more than anyone in the world. There was nothing in it for her, so why break their hearts in two?

Doryty Moon drained her glass of brandy, and for the first time in twenty years she felt strangely at peace. For by making the decision for the truth *not* to come out, she had at long, long last done something right by the child she had abandoned.

Chapter 56

'Sweet cheeks?' All Billy could hear down the line was wracking sobs and it pained his heart. 'Oh my God, what's wrong, Kerry?'

After leaving Cafè de L'Òpera, Kara had jumped in a passing taxi and asked to go straight to Barceloneta Beach. She got as near to the water's edge as she could, threw her shoes in her bag and began to paddle along the lacy edge of the small waves as they rolled gently into shore. She suddenly felt incredibly homesick. Hearing Billy's voice at the end of the phone made her feel safe, and just being by the sea reminded her of her roots.

'I saw my mum,' she managed to blubber.

'You're OK, though? Not hurt? Do you want me to come to you?' was Billy's immediate reaction.

'No, no, I'm fine, just sad. How can she be such a cow? I haven't seen her for twenty years and she couldn't say one nice word.' Kara burst into tears again.

'I'm so sorry she's upset you.'

'She just had the cheek to say that she was here for me now and I had her number and could contact her whenever I wanted to. It hurt so much seeing her, Billy.' Kara sobbed. 'I'm so sorry to call you and put this on you. I expect you're at work, too,' she sniffed, regretting her outburst. 'I don't want to ever see her again.'

'And you don't have to,' Billy replied gently, wishing he could jump through the phone and hug all her broken pieces together. 'And please stop saying sorry. It's OK. It's all going to be OK.'

'Please don't tell Dad I'm upset. Actually, no, do tell Dad and say that I'll talk to him about it when I'm back.'

'Of course, whatever you want, baby girl. I'm always here for you, you know that. I'm missing seeing that peachy aris of yours, to be fair.' Billy hoped this would cheer her up.

Kara managed a smile. 'I'll be glad to get home now. In fact, I fly home tomorrow.'

'Thank God. I thought you were away for three whole weeks. And there's me saying I'll come to you – but where the bloody hell are you?'

'I'm in Barcelona. It's such a cool place, with city and beach life. I think you might like it. I loved the tattoo book, by the way. Thank you so much.'

'Good, have you had one done yet?'

'Not yet.'

'Maybe go and transfer the pain from your mind to your body then.'

Kara now laughed. 'Maybe I will.'

'Let me text you the name of a good tattooist there. Daz's mate had one done on a stag weekend recently, said it was amazing.'

'Aw, thanks. I'll need to pluck up the courage though.'

'Do it! And make sure you get it put somewhere where I can kiss it, on demand.'

'Billy Dillon!'

The lad laughed. 'I'd better go, we're coming in to Crowsbridge. But Kerry . . .'

'Yes?'

'Don't let this ruin the remainder of your trip. You and your dad have cried enough tears over her now.'

The line went dead. Kara breathed out a huge sigh. Billy was right. She had cried enough tears over Doryty Moon, and the fact that she had offered to see her again if she wanted to was just that: an offer. One that she didn't ever have to take up, if she didn't want to. It was the nearest she would ever get to an olive branch. Her relationship with her mother was what it was and now she needed to just accept that. For years she had built up the prospect of meeting with her again. Had dreamed that it would be so different, that they would fall into each other's arms and the love would be there. But it wasn't and it never would be. It had taken her until now to realise that life is not perfect. That it never was and, like her mother's love, never would be. Life wasn't ever a fairy tale. Happy endings were rare. But this didn't have to be a bad thing. By accepting that there was no such thing as a normal life, a perfect family, a perfect body, and instead finding the freedom to live within our imperfections, suddenly everything seemed all right.

And now, it was time to move on.

Kara had never been in a tattoo parlour before. It was a different world, one full of cool people and edgy prints on the walls. A couple of topless men with more ink showing on their bodies than flesh were looking through a book of designs that were on the counter of this quirky little place. She couldn't work out where there might be space for them to have their next tattoo.

This really was a new adventure for her, something that had never been on her radar before. She showed Mateo, her assigned tattooist, the design that she wanted, and he said that although they were due to close at eight it wouldn't take long, and after filling out a form she waited dutifully for him to say he was ready. Mateo had long black hair and big brown expressive eyes. He was short and stocky and was wearing shorts and a vest that showed off the amazing tattoo art that was clearly a huge passion for him. With his muscly physique and soulful good looks, Kara imagined that he'd be extremely good in bed, too.

'That eez so nice. I love this design!' Mateo had exclaimed on her showing him the tiny rose she had chosen from the vintage book. 'Red too, the only colour for a flaming beauty like you. In fact, can I take a photo of this page?' He saw the note from Billy. 'Your boyfriend?'

'No.' She smiled.

'But you wish him to be?'

'I don't really know what I want at the moment.' Kara moved to get herself comfortable in the black leather chair and positioned her arm wrist side up, as instructed, ready for the ink to penetrate her skin.

Mateo started to prepare for his creation. 'The women usually wear their heart on their skin. I like that you have chosen a flower instead.'

'Flowers are *my* passion.'

The man took a deep breath as if he was going to deliver a grand sonnet. 'Oh, the heart – so strong, yet so delicate. Sometimes it roars,' his voice then lowered dramatically, 'but sometimes it only whispers, so you must listen closely.'

'That's so romantic.'

'Not really. I saw someone on a film say it once. I say it

to all the ladies, they love it.' He shrugged comically and as his tattoo gun started buzzing, he said, 'OK. Are you ready, steady, go, Señorita Kara?'

Chapter 57

Kara left the tattoo parlour with a spring in her step. She glanced down at her wrist. The tiny but exquisite red rose had been covered with some jelly-type substance and a plastic film over the top, but she could still make out the design. She had done something just for herself and it felt so good.

She caught a glimpse of herself in a shop window, her hair flowing behind her, the jewelled sandals she'd bought in Noosa glinting in the sun, and for the first time in many years liked what she saw. She would never usually wear white against her pale skin, but with her new light tan complemented by her pretty freckles and gleaming green eyes, and another of the dresses she had bought in Saks, it now really suited her. She also felt a sense of freedom she had never felt before. It was as if the prospect of seeing her mother again had hung over her, weighing her down, and now she had met her, she had realised that just because that woman was her mother, it didn't mean that she had to love her. In fact, if she never saw her again, right at this moment, Kara actually didn't care.

Nine p.m. and the humid, bustling streets of old-town Barcelona were humming with anticipation for the start of a night full of food, frivolity and fiesta. The incredible smells emanating from the restaurants close to where she was staying made her nose tingle. The mixture of garlic, onion, peppers and spices reminded her that she hadn't eaten all day. Kara decided she would head back to freshen up and then go straight out again to get some dinner.

As she struggled to fit her key into the big, old, wooden-panelled front door to where she was staying, she swore loudly.

'And how exactly does *that* translate into Spanish?'

She spun round and did a little dance of joy on the spot. 'Angel! What on earth are you doing here?'

'I live here.'

'For the tenth time, I'm *not* saying who paid for the booking. You will find out soon enough, I'm sure, and if you ask me again, you won't be getting any of my mama's legendary paella.'

Angel filled Kara's glass with red wine. She took a sip and shook her head at him. 'OK, I will shut up now. I would have just accepted it as a complete coincidence, seeing you, if I hadn't also seen Jack and then met Brice's older brother in Australia. I don't know what to make of it, to be honest.'

'Kara, I will say no more, apart from that I insist you stay for dinner.' Angel's voice was firm but still full of fun.

'This place is just so beautiful.' Kara felt fully relaxed. They were sitting in the courtyard in the centre of the old building that she learned had been in Angel's family for three generations. He now lived here with his fiancée Gabriella, and since his father's passing, his mother had moved into their wing of the building, too. He had started renting out rooms to tourists five years ago, which enabled his soon-to-be wife to follow her passion of being an artist and for him to pick and choose the hours he worked as a sports masseur. And of course, to give him the freedom and funds to stick pins in his map when he got the urge to travel.

It was a balmy evening in a tranquil setting. Purple bougainvillea swirled over the ancient stone wall and pergola. Kara pointed to the blooms surrounding them.

'I just love these SO much. I can see them from my bedroom window.' Her tongue, slightly loosened by her few sips of red wine, caused her to get carried away about her favourite topic. 'I've been here for just a few days but I already sense that bougainvillea represents passion. They are so colourful, so vibrant, and they reflect the passion that lies within your city.'

A young woman Kara recognised appeared to place a large platter of bread on the mosaic table at which Angel and Kara were sitting. She finished off Kara's observations in perfect English.

'I agree. The bushes remind me of flouncy flamenco dresses, all frills and ruffles, gorgeously swirling around wherever they are planted, without a care in the world. I paint so many of them that Angel says I must stop.'

'You must be Gabriella.' Kara held out her hand. 'And I say, don't listen to him.'

The woman laughed. 'Thank you. It is so lovely to meet you, Kara. Angel said he had a wonderful time with you. I must visit the south-west of England one day myself.' She spoke from lips that were full and natural, accentuated with just a swipe of gloss.

'You would be so welcome.' Kara smiled at the tall and effortlessly beautiful woman, with her long black hair, olive skin and understated diamond engagement ring. 'You're getting married, I hear.'

'*Si*, next month.' Gabriella brushed her hand through Angel's hair. 'Someone has to take the ugly ones.'

They all laughed. 'More wine?' Angel offered.

Kara put her hand over her glass. 'Something I've realised recently is that too much sunshine and Spanish wine don't mix very well for me, so just some water, please.'

Angel jumped up as his mother approached them, carrying a steaming dish of paella that was nearly as big as herself. Her wrinkled brown skin showed a life of years in the sun. With those shining brown eyes and a smile as warm as summer, Kara could tell that Angel was her son. As she was a stooped little lady, Angel's dad must have been very tall, Kara thought. Angel's mum sat her plump bottom down and poured herself a glass of wine.

'*Hola, que tal?*'

'English, Mama,' Angel prompted. 'This is Ka-rra.'

'*Hola*, how you are?' the Spanish lady said, taking a big slurp of wine. 'You are welcome to our home.'

'It is a pleasure to be here, and thank you.'

The lady nodded.

They served themselves and began to eat. Gabriella had put some soft background music on, and a slight breeze had arrived to cool down the heat. Once they had started tucking into the saffron-coloured feast in front of them, Kara regaled them with some of her travelling tales, causing great hilarity when she got to the seed story at JFK airport.

'I honestly thought I was going to be sent back home before my journey had even started.'

'It is so sweet that the customs guy gave them back to you without you knowing. I love that.' Gabriella put her hand to her heart.

'I know. I can't tell you how happy I was. It made a great start to a great trip.'

'So how did you get them back through customs?' Angel asked sensibly.

Kara giggled and confided, 'I googled "how to get illegal goods home from America". I felt like a real criminal, even though I know they're just seeds.'

'I love it.' Gabriella laughed. Angel's mum headed inside to make coffee.

'It wasn't brain science. I posted them to myself inside a birthday card that I bought. I just hope that they remain undetected.'

'Yes, it would be such a shame not to have that final gift from your *abuelo*,' Angel added.

'I thought of everything. I also stuck one to the bottom of one of my of trainers. I've got this far with it. If for any reason that is picked up, I can say I must have trodden on it.'

'You're so funny.' Gabriella got up from the table. 'There is fresh fruit, churros or Crema Catalana for dessert or you can choose it all if you wish.'

'Wow, I'm stuffed but I'd love to try a little of each, please.'

Angel's pretty fiancée went inside to help Angel's mum. Kara was suddenly quiet.

'Are you OK, Kara?' Angel's voice was caring.

'Being with you and your family, it's just so lovely. But I do have to confess it is making me feel a bit homesick.'

'I have a taxi booked to take you to the airport tomorrow evening, so that is just one more sleep.'

'I know, such a short visit, but at the same time such a big one! Like I said, I saw my mother after twenty years and I got the tattoo I've always wanted. It's crazy!'

'Yes, it is.'

'Do you know what I've learned on this trip though, Angel?'

'A lot already, I can see. But please do tell me.'

'Choice is one of the main things. I've realised that I have a choice to do whatever I want with my life. I allowed myself to be beholden to Jago, also to Lydia. I felt my voice wasn't enough. I could have booked a holiday or just taken more time out, but I allowed myself to be owned by the pair of them. As if I was in prison! As if I didn't have a choice in the matter! But I didn't feel strong enough to face up to them and take control of my own life. I think meeting my mother after all this time has also made me realise that from now on I will choose where I want to take my life and who I want to take on that journey with me. And from now on, all toxic people will be refused a ticket.

'Brava!' Angel clapped. 'This is so good to hear, Kara, and yes, it's like me and Gabriella. As you can see, our bond is strong but we respect each other's wants; we are fluid in our love and the way we live our lives, separately and together.'

'You know, Angel, I have enjoyed travelling very much. However, my yearning to be at home now is great. I can't see myself having a big adventure on my own again. I'm not sure if that is what I really want. I would love to share some of the delights of the world with a friend or partner, but maybe just as a holiday.'

'You can do that. That is exactly what I do. It's something to look forward to and we all need something to look forward to, whoever we are. And sometimes, I think that we must take adventures in order to find out where we truly belong. I know now that I belong here in Barcelona, and from the sound of it, Hartmouth is where your heart will always lie too.'

Kara nodded. 'Yes, you're right. But now I know that I can spread my wings whenever I want to, that's OK.'

'It's more than OK. You'll be sticking pins in the map, like I do, soon.' Angel took a sip of his wine and carried on, 'And as this trip to Barcelona has been so short, you must let your blindfold slip and make sure a pin is reserved just for here. You are welcome any time, and I mean that.'

Just then, Gabriella and Angel's mother appeared with trays laden with sweet treats, coffee and ornate shot glasses of sweet Ratafia.

'A toast!' Angel declared, once the clattering of service had finished. Everyone held up their glasses in anticipation.

'To Kara and her many adventures ahead.'

'*Olé!*' Angel's mum said loudly, standing up to wiggle her hips as she did so, causing all of them to fall about laughing.

Chapter 58

'O Billio, Billio, wherefore art thou, Billio?'

Kara felt almost high as she waited below her apartment for Billy to appear. She was excited and happy to feel so clear-headed about what she wanted to do, moving forward. Nor could she contain the joy she felt at being back in her own surroundings again. Three weeks had seemed like two months. She took in the smell of the sea air, the familiar clinks and clanks of the boats in the estuary harbour. Even a few night-faring seagulls cried out at her return. She put her hand to her heart as she looked down to see the street lamp illuminating the familiar *Happy Hart* tugboat, and the twinkling awning lights of Frank's. He didn't usually leave them on, Kara knew, so maybe he had done it specially for her arrival? How sweet. Giggling, she loudly repeated the Shakespearean mantra that had become a bit of a standing joke between the pair of them: 'O Billio, Billio, wherefore art thou, Billio?'

On hearing his mistress's voice, James Bond appeared in the darkness and launched himself into her arms all the way from the balcony. As Kara screamed in shock, the fearless feline let out an echoing screech, leaped to the ground and tore back down to the quay. Cora Blunt's double doors flew open and she shouted, 'I might have known it was you causing a bloody commotion at eleven o'clock at night.'

A yawning Billy Dillon, allowing himself a couple of seconds to take in the silhouette of his beloved Kerry below, then casually walked out on to the balcony, calling down, 'What's going on, sweet cheeks?'

'Aren't you going to climb down and sweep me off of my feet?'

'You don't want much, do ya?'

Still maintaining a cool persona, he ruffled his hair with his hands and strolled back into her flat. Once inside, though, he couldn't contain the grin on his face, flinging open the door, flying down the stairs at speed and out of the apartments to greet her and escort her back upstairs. Carrying her case into the spare room, he put his finger to his lips.

'You're in here tonight. There's a guest in yours.'

'Ah, OK. Man or woman?'

'I don't know. Star told me to leave a key in the key store; she had a crystal session tonight and I was working when they arrived.'

'It's very tidy in here,' Kara noted, 'and is that the smell of clean sheets I can detect?'

'I was under orders from Star.' At that moment, James Bond came careering through the cat flap. He'd obviously forgiven and forgotten the scream. Billy said, 'He's missed you, that's for sure.' And he wasn't the only one.

The pair sat in the warm summer evening, quietly drinking coffee and eating toast on the balcony bench, with James Bond purring contentedly around Kara's legs. A few Saturday-night revellers were leaving the Ferryboat and loud music was streaming across the estuary from a holiday-let yacht. Kara sighed, 'Oh my God, it's so good to be home.'

'It's so good to have you home.' Billy put his hand on her

knee. 'I missed you too. A bit – but not as much as Daniel Craig here.'

'Yeah, right. I reckon you've been gazing out to sea wistfully every evening, counting the days off the calendar until my return.'

Billy smiled inwardly, glad she didn't know just how close to the mark she was.

'You look fantastic, by the way,' he said. 'There's a glow about you and I don't just mean your Rudolph nose.'

'Oi, you. It was brilliant just to go away and get some sun and visit places I didn't even know existed.' Kara turned to him. 'I've been doing a lot of thinking, too. I've had the headspace to do that. I didn't realise I needed it until I actually was on my own – like on my own properly.'

'Well, that's a good thing.' Billy paused. 'I hope.'

'Yes, it is.' Kara was animated. 'I've had an amazing time. I've seen and done things I never normally would have done. I've met some great people too.'

'Oh yeah? Men included, I take it?'

She pushed the vision of her getting jiggy with Sam in a dune to the back of her mind.

'Yes, I met a few guys, but I'm here so I didn't run off with any of them, as you suggested I might.'

'Are you sure?'

'Billy! Stop it. But look what I did do.' She held her wrist up to him. The plastic film was still over the top of it, but you could clearly see the outline of a tiny red rose.

'Aw. That's so cool.'

Kara grinned widely. 'Yes. Thanks to you, I did do it! And I bloody love it.'

Billy took her wrist in his work-roughened hands and gently kissed it. 'Perfect place, too. It's beautiful, just like you.' Then, putting his hands to each side of her head, he pulled her in and kissed her urgently. Gasping as she pulled away, she then got hold of his head and did exactly the same back to him, but this time their lips remained on each other, hungrily searching each other's mouths as if there was so much to discover in such a small space, their tongues intertwining with their hearts, rereleasing the feelings that had been brimming up and over for so long within them.

Billy broke free first, his breathing ragged. 'I have missed you so fucking much.'

'I've realised how much I care about you, too,' Kara told him breathlessly, then blurted everything out in one go. 'Thank you for being there through all the shit with Jago. And for helping me get this place ready for guests and for dealing with me when I was in such a state the night I got drunk. And for the fact that I phoned you and you were there when I was so upset about my mother. And the tattoo book – that was just the sweetest gift. Was it you who arranged the trip for me too? Talking of which, I have a present for you.'

Billy shook his head. 'Shush, now. You don't need to thank me.' He grasped her head in his hands again. 'The gift can wait. *You* are my gift. I would do anything for you, Kerry Moon. You are the most special woman that I have ever met, inside and out.'

'And you've met a few,' Kara joked, then kissed his forehead.

'Says the woman who's just been travelling on her own.' He took a breath and then said quietly, 'Please do be honest if you did sleep with anyone. You've lived with so many lies that from now on, I want us to be honest about everything.'

Kara looked down at the floor. 'I didn't sleep with anyone, no.'

'I can feel a but coming on.' As Billy felt a surge of jealousy engulf him, Kara's grandad was in front of her, saying: *Be honest, Kerry, in whatever you do. And always let your heart decide.*

Then without any thought of consequences Kara found herself saying, 'OK, I met someone, yes. We didn't have sex, but I kissed him and other stuff, but it was what it was, a one-night stand.' She took Billy's hand in each of hers. 'But it doesn't mean I feel any less for you.'

Billy stood up and pushed his hands through his hair. 'I just thought that . . .'

'Thought what, Billy? I said I wanted to go away with an empty heart. It meant nothing. In fact, it actually cemented my feelings for you. Please don't be jealous. We didn't have sex. Just mucked about.'

'It means something to me.' Billy stood up and looked out over the estuary. Turning around, he carried on, 'The Airbnb woman who was staying here. She was hot, literally put it on a plate. Came out of the bathroom and dropped her towel. I could have easily had sex with her, but I chose not to.'

'We all have choices, Billy. Come on, smile. I'm back and I missed you and I realise that—'

'I can't smile. I changed your bed, Kerry, I got us champagne. You've ruined everything. I'm going home.'

'Billy, you're overreacting. Please don't go.'

'Fuck you. I'm off.' With that he slammed the door, thundered down the stairs and was gone. Leaving the door on the latch, Kara ran down after him, but he had already disappeared. Shouting his name into the clear night brought back an angry, 'Just leave me alone!' from way up Ferry Lane.

Doing as she was told, Kara went back upstairs, put the kettle on again and frowned. Oh, why hadn't she just kept quiet? Then she put the boot on the other foot. What if he *had* slept with the Airbnb guest? She had felt a pang of jealousy herself on learning that he was just in the flat with another woman. Who was she kidding – she would have been bloody furious too. She tried his number; his phone was turned off. She made the decision to leave him be, to let him calm down. If she ran up to his place now, she knew she would get the same reaction. She would message him before she went to sleep. Kara remembered back to the reading that Grandad Harry had recited to her from his wedding day, where love kept no record of wrongs and never failed. If that was true then tomorrow Billy would come back to her and everything would be OK.

A couple of minutes later, her phone started beeping with welcome home messages, the first from her dad and Pearl – it was so nice seeing their names together. Frank and Monique, and even Charlie and Pat Dillon sent their good wishes. When she got to the one from Star quoting her beloved Rumi, a warm feeling swept through her. *'Travel brings power and love back into your life.' Me & Skye can't wait to see you XX!* That girl was so spiritual and always seemed to know what to say at the right time.

Had the true love she had been seeking her whole life, literally been right in front of her face all along? And had she now ruined it? It hurt her tired head just thinking about it.

Looking at her Rumi print, Kara could scarcely believe it had only been a couple of months ago since Star had gifted her this and she had decided to take on Airbnb guests; so much had changed since. She murmured the last few words of the poem and marvelled at their relevance. *Be grateful for whatever comes, because each has been sent as a guide from beyond.* Yes, Rumi had been talking about thoughts – but who'd have known that Kara Moon would have travelled to the other side of the world and learned to love herself, to realise what 'freedom within' meant, and also that she had choices. Billy was right: her heart had never been empty of love. The friends and family who were true to her were just that, true and real, and she couldn't wait to find out who had taken the time and energy to send her on her way to reach this state of enlightenment and happiness.

She was just about to go to the spare bedroom when she noticed a neat pile of post on the table and her own hand-writing on one of the envelopes. 'Yes! They made it,' she said aloud, pulling out the little bag of seeds. Then she noticed two minute words in felt-tip pen, in her grandad's handwriting: *Harry's Rose.* In the letter he had said that they were a secret; maybe he'd forgotten he'd labelled the little bag.

She googled the words, just in case they had a meaning, and was delighted at what she found:

Harry's Rose is named after one of Britain's most successful nurserymen who lived from 1898 to 1977, and whose extrovert behaviour cloaked a shrewd head and a kind heart. His namesake rose is a very colourful, lively rose with enormous striped blooms of orange, red and yellow. A strong, vigorous rose, it has a good long flow- ering period plus handsome, dark green glossy foliage.

It might not be a climber, but she would ensure that Harry's rose was planted so close to Agatha Christie, that the two souls blossoming in nature would forever be together in the garden of Bee Cottage and beyond.

Her eyes widened as she spotted something yellow. Ripping it open, she pulled out a postcard, then chucked the envelope onto the floor, causing an excited James Bond to scrabble at it then toss it up into the air. The postcard had a picture of a love heart and a bunch of flowers, and it simply read;

TOMORROW

The wanderer returns.

How greatly we all care.

Passion Flowers at eleven.

Be there, Kara, please – or be square!

Chapter 59

Kara woke at nine thirty to a snoring James Bond; his tail curled loosely around her neck. She gently moved her funny feline out of the way and eased herself up. Yawning loudly, she checked her phone to see if Billy had messaged her back, but on seeing that he hadn't, she let out a little groaning noise of frustration mingled with sadness. If only she'd kept her mouth shut, last night. Her dalliance with Sam had been exactly that: a dalliance. Just two people enjoying each other's company and bodies. In fact, as she had said to Billy, being with someone else had made her realise just how much he did mean to her; had made her realise what she really did want. She had made Billy no promises before she had left. It was a choice for her to make out with the cute Australian on the beach. And the fact that Billy had made the choice not to get it on with the Airbnb guest – well, that was his decision, too. She thought again about him having sex with the woman in her flat. It would have bothered her, bothered her a lot.

'Fuck,' Kara said aloud, then let out a deep sigh. In the cold light of day, she realised she did have some making up to do. The feeling of elation she had felt knowing how much Billy must care for her was overridden by the fact that she had hurt him, whether intentionally or not.

Remembering at the last minute that she had a guest in the other room, she pulled on her joggers and a T-shirt and

331

tiptoed out to the bathroom. Then, relieved to see that they had either gone out or left already, she yawned, filled the kettle and opened the balcony door.

It was a drizzling August day, but she didn't care. It was lovely to feel some fresh sea air flowing through the flat. She looked across the estuary to see the ferry making its first drop-off over at Crowsbridge Quay. It was Sunday so both Darren and Billy would be working. She craned to see if she could see him, to gauge what his body language might be saying, but they were too far away. Just seeing the *Happy Hart* also made her realise that she couldn't wait to see and give her dad a big hug, too. Last night had proved that being honest about everything wasn't always the right way forward – especially if it was going to hurt someone else in the process. But she had done it now and hoped that Billy's emotional intelligence would come to the rescue on this one. Because what Kara was now certain of was that the one thing in life that never ever lied was a kiss.

She had messaged everyone this morning to see what they were up to, but weirdly she'd had not one reply. She was too focused on her last instruction, though, to give it too much thought. Eleven o'clock, the postcard had said. She hoped that then, at last, she would know who had arranged her trip. The only thing that was bothering her was meeting at Passion Flowers. What if Lydia had arranged everything? She gave a little shudder. Surely not. That idea hadn't even crossed her mind before! And if not, why there at the shop? It was all very confusing.

She had wondered on reading the words 'we all care' if her trip away could have been a joint effort by everyone she loved. She drank her tea, then ran herself a deep bubble bath. Soon, she would know.

Lying back in the soothing bubbles, she shut her eyes. The excitement she felt was tarnished by a sense of sadness. Oh, how she would miss going up the garden to sit and chat to Grandad Harry in his shed. He would have loved to have heard about all her adventures and to know that she was feeling so free, and how at last she had broken her boundaries and travelled abroad. She thought of his funeral and the strength it had taken for her to get up and read the carefully thought-out words she had written about him. She would, of course, continue to grieve, but on Harry's insistence that she was to follow her heart and dreams, she would also continue to love and to strive for happiness.

She would never forget her kind and humorous grandfather. In fact, she already felt comforted by the conviction that the blooming of Harry's Rose would be a homage, not only to Harry Moon, but also to his strong belief that every soul is a flower blossoming in nature.

The thoughts of both her dear grandad and the fact that she may have ruined everything with Billy caused tears to run down her cheeks. Billy Dillon was a good man. Kind, strong, genuine, one of a kind, in fact. And as she lay back in the bubbles, letting out an involuntary wracking sob as she did so, she thought that if as a child you were taught how intricate and complicated the game of love was, then only the very brave would dare to play.

Chapter 60

'Quick! We need to get the *Welcome Home* banner up. She'll be here in a minute.' Joe Moon placed a ladder up against the large front window of Passion Flowers.

'You'll need me the other side, mate, or it'll take for ever,' Charlie Dillon put in, rushing to the back of his shop to fetch his stepladder.

'C'mere, I'll do it,' Big Frank Brady said in his deep Irish accent as he sauntered up towards them, raised his long arm and tied one side securely without either a step up or fuss.

Pearl, her vast backside wobbling more than the ladder, fearlessly made her way rung by rung up the other side, causing Joe to rush round and balance her with all his might at the bottom. Big Frank had to contain his laughter at the sight.

'Oi, 'ave you got the champagne, Pat?' Charlie bawled down to his wife as he secured his end of the banner.

'Chilled – and glasses laid out.'

Star appeared with a length of pink ribbon. 'I was thinking I'll put the ribbon over the door, we all hide inside, and a bit like the Mad Hatter's tea party, instead of a sign saying *Drink me!* I just leave some scissors hanging on a string with her name on them, saying *Cut me!* So exciting!'

'Crazy, but yes – do it, duckie.' Pat Dillon smiled.

'Auntie Kara will love it,' Skye said almost shyly. The teenager had understood that getting up before midday today had been essential as she loved a party as much as her mum's best friend.

'Time check,' Joe Moon boomed.

'Ten forty-five,' Big Frank replied, looking down at his gold Rolex.

'No Monique today, then?' Joe enquired.

'Sadly not. She's working on a show on Broadway for a couple of weeks.'

Star handed her daughter a bag full of star and moon tree ornaments. 'I forgot these, quick. Pearl and Skye, can you hang these on the tree in the window, please?'

'Shit!' Pat Dillon stated, after her phone buzzed. 'Darren's just texted from the ferry quay. She's on her way up Ferry Lane now.'

Everyone rushed inside, leaving Star to quickly hook up the ribbon, secure the scissors, duck beneath it and hide under the flower-arranging counters with everyone else. They all then jumped as Darren, who had sprinted up, dashed inside the back door and hid amongst them, too.

'Where's your brother?' Pat whispered.

'He's—'

'SURPRISE!' Joe Moon led the welcoming party in jumping up as his daughter, with a look of astonishment on her face, cut through the pink ribbon and made her way into the shop, which for the first time in its history was empty of blooms.

'What the . . . ?' Kara gasped in disbelief as eight sets of smiling eyes stared back at her. Star pushed a huge bundle of fragrant flowers into her arms. Pearl began to pour the champagne and started to hand it around. Hot pasties and home-made cupcakes were piled up on plates.

'I should be the one buying all you lot flowers as I assume you all had something to do with sending me away on such an amazing trip,' Kara told them, her cheeks pink with pleasure, as she placed the magnificent bouquet carefully down on the counter.

Joe Moon shook his head. 'Nothing to do with us.'

'Stop messing with me. It had to be all of you.'

The group fidgeted. The silence seemed interminable. And then all of a sudden, a figure appeared from the office and another set of familiar eyes was looking directly at Kara. And then a voice said quietly, 'It was me.'

There was a silence as Kara took in the news and family and friends waited with bated breath for her reaction. Putting a hand to her chest and with tears pricking her eyes, she managed to reply, 'You? You did it all – the travel, the postcards. You did it for *me*?'

Jenifer Moon nodded slowly, walked towards her younger sister and pulled her into an awkward hug. She broke away, reached for her glass, took a large slug of champagne and started to address the group as if she was addressing a corporate audience.

'Really, we need to give Grandad Harry the credit for your trip away. He woke me up to the fact that I've been the most dreadful sister *and* daughter. I had no idea that you had been offered a place at college to study floristry and turned it down, all those years ago. You put love for our dad first. Whereas, I was all right, selfishly at university, having a right good time.'

Hearing this, Joe bit his lip and Pearl put an arm reassuringly on his.

337

'I am so sorry, Kara,' Jen went on, 'for the way that I've treated you and have spoken to you, your whole life. Who am I to say you can't stay in Hartmouth? After being back here for a few days, I can see now why you love it so much. I was away too long, and forgot how much heart it has. London is so fraught and busy and smelly.'

Kara wiped her eyes and took a deep breath. 'I don't know what to say.'

'You don't have to say anything, little sis. Doing this for you has helped me so much, too. I may have got the big flat in London, money and all the materialistic bullshit that comes with that, but true riches are what you have here, Kara. You are so loved.'

There was a ripple of applause then Frank said, 'Sure, yes you are, Kara Moon.'

Jen went on. 'You have Frank and Monique to thank for the use of their apartment in New York and for arranging the Orchid Tour for you.'

'Oh my God, the burlesque mugs and the Audrey Hepburn picture – now you tell me! That is so Monique!' Kara exclaimed. 'I had no idea.'

'Ha! Yes, I knew you'd love Dahlia, too,' Frank said, pleased as could be. 'I didn't want to do a feckin' tour round some gardens, but my love insisted when I went over there to visit once – and well, as you saw, it is a magical place and she is a wonderful guide.'

'It was stunning, and I'm staying in touch with her, for sure. It also made me realise that my heart is not only here in Hartmouth, but in my passion for flowers.' Kara stopped to think. 'I have so many questions now! The personal shopper in Saks? Oh Jen, that was you too, I guess? It was such a wonderful experience. And Luis, my driver, was such a lovely man.'

'Well, when I saw you in that dreadful non-matching suit at Grandad Harry's funeral, I just had too. You have a beautiful figure, Kara. You just needed a little push to not only show you how to spoil yourself sometimes, but also to realise you never need be shy about your body shape again. Show off those assets, girl. I'd be proud of those voluptuous curves, especially those puppies of yours. Women pay a fortune to look like you. Unfortunately for me, I got blessed with the figure of an ironing board and couple of Grandad Harry's bee stings.'

Joe glowed pink as everyone else laughed.

'But what about Jack and Angel – and I'm sure I met Brice's brother.' Kara had a sudden flashback to her and Sam writhing about in the sand, but pushed it away. 'Where do they all fit in?' she asked the group as they began to help themselves to more drinks and warm pasties.

'I was working on a finance project with Jack,' Jen said. Star's face lit up. She listened intently as Jenifer carried on. 'I can't believe I'm admitting this and I am truly sorry and ashamed, Pearl, but I knew Dad was seeing someone else and rather than me travel down, Jack was coming over anyway and needed a break so I sent him to check up on who this new woman was and what her motives were. Again, I'm so sorry, Pearl. I realise now that I'm getting to know you that you are the best thing that has ever happened to our dad. I can't believe I even thought it.'

Kara looked at Pearl, who said, 'It's OK, child. We've had it out and I wasn't happy, but your dad's best interests are mine too, so I get it. It's all forgiven and forgotten.'

Kara looked deep into the kind woman's eyes and saw with relief that not only was this wonderful woman telling the truth, she was proving further strength in the forgiveness of her elder sister.

'Anyway,' Jenifer continued, 'after I'd decided to fix up the holiday for you, Kara, it was the obvious choice to send you to New York as I knew Jack could be trusted to deliver the second postcard. I just had to get the first one to you, which was the easy bit, eh Dad.'

Joe nodded. 'That bloody Cora Blunt nearly caught me, though – that's why it was hanging out of the door. I had to do a runner.'

Kara laughed. Star's face looked pained. Jen had declared ignorance when she had asked about Jack and she had still had no reply to the message or email she had sent him, even since Kara had told her of the state he was in.

'But why the John Lennon Memorial?' Kara inputted.

'In a weird way I wanted you to realise that you had come further than you thought after chucking out Jago, but not just in distance. Also, "Imagine" is the word in the middle of the mosaic and the stoned guitarist is often there singing it. I hoped you would hear him. I wanted you to imagine a new world ahead of you.'

'That's a bit deep, love,' Joe inputted.

'It was actually a really memorable part of my trip.' Kara smiled tearfully. 'And the flowers and the shopping spree and also seeing the sights of New York – well, it was magical, I felt like I was on a film set half the time.'

'Good.' Jen felt herself welling up. She coughed.

'So, for the rest of the trip, Dad had told me that you'd had a couple of other visitors and Star has your Airbnb account details so to make it all the more personal, it made sense to use the contacts you had already, plus it guaranteed that all the clues were delivered safely and on time. Isn't Angel such a diamond?'

'He really is.' Kara smiled.

'However, it seems now that Brice was the only one who kept undercover!'

Everyone laughed.

'I can't believe you did this for me.' Kara was now serious. She looked around her. Where was Billy? 'Thank you, thank you all. Now come on, more drinks, more food everyone.'

Jen refilled her glass as Kara, who had now pulled herself together a bit, said, 'Actually, hang on a minute. Why are we in here? And why is it empty? What's been going on?'

'I'm so glad you said earlier that you realised that your passion is still flowers.' Jen addressed the small crowd again. 'Lydia has gone back to Berkshire to be near her son, I think. Something happened here, I don't know what, but it upset her so greatly she had to get away.'

Daz Dillon squirmed uncomfortably. He hadn't realised just how much Lydia Twist had fallen for him. When she found out that he was shagging Rachel Penhaligon, she had gone crazy at him, really ripped into him. And when he had said that he could offer her nothing more than his body, the next day she had upped and left, just like that. It had upset him to see her like that, but he had never promised her anything and she had always insinuated that what they had was no more than just sex. He would never understand women, and that was a fact.

'I hope it wasn't my fault,' Kara said in a subdued voice, feeling sad at this and also that Billy was still not here.

'It wasn't,' Darren promised meaningfully.

Kara nodded at him in understanding and mouthed, 'Thank you.'

'Come on, Jen, pull your finger out and get on with it,' Charlie Dillon nagged cheerfully, 'I've got a shop to run, love.'

'You clear off back to it if you're so keen, you silly old sod,' Pat Dillon chastised her husband.

Jen cleared her throat. 'Thank you, Charlie. So basically, I've taken over the lease for a year here. I really hope it's what you want, Kara, but if not, it's not a problem as I hear property on Ferry Lane Market is like gold dust. It is your choice. And if you do want to take it on, then I will have nothing to do with the business, it will all be yours. I just know you will make a success of it and will eventually be able to pay the monthly rent yourself before the year is out.'

Kara's eyes were wide. Could she take any more surprises? Her heart was beating so fast. 'Oh my God, of course I want to do it! This is like a dream come true.' She grinned at her sister. 'Bloody hell, Jen, you didn't upset me that much.'

Everyone laughed again and then pretty blond Jen went on: 'And as I didn't realise that you'd missed out on getting a proper floristry qualification at Bishop Burton all those years ago, I've pulled some brochures together of some online courses that may be of interest with regards to both floristry and business that would give you further skills to maximise your potential here. Again, obviously that's down to you. Everything's in the office here for you to look at when you're ready. And I kept the money back from Grandad Harry for this, so I will gladly finance that for you, too.' Jen paused. 'But that's for you to think about and decide in your own time.'

'And also,' Star gently pushed her daughter in front of

her, 'Skye said that when she's finished in the college, she'd love to be your apprentice, if you'll have her.'

'I don't know what to say.' Kara put her hands over her face, causing her to miss a lone figure walking in through the back door of the florist's.

'Well, I hope you are going to say yes,' Jen said abruptly, then laughed.

'Yes, and yes!' Kara beamed, ruffling Skye's long blond hair, causing everyone to cheer and her father to raise his glass.

'To Kara Moon, my beautiful second daughter and the proud new owner of Passion Flowers.'

'To Kara Moon.' Everyone lifted their glasses.

Somebody then tapped on their glass with a pen. 'There's one more thing that needs a yes, though.'

'Billy, son, where you been hiding?' Charlie piped up. 'You've missed the whole bleeding shebang.'

'I've been standing behind Big Frank all the time.' The young ferryman winked at his dad, then at the gigantic Irishman.

Kara's heart began to beat at one hundred miles an hour. Her sense of relief was overwhelming. She put her hand to her chest and started to blurt, 'Before you say anything. I am so sorry, Billy. I was so flippant last night, I was tired and . . . I was wrong in the way I reacted. It wasn't fair.'

'What 'appened?' Pat Dillon mouthed to Darren, who screwed up his face and shook his head.

Billy walked towards the pretty redhead and took both of her hands in his. Just looking at his cheeky face caused a big grin to spread across hers. 'And I *over*reacted. You didn't do anything wrong, I upset myself and how could I not forgive somebody as lovely and perfect as you.' Kara smiled a watery smile.

343

'What else has she got to say yes to, then, lad?' Charlie Dillon shouted.

Turning an empty flower bucket upside down, the smiling ferryman stepped up onto it and cleared his throat purposefully, 'Kerry Moon, will you *please* go on that bloody date with me!'

Joe Moon had a tear in his eye. 'Never mind, Billy Dillon, I reckon this is better than when old Tom Bawcock came back from the sea that day.'

'Who the hell is Tom Bawcock?' Kara, Jen and Pearl said loudly in unison.

EPILOGUE

'It's not quite the first date I'd imagined, but I can honestly say there's nowhere I'd rather be.'

'Do you really mean that?' Billy handed Kara a chilled glass of champagne. 'I was worried that now you're officially an experienced globetrotter, it might not be enough.'

Kara looked deep into his indigo-blue eyes. 'You, just *you*, Billy Dillon, would be enough, without all these added extras.'

'The boy done good then,' Billy congratulated himself, before leaning down to turn on the Bose speaker under the bench to allow soft chill-out music to envelop their space. 'Well, with a little help from our friends.'

He smiled at Kara. 'It was my idea to do the old tug up. Your dad helped with the fairy lights and it was Daz who sneaked this and the mattress on board.' He patted the long cushion on the bench they were sitting on. 'Oh, and Frank insisted on the icebox complete with champagne and glasses.' He added shyly, 'The roses are your favourites – Agatha Christie. Pearl helped me pick them this afternoon.' Billy took a sip of his drink and turned the music up a little, saying, 'I do hope it's to Modom's satisfaction and comfort.'

'All I can say is, it's not the only *Happy Hart* on the water tonight.' Kara put her hand to her chest. Not only was it the sweetest thing to learn that everyone had been involved in making their night so special, but she had also only just noticed the beautiful pink blooms intertwined amongst the fairy lights. Tears pricked her eyes. 'You are so thoughtful. I love it. To be under the stars on a balmy summer's night with somebody as gorgeous as you – what more could a girl want?'

'Flattery will get you everywhere.'

'Will it really?' Kara smirked.

'They call this place Lovers' Cove, you know.'

'Do they now?' Kara took in the familiar sounds of the sea lapping against the decorated tug, which had been a part of her family's story for so long. The still blackness of the small beach against the glimmering moonlight made for a dreamy setting, and the drifting perfume from the roses filled her with peace.

'I hope I can do it,' she said suddenly. 'Run Passion Flowers by myself, I mean.'

'Of course you can.'

'And I don't want to go to college. I don't feel I need to now.'

'And that's fine. It's your choice, so good for you.'

'I might be a bit grumpy,' she warned him.

'I can handle it. A bad day with Kerry Moon will be better than a good day with most people, I reckon.'

Kara took Billy's hand. 'You look so bloody handsome tonight.'

He tutted. 'Like I've said before, you've got the monopoly on most things beautiful in this world. I think you are stunning, Kerry Moon. And I can't explain just how much I missed you when you were away.'

'I'm pleased and – shit, well-reminded.' Kara reached

down for her handbag. 'I got you something. If you hadn't stormed off, you'd have got it the night I came back from my travels.'

'I was so hurt.' Billy looked straight out towards the little cove.

Kara shut her eyes and took a deep breath. 'I know and I'm truly sorry I upset you. But sometimes I think that things need to happen to make us see the true picture. To make us realise what it is that we truly want. And I have not one single doubt that all I want is you.'

A quiet, 'Good,' was all that Billy could manage as Kara handed him a small green box.

'Jesus, it's a bit early for a proposal, innit?' He laughed, quickly opening his gift. Inside was a small silver key ring in the shape of a boomerang. Kara cleared her throat and, as if delivering a line from a rehearsed play, she announced, 'Just like a boomerang, I came back to you. And I will always come back to you for evermore.'

Billy swallowed. 'That is cool, so very cool,' he managed.

'Turn it over,' Kara urged.

'What are you doing to me?' Billy's grin widened as he read aloud: 'To Romeo from your Juliet.' He shook his head. 'You are incredible.'

'I have my moments.' Kara was grinning now too. 'It was amazing to get away, but Hartmouth is home, isn't it? Where I belong.'

'Where *we* belong,' Billy corrected her. 'And while we're at it, I have a little gift for you, too. Don't get too excited, it's nothing much.' He felt in his jeans pocket and pulled out a tiny square envelope. Inside was a card with an illustration of a woman with long, shiny, bright red hair wearing a crown of pink roses.

'She looks like me,' Kara said.

'Look at the back,' Billy instructed.

Kara did as she was told, then said, '"Nothing much", you said? Billy, this trumps the tattoo book and then some.'

'Really?' Billy gently turned her wrist over and kissed the little red rose on it.

'"Flora, the Goddess of Flowers and Fertility",' Kara read from the back of the card.

'That is you, you see,' Billy hastened to explain. 'My very own Goddess of Flowers. And I know how important a family is to you so, well, we can work on the fertility bit as soon as you're ready . . .'

'I see no harm in practising right now, actually,' Kara said boldly.

Billy bit his lip. 'I didn't want you to assume that because the mattress was there that we had to – you know. It was more for looking up at the stars and—'

Kara put her finger to her beau's lips, placed both their glasses back in the icebox and lay down next to him on the comfy duvet. Then, grabbing him tightly to her, she kissed him. Her handsome partner needed no persuasion to kiss her right back. She felt that same rush of euphoria she had felt when she had grabbed him at Crowsbridge Hall, the same soft, yielding that kissing this man always brought.

He kissed her lightly at first, and then with such intensity that she began to lose herself. Feeling slightly disorientated, she pulled away.

Billy gently touched her nose and whispered in her ear, 'I love you.'

'You do?' Kara felt her eyes stinging.

Billy nodded, then grinning mischievously, he said, 'To the other side of the River Hart and back,' and when she tutted and slapped him, he laughed. 'Oi! I meant to say that I love you, my darling Kerensa Anne, to the Moon and back – and don't you ever forget that.'

Read on for an extract from

STARRY SKIES IN FERRY LANE MARKET

The second book in Nicola May's brilliant new series . . .

HODDER

'If you do not love too much, you do not love enough'
— Blaise Pascal

CHAPTER ONE

'I've told you before, Mum,' Star Bligh said irritably. 'I don't want you doing this if you're stoned.'

Ignoring her daughter, the woman with braided hair carried on laying out the well-worn Tarot cards.

'I can see a man,' Estelle said slowly. 'In fact, I can see two.' Her long, slim fingers began to circle the crystal ball in front of her.

'Huh. Isn't that just your wishful thinking?' Reverting back to her sulky five-year-old self, Star began to twirl a strand of her long blonde hair around her finger.

'Shhh,' her mother hissed, then went on. 'Choose wisely, for one of them may break your heart –' a dramatic paused ensued – 'and the other may *shake* it to the core.' Her Cornish accent trailed off in an ominous whisper.

'I don't suppose you saw Skye in your crystal ball, did you?' Star sounded weary. 'I mean, that was the reason for my coming up here this early – thinking that my wayward daughter might have sought solace with her even more wayward grandmother.'

Estelle tutted. 'She's a big girl now, Steren. You really do need to let her go.'

'Let her go? She's only eighteen, Mum.'

'And at that age, you were a single mother with a two-year-old and you were already out working all hours at Sibley's.'

Star looked up at the metal clock in the shape of a black cat hanging on the wall. 'Ooh no, is that the time?' She shimmied sideways out of the bench seat in her mother's kitchen and went to fetch her coat and hat. 'I need to get back to the market,' she said, then she shivered. 'It's bloody freezing in here. How do you stand it?'

'Oh, to me it brings back lovely memories of all three of us cuddling up under a blanket when our Skye was a baby.'

'Yeah, right. Those happy days when we had no money to mention and you still convinced me that having a baby when I was in my last year at school was the right thing to do.' Star couldn't keep the bitterness out of her voice.

'That's not fair.' Estelle looked pained. 'Do you regret it now?'

'Of course not,' Star snapped. 'I just don't want to see Skye following in my footsteps. She needs to have a life before she even thinks of starting a family.'

'You're a great mother to her, love. A much better mum than I ever was to you.' Estelle gave a sigh.

Star looked up at the ceiling to suppress the tears she could feel welling in her eyes. 'Anyway, don't you want to be moving to a proper house, now that you're getting older?'

'And leave this perfect little commune – are you mad? As for the temperature, I've got proper electric heater things now. Haven't sussed out how to work the timers on them, that's all.'

Star looked out across the amazing cliff-top view to see the horizon cutting the white November sky and steel-grey sea perfectly in two. Seabirds on the wing, ready to dive down and catch their fishy lunch, squawked in anticipation. There was no denying that the Hartmouth Head residential static home park was set in an incredible location. And despite it having being subject to 'trailer trash' taunts from some of the kids in her school days, Star thought that being brought up in such a close-knit community, and against such a stunning back-drop, had had its advantages.

'Can't your new boyfriend do it?' she asked, grateful for Skye's regular updates on her grandmother's unpredictable love-life.

'Sort the heaters, you mean?' Estelle raised her eyebrows meaningfully, then laughed. 'Harley's about as useful on the DIY front as a chocolate teapot.'

'Maybe if you dated someone who wasn't just out of college . . .'

'For your information, he's forty-two.'

'Oh, just the twenty-year age gap this time, then.'

'You're just jealous. When's the last time you had any fun, eh, my girl?' Opening the door to her static home, painted a dark green that reflected her pagan love of nature, Estelle picked up and lit the half-smoked joint that was resting in an ashtray on the steps of the decking area. Then, after taking a large drag on the fragrant tobacco, she said gently, 'I named you Steren because it means Star. Now that your daughter is grown and can stand on her own two feet, don't you think it's time for *you* to start shining?'

CHAPTER TWO

'Try this.' Frank Brady placed a small sugar-dusted pie in front of the woman who was sitting on a high stool across the café counter from him.

The clattering of cutlery as a couple finished off a huge fried breakfast and the shrieking of a two-year-old having a tantrum in the corner were only slightly drowned out by Audrey Hepburn singing 'Moon River'.

'She's singing your song, Kara Moon,' Frank teased the pretty redhead. Then the towering, dark-haired Irishman, who had owned and run Frank's Café on the Hartmouth Estuary seafront for the past eleven years, went over and twiddled with his beloved jukebox in the corner.

'So,' he said, coming back to the counter, 'what do you think of the mince pie? I'm testing it out ready for the Christmas trade.'

Licking her lips, Kara took a big bite out of the succulent-looking pastry. She began chewing then shuddered, stuck her tongue out and made an ugly face. 'Ew! That taste, it's so bitter.' She reached for the water bottle in her bag and washed down the alien-tasting filling fast. 'What the hell have you put in there?'

'I'm just testing out an age-old, revered mince-pie recipe. You are my guinea pig.'

'It's only November the fourth,' Kara's faint Cornish accent trilled.

'You know me – I like to be ahead of the game. I found it in a drawer at my old Mammy's place after she died, God bless her, and then came across it by chance yesterday in the back kitchen. It had mice teeth-marks all around the edge.'

'What – the mince pie or the recipe sheet?' Frank laughed his deep throaty laugh as Kara continued, with a huge grin, 'Or maybe you just put the bloody dead mice in it?'

'No, just a slosh of Guinness, as well as the usual brandy.' He took a bite himself, then gagged. 'Jesus! Me old dear must have been on the black stuff herself when she made these, so she must,' They both laughed. 'My Monique already said to just get some of the homemade mincemeat from Alicia's market stall. I think she's right; it'll be a lot easier.'

'Your Monique is *always* right,' Kara said, 'and sensible too. I'd follow her advice, if you want to keep any of your customers.' She swallowed a bit more water before exclaiming, 'Shit! I need to get going. I've been waiting on an extra delivery of gypsophila and it should be arriving soon.'

'How's it going up there at the shop, now that you're Miss Passion Flowers herself?'

'Really good, thanks,' Kara said happily. 'I'm so lucky to be working at something I love, and now that the business belongs to me I cannot tell you how good it is, not being ordered around by old Twisty Knickers.'

'Living the dream, young Kara. And you deserve it, you really do.'

Kara glanced through the café window and saw the *Happy Hart* car ferry heading across from Crowsbridge to the Hartmouth quay.

'Talking of things I love, I'd better take Dad and my Billy a coffee whilst they load on the cars,' she said. 'It's cold work on that crossing this time of year.'

Frank placed four take-out cups in front of her in a holder. 'So, that's you, your dad, your fella and Skye sorted. I think I've got the milk and sugars right.'

'Brilliant, thanks.' Kara paid and made her way to the door. Frank ran around the counter to hold it open for her.

'Feck it!' the big man suddenly exclaimed.

'What's up?'

'There's me, wittering on about the mince pies and forgetting I needed to talk to you about something important.'

'That's OK. Let me quickly message Skye and ask her to open the shop up a bit earlier and take the order in.'

While Kara did that, Frank served two new customers with coffee, then came to sit down opposite her in one of the American diner-style booths. Checking her phone, Kara was relieved to see a thumbs-up emoji from her apprentice.

'It's about my brother's boy, Conor,' Big Frank revealed. 'To cut a long story short, he needs somewhere to stay, just for a little while, and I wondered if he could rent your flat – the one above the flower shop, I mean. It is still empty, isn't it?'

'Is he in trouble?' Kara asked instinctively, knowing full well what a colourful family Frank heralded from. In fact, Monique moving him down to the south-west of England had probably saved the big fella from a life of crime. Selling hooky booze in the guise of a 'blackcurrant cordial' or 'special iced tea' was now his only vice.

Not even flinching at her comment, Frank replied, 'He's not now.' Then he put his huge hand on top of Kara's pale freckly one and added, 'And you know I would never put you in a difficult position. He's a good lad, I promise you.'

Kara trusted Frank like family. 'The flat is empty, yes. I use it more as a stockroom, hadn't even thought about renting it out, to be honest. But why's he not staying at yours?' she asked.

'He's a youngster, like you – he'd be bored stiff living way up on the moor with me and Monique. Let me know how much you want, and I'll pay you three months upfront. Cash, of course.'

Kara thought about it. 'It's not very plush and I've only got a sofa up there at the moment, so we'll need to get a bed . . . and it needs a good clean throughout . . .'

Frank patted Kara's arm gently. 'Just tell me what you need, little lady, and I'll get it sorted.'

'OK, if you're sure. Any idea when he wants it from?'

'Yesterday.' Frank grinned his lop-sided grin. 'You know us Brady boys, we don't muck around.' He stood up. 'Come on, let me get you some fresh coffees. These will be cold.'

Kara took a sip of hers. 'They're still OK. Don't worry.'

'Grand, grand. Right, I've got to get myself sorted for tomorrow's fireworks on the quay, so I'll catch up with you later about the logistics of it all. And thanks a million, Kara.'

As Star drove to the end of Ferry Lane, she noticed Kara about to hot-foot it up the hill towards the market. Tooting loudly right behind her, she stopped and beckoned her friend over to her Smart car. 'Get in,' she called. 'I'll take you.'

'You scared the life out of me,' Kara laughed, climbing in carefully so as not to spill the coffees. 'What are you up to, tearing around this early, anyway?'

Star let out a big sigh. 'Skye didn't come home last night.

I know she's officially a grown-up now, Kar, but I wish she'd had the decency to let me know where she was. I didn't sleep a bloody wink.'

'Oh, love. Well, she's at the shop now. She's just messaged me. Is this the first time she's done this – stayed out all night, I mean?'

'Yes, but – fuck!' Star braked suddenly as a stray melon toppled from a box that Charlie Dillon was carrying, just avoiding being crushed under her wheel.

Kara fell forward, causing hot coffee spill out of the cups she was clutching and onto her jeans. 'Bloody hell, mate. Be careful!'

'Don't you be having a go at me, too.' Star suppressed a sob as she pulled up outside the florists. Oblivious to all this, Charlie Dillon blew them both a massive kiss, bent to retrieve the runaway fruit and stuck it up his jumper, along with another one. 'Don't get many of these to the kilo,' he laughed and then catching sight of an old lady looking in his shop window, he quickly put them back in the box.

'Oh, Star, I'm so not having a go. I've got to do an early hotel drop, so how about we meet for lunch at Tasty Pasties and you can tell me what's really the matter. Say twelve thirty, all right?'

'You know me so well.' Star smiled weakly.

'What is it they say? Sister from another mister, or something like that.' Kara touched her best friend's cheek gently. She put one of the coffees in the car's drinks holder and got out. 'Get that in you,' she said. 'I've already had a sip and it's got sugar in it, but it's wet and warm.' Then waving goodbye, she turned and made her way through the glass-fronted door to her personal domain: the beautiful, sweet-smelling florists called Passion Flowers.

CHAPTER THREE

Star yawned as she made her way inside STAR Crystals & Jewellery, the shop she had rented and run in Ferry Lane Market for the past six years. Taking a sip of the sweetened coffee, she grimaced then cranked up the heating. She hated the winter, mainly because it reminded her of those freezing days living in the static home with her mother and a young baby. The memories of all three of them cuddling together under a blanket were not quite as romantic as the version her mother had fondly recalled. Probably because Estelle Bligh had been warmed through with brandy or pot, Star thought grimly. The experience had, however, made her determined that as soon as she could afford a place of her own, she and her beloved only child Skye would never be cold again.

Oh, how hard she had worked to create her own little business and forge her way in the world. Steren Bligh had always been a grafter. As soon as she was old enough, she had put herself on the bus to work on Saturdays and after school at Sibley's, the newsagents in Penrigan, owned by her Great-aunt Florrie and her Great-uncle Jim Sibley.

The childless churchgoers had always looked out for their pretty little fair-haired assistant. And when she became pregnant at just sixteen years old, despite their Christian beliefs – or perhaps because of them – they had not turned their

Nicola May

backs on her; on the contrary, they had taken care of both her and the baby. The couple had kept Star's job open, and they'd also made sure that, when Estelle was working at her 'witchcraft' as they called it, Skye was fed and cuddled in the flat upstairs. Their great kindness allowed Star to carry on working her regular shifts and never having to find money for childcare.

This also meant that Star could save up her wages to buy beads, silk threads and fastenings. Then, staying up as late into the night as possible before her eyes shut without her permission, she would make bracelets and necklaces to sell along Penrigan Beach on a Sunday to the many visiting holidaymakers. Putting Skye in a makeshift papoose and ably managing to dodge the council do-gooders, the young entrepreneur did excellent business, with her little white-haired bairn proved a valuable attraction. To the coos of 'what a gorgeous baby', her basket full of trinkets was soon empty, and her money belt was full.

This routine continued until she finished her exams and began helping out more in the newsagents. By now, Florrie and Jim were allowing her to sell her handmade jewellery from a stand next to the magazine rack, and she also sold at as many arts and craft fairs as she could fit in around her shift.

Everything changed when her beloved great-uncle Jim dropped down dead the day before he and Florrie were due to retire. He had been just seventy-five.

Not being greedy folk, the Sibleys' retirement plan had been for the pair to fold their business, stay living in their modest flat above the newsagents and donate the space below for charitable and church causes. It wasn't until they both passed that their heirs would be Star, Skye, the RSPB and the local church.

366

But with his untimely passing came an unexpected gift: the generous legacy of twenty-thousand pounds which Jim, with the full support of his wife, had left Star in his will.

Thus, when the lease of the much sought-after unit on Ferry Lane Market came up for sealed bids, Star's dream to have a shop and a home of her own came to fruition far sooner than she could ever have imagined.

Star often thought that, if it hadn't been for the passing of her employer, three generations of Bligh girls would still be living all on top of one another in the small park home on top of Hartmouth Hill. When she had inherited the gift of money from a man she had looked up to and loved, and with the blessing of his dear wife, she had felt that the universe had been listening to her dreams and that she really did have a guardian angel.

Turning on the display window lights against the gloomy November day, Star's phone beeped with a text. *My battery went last night, sorry mum. At work, can't talk. See u later. xx*

Star took a deep breath of relief. If the world were powered by the angst teenagers caused their parents, there would be no need to worry about global warming ever again, that was for sure. As the heater at her feet began warming her up, she set about unpacking the new order of precious stones and crystals, which she would use to make jewellery for her sparkly new Christmas gift collection.

To find out more, order *Starry Skies in Ferry Lane Market* by Nicola May now!

Looking for more from Nicola May?

Sign up to the Nicola May
newsletter for exclusive updates,
extracts, competitions and news at
WWW.HODDER.CO.UK/LANDING-PAGE/NICOLA-MAY/

OR SCAN THE QR CODE BELOW

Stay Social and Follow Nicola:

@NICOLAMAY1

@AUTHOR_NICOLA

@NICOLAMAYAUTHOR

WWW.NICOLAMAY.COM

When one book ends, another begins...

Bookends is a vibrant new reading community to help you ensure you're never without a good book.

You'll find exclusive previews of the brilliant new books from your favourite authors as well as exciting debuts and past classics. Read our blog, check out our recommendations for your reading group, enter great competitions and much more!

Visit our website to see which great books we're recommending this month.

Join the Bookends community:
www.welcometobookends.co.uk

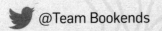 @Team Bookends   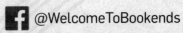 @WelcomeToBookends

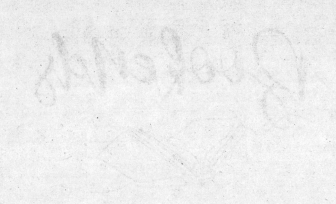